A CHERISHED FREEDOM

A CHERISHED FREEDOM

Joyce Stranger

This first world edition published in Great Britain 2000 by
SEVERN HOUSE PUBLISHERS LTD of
9–15 High Street, Sutton, Surrey SM1 1DF.
This first world edition published in the USA 2001 by
SEVERN HOUSE PUBLISHERS INC of
595 Madison Avenue, New York, N.Y. 10022.

British Library Cataloguing in Publication Data

Stranger, Joyce
    A cherished freedom
    1.   Farm life - Wales
    I.   Title
    823.9'14 [F]

    ISBN 0-7278-5682-0

Typeset by Hewer Text Ltd.,
Edinburgh, Scotland.
Printed and bound in Great Britain by
MPG Books Ltd., Bodmin, Cornwall.

This book is written for the many readers
who have asked for another of
Joyce Stranger's country-based stories.

One

L ouise Pritchard was sitting on the low stone wall surrounding the farmyard, taking a brief rest from the
chores that overwhelmed her. Above her the mountains
towered into a blue sky. Beyond the farm, lower down the
slope, was Kane Merrit's cottage. The mystery man, Mervyn,
her husband, had called him, because he shunned company
and spoke so little about himself. He had retired there two
years before, and almost at once had begun to collect an
assortment of stray and injured animals. A shy man, he was
happier talking to Mervyn rather than Louise, but their
encounters were only in passing. They did not visit.

She could see the paddock by his house where his newest
acquisition grazed. Her elegant head and neck told of her
thoroughbred ancestry, though her shape was now marred by
the foal she was carrying, due very soon. It would be wonderful to have a foal to watch. Louise loved them above all young
animals; they were so delicate, so dainty, so filled with life as
they pranced and jumped and tried to race the wind.

She sympathised with the mare. Her own baby was due
early in January. She was already uncomfortable. Though, as
she had been married for twelve years and given up hope of a
child, she was not going to complain about that.

"Well, not much," she said, talking to the air.

She tired quickly, which irritated her but the rest had
refreshed her. Bending over was difficult and you needed
to do that so often when looking after animals.

She eased herself to her feet. Demon, the drake that

1

terrorised the ducks, was watching her, hoping for a handout of bread. She had forgotten it. Exasperated, he pecked her leg. She looked down at him. He, in his turn, looked up at her, his bright beady eyes almost amused, she thought. They glittered in his small head. His yellow beak was brilliant against his white feathers.

"I hate you," she said, and laughed at him. "Watch it, or you'll be cooked for my dinner one day."

Giving up, realising she had no food on her, and no intention whatever of remedying that, he waddled over to the pond, where, moments later, he dipped his head, tail in the air, dabbling under the water.

The brief encounter lightened her mood. The drake could be relied on to amuse her from the time he woke up and was released from his pen, when he waddled up to the kitchen door and stood waiting for his morning slice of bread. If she ignored him, he followed her, impatient, or quacked at the two dogs, whose responding bark told her she was wanted.

She always marvelled at his awareness of the approach of darkness and the need to hide himself and his harem from the foxes. If she and the dogs were late, he waddled expectantly to the shelter, waiting for the door to open. If she were late in the morning he quacked imperiously, summoning her to her duty, expecting the door to be opened as soon as it was light.

It was time to check on her pride and treasure, Tarquin, the ram lamb that had been born to a ewe Mervyn had bought in the year before. That day was vivid in her mind. It had been a jewel of a day, a day to treasure, and one she hugged to her now, when everything had changed. It had been their twelfth wedding anniversary, just a month before Christmas. They had married in the least busy season: summer weddings were not a good idea on a busy farm.

"I'm celebrating by buying the present of a lifetime," Mervyn had said as he climbed into the Land Rover that morning.

"Not jewellery." Louise was suddenly anxious. She did not

wear anything but her wedding ring when she was working and there was little time when she wasn't. She didn't want adornments. Money was never plentiful and she preferred it to be invested in the farm which was their livelihood.

He laughed, teasing her. "What do you think?"

She could not imagine what he had in mind. She wondered all day. The year before he had bought her a Welsh Black cow, the start of a new breeding herd.

They had sold their dairy cattle and milk quota, which had rid them of the twice daily milking routine. Their cowman had been nearing seventy and they had not been sure they could replace him when he retired. In future, they'd decided to concentrate on sheep and beef cattle. "We'll invest it," Mervyn had said when they received the cheques.

Mervyn had driven back to the farm that evening, and had hooted five times as the Land Rover came to a standstill. He had jumped out of the driver's seat into the yard when she came out of the kitchen, where she had been preparing a special meal. The table was laid with a lace cloth, one of her mother-in-law's treasured possessions, the best cutlery and a centrepiece of flowers flanked by candles. Mervyn had bought a rare bottle of wine.

He was not a big man, though he topped her five foot three. Some unknown ancestor had given him a thatch of curly chestnut hair. Brown eyes laughed at her, and he hugged her, his excitement spilling out of him. As always, his right eyebrow shot up as he began to talk.

"Happy anniversary," he said. "Come and see our investment."

He opened the back of the Land Rover, and brought out the ramp. Louise looked at the ewe that marched down into the yard, and fell in love.

"A Suffolk," she said. "Are we crossing with our Welsh Mountains if she has a ram lamb?"

She was a child's toy of a sheep, with white close fleece, a black face and black legs. She seemed quite unworried at finding herself in a totally new environment, and followed Mervyn to the little paddock he kept for newcomers. As soon as she was inside the gate she began to graze.

Louise leaned on the gate, revelling.

"She's been covered by a ram worth £38,000," Mervyn said. "I'm praying for a ram lamb. He'll be worth his weight in gold. We'll start our own flock of Suffolks. And he'll be in demand. I know of at least four other farms that are breeding them now and one hobby farmer. They'll jump at the chance of using a ram with his heredity."

Louise stared at him, startled.

"All that money in one animal. Suppose she loses the lamb?"

"Suppose she has twin rams? Both worth a fortune . . . this is our future, my girl. Meanwhile, we have to wait. And that's not going to be easy. Mind you, she didn't cost all that. Cy owed me a favour, and sold her to us at well below her market value. Remember that cow we sold him? She went Best in Show and he made a huge profit and he's always felt guilty." He laughed. "I'll be more careful in the future when I sell. But Daisy May didn't look like a champion at the time."

"She was a pain," Louise said, remembering her habit of nasty little sideways kicks. "Still, she's done us some good." She corrected herself. "If we get a ram lamb, an enormous amount of good."

They agonised together in the weeks that followed, brooding over the ewe, who Louise named Belle. Mervyn became neurotic about her, hearing heart murmurs, and coughs, sure she had almost every problem that could plague a sheep. Suppose she lost the lamb? As the weeks went by he became more and more anxious.

Belle, unaware of human folly, saw no reason whatever for their anxiety and produced a sturdy ram lamb in early April without any problems at all. Within minutes he was up and sucking.

In the next few months the baby, named Tarquin, proved to

be a character, another entertainer on the farm, and enchanted all of them with his mischief. He was an explorer and an escaper, and his goal was the farmhouse kitchen. Once there he would stand on his hind legs and steal anything that was on the table, having a most un-sheep-like appetite for bread and cooling cakes.

At first the lamb found gaps and crawled under the gate, but that stopped as he grew. But then gates only kept him safe if they remembered to secure them with a chain and padlock. He could open any catch they tried. If either of them were out in the yard and he was free, he followed them like a dog and within two months they decided they actually did have three dogs and not two, especially as he came, like the collies, when they called to him. When they were not too busy they let him into the yard, enjoying his firm determination to follow the dogs everywhere.

"Maybe we *could* teach him to herd the other sheep," Louise said one evening, as the little ram helped Fern drive Demon and the ducks into their night-time quarters.

"It's just as well we don't have many visitors," Mervyn said a few days later, as she stood by the kitchen door holding out a mug of coffee. He grinned at his entourage: a small Suffolk ram, two collies and a quacking drake.

"They'd think we were mad." Nicely mad, though, she thought, savouring the sight.

Tarquin adored scones and griddle cakes, and was able to smell them from a distance. He always appeared fast when Louise was baking. He learned to open the kitchen door by butting up the latch with his nose. Callers looked in surprise at a kitchen door which had a bolt outside at eye level.

Louise smiled to herself. She needed her memories and she needed to keep busy. She was alone now, and everything depended on her. The animals, the farm's future and the baby growing inside her.

She looked around at her small realm. This was no rich farm. The solid stone building, as simple as a child's drawing, stood on the side of a mountain, high in the Welsh uplands, clinging to a rocky base. Only the old chimneys betrayed its age. It had been built for a huge family, and for servants, two centuries before. Now she felt lost in the emptiness of vacant rooms where no one ever slept.

Her husband's father had been Welsh but his mother had been English. The old man had had a fatal heart attack and his wife had followed him a year later when influenza turned to pneumonia. Louise thought her mother-in-law had lost all desire to live after her husband had died.

She stood for a moment, easing her aching legs, looking at the sky. She walked over to the paddock, where Tarquin ran to the gate, bleating his excitement. Belle, in the distance, turned her head, but did not worry about her offspring .

It was becoming increasingly difficult to manage the necessary work on her own. The baby that her husband had never even known about was growing fast. Its expected birth date was very soon after Christmas. Only twelve weeks before, Mervyn had been beside her, laughing with her, planning with her, making light of all their many problems. He could never pass the paddock without calling to Tarquin, and letting him out to play follow-my-leader round the yard.

"Bring him to bed," she had suggested one day and had been rewarded with a quirky raised right eyebrow and a grin.

"Might be an idea at that. At least he wouldn't have cold feet."

Life never stopped changing. A year ago she had felt she was failing Mervyn because the longed for baby refused to become reality. Twelve years of waiting. The day she had waved him goodbye had been the first faint stirrings of hope, so faint as to make her wait before telling him. Time enough when he came home, she'd thought. He would only be gone a week, and would be back the day before her thirty-third birthday. There had been too many disappointments. She had miscarried twice before. She would wait until she was sure before she told him.

Now she leaned against the low farmyard wall, the two sheepdogs, her shadows, watching her. They leaped up whenever any car came near the farmyard, sure it must be Mervyn. When their expectations were not rewarded they came back to her, tails down, ears drooping. They, like her, still hoped. She knew how they felt.

She had put on her husband's jacket, as all hers were now too tight. Its closeness to her face, and the faint smell from it of sheep, caused her thoughts to betray her again. She tried to deny the memory but it demanded attention. It dominated her dreams, a torture of Tantalus, ever recurring.

Daytime was fine. She could keep well occupied. There was no difficulty about that. The nights were the problem. She half solved that by taking the dogs up to bed with her, with guilty feelings because Mervyn would have been horrified. Sheepdogs belonged outside, he said time and again when her soft heart wanted to bring them indoors out of the cold. "Thick straw keeps them warm."

The memories would not be stifled. In her mind's eye she saw the police car drive into the yard, watched the policeman and the woman police constable stand beside it, as if unwilling to walk towards the house, and had known without being told that Mervyn was dead. She called the dogs to her, stilling their barks.

"It's safe, silly," he had said, the week before, laughing at her. "I know Bosnia was a war zone, but it's peaceful now. There's been no trouble for months. I can't let Chris down. He needs a co-driver and the man who should have gone with him is in hospital with appendicitis. Those people need that food. Besides, it gives me a chance to travel abroad that I'd never get otherwise. All expenses paid."

A change from the unremitting work.

She was not sure whether the news the police had brought was worse than news of death would have been.

The uneasy policewoman told her that the lorry had been hijacked by bandits, or worse, terrorists . . . nobody knew . . .

who stole the food brought to help starving children. No one had any idea whether the driver and co-driver were alive; they had been driven away with the lorry. There was no sign of either. They might be hostages, or might lie in unmarked graves far from any place where they would be found.

Louise did not know whether to grieve or hope and the solemn men from the government office who came to see her could offer little comfort. There were days when she was sure that Mervyn would walk in through the door, and days when she was haunted by the fear that he lay far away and unmourned, brutally killed on some mountainous hillside, and left unburied at the mercy of wild animals.

Often in the night she talked to the baby inside her, telling him he must grow and be strong and a comfort to her.

"Your father will come home and see you," she said, trying hard to believe her own words.

At least her health was good and after those first few weeks of morning sickness, aggravated by despair, she was fitter than she had ever been. That was just as well, as she had more work and responsibility than she had ever had, as well as the fears of any woman who found herself unexpectedly alone in the world to bring up a child without a father's backing and care. She had never imagined that it would happen to her.

There were so many worries. The BSE crisis had ruined the major part of their business. Their income was cut to the bone, so that she wondered at times how on earth she could survive.

Mervyn had taken out a huge life insurance to go to her if he died, but he had never envisaged a kidnapping and there was no proof that he was dead. She had to borrow, and that cost her far more in interest than she felt reasonable. Also, she was not sure how much longer the bank manager would remain supportive.

Pregnant, without Mervyn, with the fear that he might never come home, the long nights gave her too much time for thought. She was glad when they were interrupted, when some animal was unwell and needed extra care.

8

Just to add to her woes, Huw, their farmhand, who had been her right hand and an immense comfort, had, at seventy, at the end of the month before, been forced to retire, as his back, which frequently protested, told him in no uncertain terms that his working days were over. He needed treatment, and there was no chance at all that he would be able to work again at such a heavy job. The doctor told him he should have given up long ago.

How did she find a reliable farmhand? Advertising had not produced one single reply. Few men wanted to work in such an isolated place. The journey from the village below was tiresome, especially in bad weather. The access lane was narrow, steep, rutted and badly in need of repair. She needed help, soon. Time was short. Someone had to care for the animals when the baby came. She would not be able to do it herself for at least a week, if not longer.

There were no other farms near and she did not know many people in the area. They had always been too busy for social affairs. She had not needed anyone when Mervyn was there; they were busy and happy together. Now, she longed for human company; she was desperately lonely.

She looked up at the clouding sky. There was a thin band of gold amid the black. It spoke of hope. Mervyn would return and life would be normal again. Never give up.

She ought to be working, but there was always pleasure in watching the animals. Mervyn would love Tarquin now, more than ever. The ram was their future, but he was also the most endearing character. Mervyn, almost neurotic about his investment, had extended one of the stables, reinforced the door and padlocked the latch. He had been afraid of thieves so Tarquin was locked away at night. Louise was eternally grateful for the extra security now she was on her own.

There was a niggling wind that would soon rise to half a gale. A kestrel stood on the air above them. Dusk was coming. Demon, butting at her leg with his closed beak, was saying that it was time to put him and his companions safe indoors for the night.

The dogs had told her that a fox had come past the night before. They had woken her, racing to her window and barking. She had looked out, afraid that there might be a human intruder. She had seen the lean red body trigger the security lights, stand a moment to stare, and then depart, jumping the low wall. Luckily the runs were all secure. Mervyn had strengthened them the week before he went away.

Dear God, don't let anything more go wrong, she prayed. They were isolated here in the hills. When Mervyn had been with her that had not mattered. There had been laughter and plans to make, and the constant interest as he raced to call her to see a new calf, to admire the latest kid, or brought a lamb to be bottle fed and cared for because the ewe had died or had not enough milk for twins.

She heard his voice now in her dreams. "Come and see. Doe Eyes has a new calf . . . she's fantastic . . . eyes just like her mother's."

She closed the doors on the ducks and chickens, the dogs helping to round them up. Belle and Tarquin were already safely locked in. She could relax and go in and have her evening meal.

She heard a sound from the barn and sighed.

Not now, she wished, a fervent wish she knew would be denied. She walked across the yard, longing for rest, for a chance to sit and drink a cup of tea and maybe eat a sandwich. She was always so hungry. There was never time now she was on her own to do a big baking that would save her from the need to make frequent small meals.

She switched on the light in the big barn where Mervyn had built a farrowing pen. She ran, wishing she was not so clumsy. Ceri was a sow to end all sows, stupid to the point of utter idiocy. The first piglet was almost born, his head and shoulders protruding. His presence was plainly irritating his mother. As she tried to slap the itch under her tail against the side of her pen, Louise was just in time to catch the mite and save it from certain death. She put it down in the straw. She could never watch the sows give birth without laughing at the little pigs, who, as soon as they arrived, bright eyed, stood, then raced round this huge creature that had just brought them into the world staring at her in total amazement.

This was Ceri's fifth litter. She always started the same way, uneasy and almost panicking. If her owners were not quick the firstborn often died, but the presence of a human beside her pen seemed to settle her. She dropped in the straw.

She looked up at Louise, taking her presence for granted. She grunted.

"I loathe you, do you know that?" Louise told her, some hours later, after looking at her watch. Three in the morning. Farmers must all be mad. Other people worked nine to five for five days a week and then went home and slept. There was one blessing – another night had passed. Maybe tomorrow Mervyn would walk in, laughing as if he had never been away.

Hunger called her, but there might be another little pig to make its way into the world whose life could end immediately if she left the sow. Once they were all born their mother was safe with them. Louise needed the money they would bring. Even one piglet dying was not only a small disaster but a commercial tragedy. She had never been so penny conscious.

Mervyn had arranged the pen so that Ceri could not lie on her young. Unless they crawled beneath her. They would be transferred to roomier quarters when the little pigs were three days old and less likely to be accidentally smothered by the giant sow.

"You're the stupidest animal I've ever known and quite the worst mother. Get on with it. I'm starving."

There were eleven small piglets now lying in the straw, fighting for teats. Ceri had had fifteen before now. Louise yawned, and then was startled as a strange noise in the darkest corner of the barn, among the piled bales, suddenly exploded into a joyous uncontrollable laugh.

She grabbed a pitchfork, which was the nearest thing to a weapon she could see. She was alone and heaven only knew who was hidden in the hay.

Two

F ear seemed to have dried Louise's throat.
       Her voice sounded strange as she called out,
"Who's there? What are you doing? Come out, and let me
see you."

A large figure emerged from behind the piled bales that she
had brought in from the fields. These were not wrapped in
plastic which had made her task of moving the hay easier.

"I'm sorry. I'm Jason Grant . . . I didn't mean any harm. It
was warm in the straw and doorways are chilly these September nights. I've been abusing your hospitality at night for
the past three weeks. I couldn't help laughing. Do you always
talk to pigs?"

Although he was tall and solidly built, he was only a boy,
about sixteen, Louise guessed. The dark hair had been
roughly trimmed. There was no threat in the long almond-
shaped brown eyes. The bones of his face promised a man who
would attract many a woman and make her yearn and dream.

"Have you no home to go to?" Louise asked.

"Another piglet coming," he said, and watched as Louise
supervised, making sure the little one was safe from his
mother's clumsiness.

"Look, will you trust me? I can't do anything for your
sow . . . I don't know enough, but you've been here for hours,
and with the baby coming you must be half dead. Everyone
knows about your husband . . . it's tough. I could make you a
drink and a sandwich if you let me have the run of your
kitchen. I'm clean and tidy and I've been running my gran's

home and then my dad's for the past four years. I'm not going to take anything from you and then run off."

She stared at him in astonishment, listening to the words that spilled from his mouth, as if he had urgent need of speech. Had he been alone up here all this time, she wondered? If so, what had he eaten?

The large canvas chair that Louise had put beside the pen the day before was becoming uncomfortable. Thank goodness it wasn't a deckchair. That would be impossible. She'd never have got out of it. She smiled at the thought of herself struggling in vain. She dared not sit on the low settee any more. It required a major gymnastic effort to get up from it.

Her father-in-law had bought the chair when he retired. A director's chair, he said, and I'm going to be telling you what to do. In fact, he had rarely made any suggestions and they had been glad to ask him for advice, of which he had a vast store after years of experience. She still missed him, and her mother-in-law too. They had been a great team. Her own parents had both died soon after she and Mervyn married, lost in a plane crash coming home from their first holiday abroad. At least they'd had the holiday. They had just sold their farm and retired.

Her mother-in-law had been a great comfort, and they had got on very well together. The younger couple had their own flat over the cow byres until the old man died, and then they moved into the house, making two rooms into a separate apartment for Mervyn's mother. She'd have been so delighted at the thought of a baby. Ah well, Louise thought. No use regretting.

Another piglet made his way into the world and gazed at her. She had an absurd notion that he probably thought she was his mother and grinned, wondering if she would have a little pig to add to the small menagerie that followed her when she let them. Pigs were so intelligent. Mervyn had taught one youngster to jump tiny hurdles in the early years of their marriage. He had also ridden one of the bullocks.

"You've married a crazy man," her father-in-law, old Ceredig had said, but he was, she suspected, secretly proud of his son's strange antics.

The sow wasn't finished yet. Louise longed for sleep and needed food badly. The boy was company. Maybe she was a fool but she had to trust him.

Jason was back in an amazingly short time. The kettle was always hot, sitting on the Aga, and he had brought mugs of coffee for both of them. He had found a tray and on it was milk and sugar as well as some of the neatest ham sandwiches, made from the ham she had cooked the night before, and there was mustard in an egg cup as well.

"I didn't know if you liked it."

He had also brought a rug which he put round her.

"It's not very warm and you can't afford a chill," he said. He grinned at her expression. "My gran brought me up; I had to care for her after her stroke. She made sure I knew when she felt cold and needed an extra rug. Second nature. I once thought I'd be a nurse, but nurses don't get well paid, and people still consider it an odd profession for a man. Can't think why."

He was unlike any lad of his age Louise had ever met. Responsibility made you grow up fast, she thought.

She spread the mustard liberally. She had the oddest cravings these days.

"You've done very well," she said, wondering at the speed and dexterity with which he had cut bread and meat.

"I've been doing part-time work as a chef . . . well sort of chef, in a tiny caff run by a friend of my gran's," he said. "It's just a lorry pull up, really. Nothing grand, but the boss always says they deserve well-cooked food all the same, like anybody else. She's a tartar, but the money helped no end, especially since I had to look after my dad."

"Is he an invalid?"

"No. He's an alcoholic."

He obviously did not want to pursue the subject. He seemed to have no intention whatever of going home.

"Can you leave her when she's had them all? Are there any more to come? Can you tell?" he asked, and hesitated, eyeing the plate which contained more than enough for two people. He had not attempted to take any of the food.

"Go on. Help yourself," she said, with her mouth full, wondering if all pregnant women felt the need to eat as if they had not been fed for months.

She was rewarded with a brilliant smile that lit his face.

"I hoped you'd say that."

"May I ask just what you're doing in my barn and why you have nowhere to go?" Louise asked.

"It's a long story."

"We seem to have the rest of the night." Louise yawned as she supervised yet another little pig as it emerged.

"My mum had me when she was sixteen. She did marry my dad, but the two of them were a disaster. Went dancing and drinking and left me alone when I was only a few weeks old. So my gran brought me up. Only she died eighteen months ago. She'd had a stroke and only me to look after her, mostly. She could get about the house and garden a bit and didn't want to go into a home, and I didn't want her to." He stopped, frowning as if he did not like the memory. "Not nice for my gran. It was a council house and when she died I had to go to my dad. Nowhere else to go. He didn't want me . . . but it was that or nowhere. I'm too old to be taken into care. Nobody bothers about you. I wasn't going into town and a hostel. My mum upped and left long ago."

As he bent forward, Louise noticed the fading bruise around his left eye. Though there was lighting in the barn, it was dim, one of the bulbs having failed. She dared not risk climbing a ladder to replace it. She had brought in an extra hand lamp to ensure that she could see well.

"I've spent eighteen months clearing up after a hopeless drunk. Three weeks ago I'd had enough. I left school as soon as I was sixteen. Had to, or I wouldn't have eaten. Dad didn't want me, and never gave me a penny, though he was glad

16

enough to have me clean up the house and cook when he felt like eating."

He ate another sandwich and Louise wondered if he had been feeding himself properly. He was far too thin.

"I cooked for him but he never ate it. Sometimes he threw it at me. I'd had enough. I saw your barn when I was walking on the moors. Have you seen the mare? She's wonderful."

He had an odd habit of skipping suddenly to some unrelated subject. Conversations with Jason, she was to discover, could be very odd indeed.

The night and the isolation bred confidences. Jason had convinced her of his honesty and also of his competence.

"She's wonderful," Louise said. "I always stop to talk to her when I go to the Keepgate for the post. She knows me and shouts to me. You can't ignore her."

"She greets me too," Jason said. "Her foal must be about due."

"Within the month, I think. How old are you?"

"I'll be seventeen in January. Gran wanted me to stay on, try for university, make something of my life but there was no chance of me getting decent marks. Not with her and then my dad to look after. I had a chat with the headmaster. He thinks I'm caring for the old man. I told him he had Alzheimer's. But after that last week . . . he can rot, for all I care. It's not my job to look after him."

"Are you looking for work?"

His lips twitched.

"Yes, ma'am. As your farmhand. I can learn anything you teach me, and you can't stay up here alone with a baby coming . . . I'm sorry, but it's obvious, isn't it? By the time it does come I ought to be able to caretake while you're away. Had you thought of that? And who's going to send for an ambulance? Or maybe a helicopter, when the birth begins? Winter here can be dodgy . . . especially if it snows."

Louise stared at him, wondering if he had had all this worked out before he revealed himself, perhaps planning to

17

apply one day. The village was small and everyone seemed to know everyone else's business.

"Whoops," Jason said. "Her ladyship's going to brain that one."

Ceri was on her legs again. Surely this must be the last? Louise removed the offending piglet before the sow could swing her hindquarters round, and sighed.

Jason intended to make the most of his opportunity. Though born in the village, he loved the countryside. He was determined to make a good impression.

"You need sleep. I can do things like cleaning out sties without being taught, and save you the bother. And you can tell me where the chicken feed is. I can take that chore over and collect the eggs. Bet it's not comfortable, bending down. I can go on sleeping in the barn." He grinned at her, desperate to make her agree. "I'm clean, tidy, good about the house. I learn fast, work hard and I'm strong as Samson, ma'am. You can't afford not to have me stay."

"If you do, there's a flat above the cowsheds." Louise said. "We lived there when we first married. It's in fairly good condition and the roof doesn't leak."

He could decorate it, she thought, which he would enjoy, and have furniture from our spare rooms. Maybe she was crazy but she was going to give him the job. Huw would have said that beggars couldn't be choosers. She needed help so desperately and this boy was old for his age and seemed responsible. Also he was cheerful and made her laugh. She needed that too.

"Look," he said. "You don't know me, but I can bring references; or you can go and see the people I've worked for. I'm a good gardener and a good cook. I'm honest and hard working. I was my gran's carer for twelve months when she could barely move. I cooked and cleaned for both of them." He grinned at her again, but his eyes were pleading. "I've dreamed of working on a farm, all my life. I love animals. I can look after dogs and cats, but I've not tried any of this lot. My dad's put me off drink for life and I don't drug."

"You're on," Louise said. "Why didn't the dogs bark at you?"

Their announcement of visitors was usually vociferous, and anyone coming to the farmyard was greeted with a raucous welcome that many distrusted.

"I took care to come here only at night," he said. "I watched till your lights went out. I've been working in the caff all day. And they fed me. I come over the fields, well away from the house. The dogs haven't heard me. They've been safely indoors."

Her room was at the back of the house, away from this barn. She suddenly felt vulnerable. She could think of nothing to say. He seemed to have worked everything out, and to be a survivor.

"I'll rig up an alarm so you can call me if you need me. I'm good with electrics. And I can cook for both of us. I thought at one time I'd try hotel work and be a chef . . . but it means living in and I don't like too many people around me. Crushing me in. You've space here."

"There's an intercom phone in the flat. It's probably still connected. I can get through to you so we don't need an alarm."

It was daybreak before Louise dared to leave Ceri on her own. Jason cooked bacon and eggs and fried bread and made her promise to sleep.

"Can I ring the caff? Tell them I won't be in any more. My boss knew I hoped to try and get a job here. Thought it was a good idea, with you on your own and the baby coming, like. Told her I was coming up here. Didn't tell her I slept here, though."

An hour later, Louise lay, listening to sounds from the yard: to Jason's voice as he spoke to the dogs, who followed him as if they had known him all their lives, to the trundle of the wheelbarrow, and then a snatch of song, hurriedly choked off as he remembered that she was resting. Life was very odd, she thought, and wondered if perhaps a guardian angel had been watching over her and had provided her with such unlikely help. If he proved really useful, he could stay on when Mervyn came home. She refused to contemplate any other alternative.

Jason, noting jobs that needed doing, the tractor that he would have to learn to drive, the end stable that needed repair, and the animals that surrounded him, felt as if his own dreams had come true. This was the life he had longed for. He had every intention of making himself so indispensable that Louise would employ him permanently. His father would never think of looking for him here.

Three

T here was, Jason quickly discovered, a great deal more to farming than feeding animals and cleaning up. There was so much he had not seen, and did not know. The farm, by day, was new territory. He had taken great care never to arrive at the barn before midnight and to leave just before five a.m., in case Louise appeared. Farmers always got up at dawn, and he did not know if there was a milking herd. It was a three-mile walk to the village, which had taken him just under an hour. Jason's employer had provided him with all his meals, in return for which he had been paid somewhat less than the average wage.

The village was a tiny place, with only two thousand inhabitants. There was a doctor's surgery, a lock up, manned every morning, at one end of the main street of drab grey houses while the vet was at the other end. Apart from the post office, there was only the village shop, which boasted the name of the Mini Mart, and sold staple goods and had a deep freeze, but its stock was limited, and it could not compete with the supermarket which was ten miles away. It was open from six a.m., when the papers were delivered, until ten p.m. Next door to it was the little café where Jason had worked. The doctors had their own dispensary, which ensured that those without transport could be supplied with medicines without difficulty. Most people drove to the small town twelve miles away, although there was a bus service every morning and evening. A library van, a travelling butcher and a fish van called weekly, stopping outside the

21

café which was helped by their presence. There was a small estate of bungalows, inhabited by those who, for the most part, had retired from English towns, and two rows of council houses.

In spite of the long night, Louise was up after only two hours' rest. Jason had been exploring and was puzzled. There was a din from one of the sheds, but he had no key for the padlock. The noise rose to a level he hadn't believed possible, caused, he thought, by a number of ducks.

Jason cleaned out an empty pigsty, which had housed Ceri the day before. She had been moved into the barn before he had arrived back from the café, and he had been surprised to see her there. He felt that mucking out was one job at least that couldn't be done wrongly. He did not know the routine and had no desire to make a serious mistake on his first day.

Louise was dressed in dark trousers and a loose smock, her curly chestnut hair caught back into a pony tail by a rubber band. A small woman, just over five foot three, and normally very slim, she looked out of proportion when the smock clung to her body. It would get worse, she thought, as she looked in the mirror. She could not afford clothes that would hide her shape; she had to make do with trousers and smocks as she dared not waste money.

She opened the chicken-house door and let the hens into the yard, scattering corn for them. They were hungry, feeding time being long overdue, and within seconds were fighting for the food. The dogs, sitting quietly by the kitchen door, watched, Fern with her tongue hanging out, Mott with his head on one side. They also needed food. They joined her as she crossed the yard again to another shed and opened the door, fastening the padlock to its chain.

This was plainly a daily occurrence as out came a half-grown lamb with black legs that matched his black head, followed more sedately by a large ewe, who stopped to nose Fern as she came through the door.

The greeting over, Jason was amused to see Louise hugging the ram lamb, who butted her for attention. Fern followed behind the ewe, and then came the ram, who ran up to his mother and tried to feed. Mott guarded the rear, making sure none of them turned and escaped across the yard.

Belle butted her son irritably and moved across to the far edge of the grass and began to graze.

"I waste too much time watching them," Louise said, turning away reluctantly.

She led the way down the yard. Jason had not realised how big this was. There was room for at least a hundred cows in the huge area. The second barn was smaller, and a temporary pen had been made by the simple expedient of surrounding the sleeping area with piled bales of straw.

"Meet Dopey. She never knows which are her babies and which aren't. Also, she never has more than a couple. She's a wonderful mother, unlike Ceri, who appears to suffer them stoically. Dopey's never happier than when she has tiny piglets around her."

"But she's a pot-bellied pig. And why Dopey? It's an awful name."

"I didn't choose it. Someone in the village bought her for the children and she grew too big for their home, to their surprise, but not to anyone else's!" Louise laughed. "When she's free from her family cares she's another of my followers; she's as clever as the dogs, and follows me whenever she can."

The two tiny pot-bellied piglets were a week older than Ceri's youngsters, and dwarfed them. Dopey, quite happy to let the extra three suckle, looked up at Louise and grunted. Louise grunted back.

"She's used to people and very chatty. Would you believe they made her a den in the house, in the corner of the dining room, where she had a large kennel and straw."

"Doesn't sound hygienic," Jason said.

"She's house trained. Pigs are as clean as any well-taught dog. We have to let her out five times a day into the paddock beyond the barn. She wouldn't dream of soiling her quarters." She scratched Dopey on the nose. "It doesn't sound much of a job but it does take time, and she often wants to wander round and have a nose into everything instead of doing all she should. Worse than a dog. I keep her outside in summer, and she's out in the yard all day when she doesn't have babies to look after."

They went out, Louise shutting the door behind her. Fern, agitated, pawed at her mistress's leg.

"Oh, Lord," she said. "I haven't let the ducks out. And they need feeding. And I've no bread for Demon. So watch out."

Fern and Mott were both waiting by the door as she opened the shelter. The ducks exploded into the yard, racing for the pond. Demon, eyes only for Louise, ran to her and pecked determinedly at her wellingtons. Mott barked at him, trying to drive him off and he flew at the dog and then returned to his original target, who was leaning against the gate by the pond, laughing, as the drake continue to rain blows on her leg. Not only had she failed to let him out hours before, but she was also intent on starving him. He did not intend to forgive her.

Jason, deciding that matters needed remedying fast, ran to the kitchen and brought a large chunk of bread from the table. He threw it, and Demon, seeing it soar through the air, half flew, half ran and began to attack it with as much fervour as he had attacked Louise's boot.

"Thanks. I think we'll eat. I didn't bother with breakfast, as we ate during the night, but I'm starving now. This fellow is always demanding food." She patted her tummy.

"Doesn't the drake hurt?" Jason asked.

"He's not usually as bad as that, and he does it with a closed beak. I'll probably have a bruise or two. We were to blame, forgetting to let them out."

They went into the kitchen. Louise took two packs of

sandwiches from the freezer and put them in the micro-wave.

"Easiest way of coping when I'm alone," she said. "It's simple to make up packs like this, it takes much more time to bake pies and pasties. I used to do that when Huw and Mervyn were here. There was more than enough work for three of us."

"Things change fast." Jason took the sandwiches out of the microwave and put them on a plate while Louise made coffee for both of them.

"If there's time I'll make you a Sunday evening meal to remember," he said. "Never had the chance to spread my wings."

Louise shelled a hard-boiled egg that she had taken from the refrigerator and passed another to Jason.

"I need to shop. We've run out of fresh fruit, and I like to have some on hand when hunger strikes. With you here we'll need more bread, as well as everything else."

Jason wanted to learn everything he could about the farm.

"Do you sell your eggs? You must sometimes have surplus eggs when they're all laying?"

"There's never time to grade and box them and take them to the shop. I feed them to the pigs and the dogs. I can make loads of omelettes for us. Never any shortage of empty mouths here. I keep a dozen or so hard-boiled in the fridge and then if I'm tired I have an easy meal, or make sandwiches. Luckily I adore egg mayonnaise."

"What about milk? You don't have a milking cow?"

"I milk the goats and any cow that has a calf and lets me. Mostly we breed calves to sell on. We gave up our milking herd last year and thank heavens we did, or I'd be in real trouble. There aren't enough hours in any day as it is."

"Don't you have any more pigs?"

"Russell . . . he's our vet . . . arranged for most of my sows to go to a farm across the valley to foster for me. The

25

farmer has the piglets as his fee. Both goats have kids so it doesn't matter if they aren't milked and all the cows have calves, so that's another unnecessary chore, unless one of them has mastitis. There's one we call Trouble for very good reason."

"What earned her the name?"

Louise laughed.

"Her mother had immense trouble calving and had to have a Caesarian. The calf didn't thrive and we had a huge vet bill before she was well. She had practically every ailment a calf can get. She even managed to have pneumonia. I spent hours nursing her. I hate animals dying on me."

She paused to make two more mugs of coffee. Jason liked three spoonfuls of sugar, and Louise remembered to add it before she passed the mug to him.

"Trouble went on as she began. The difficult calving must be inherited as she had immense problems with her own first calf, but she wouldn't allow anyone near her. I ought to cull her, but somehow . . ."

"You're too soft hearted," Jason said.

"Not really. It's just that I hate getting rid of any of the animals while Mervyn's away. I want them here when he comes home again."

The animal feed stocks needed constant checking, Louise told Jason.

"We used to make a lot of our own." She sighed. "I've had to get commercial feeds in. Mervyn has a recipe of his grandfather's for cattle feed. It contains molasses. The cows go mad for it. I won't be able to make it this winter, and we won't have enough hay. Luckily the grass is still growing and we don't need to supplement yet."

"Do you collect swill for the pigs?"

"No. That's not done any more. There are so many new regulations, mostly from Brussels. It's hard to keep track. I feed potatoes to them if I've time to deal with them . . . and cooked peelings. But they really do need a balanced diet, or you have a lack of vitamins and minerals and then get a lot of trouble."

"Like us," Jason said. "I hope you're eating properly. My gran used to be really pernickety about food. 'Plenty of fruit and vegetables and only the best meat, my boy, and no skimping meals.'"

"Your gran sounds a character," Louise said.

"She was. How do you get to the village? Can you still drive?"

"Just about. I soon won't fit behind the steering wheel. Mervyn has a mountain bike . . . you could use that. It wouldn't take long to cycle from here. Can you ride a bike?"

Jason's eyes showed his excitement.

"A mountain bike? Could I? I can fit panniers and take over a lot of the shopping. Maybe you could get a taxi once a month for the rest. We can get meat on Mondays from the travelling butcher and fish on Fridays. I know the fishmonger . . . he was a pal of my gran's. He'd bring in any vegetables and fruit we ordered. Her at the caff would keep it in her fridge for me to collect."

"Can you feed Dopey?" Louise asked some time later, having battled with Ceri, who had developed a ravenous appetite and sent the feed flying out of Louise's hands all over her piglets.

Jason went into the barn, and climbed over the bales, intending to put down the bucket and empty it into the trough. Dopey did not know him, and as he approached she charged, afraid he had designs on her small family. He fell backwards against one of the bales, hitting his head against the corner of a table that held hand lamps and a large sealed cardboard box. He clambered hastily out of range, leaving the pail on the ground. Dopey knocked it over, and began to feed.

While she was busy he retrieved the bucket, and went back to the farmhouse, wondering how he could tackle that problem in the future. Farm animals seemed to produce hazards for the unwary. He had a headache and a lump on his forehead.

"I forgot she didn't know you," Louise said, filled with remorse. "I'd better feed her next time. Meanwhile, talk to her every day. Once you start grunting at her, she'll accept you as a friend."

And I'll be as nutty as you are, Jason thought, grinning to himself, imagining the scene, as he watched the night-time procession of ducks and drake led into their shelter, and safely locked up.

Tarquin was not eager to be penned, and dodged behind Louise, apparently convinced that the dogs would play tag with him too.

Fern nipped him, and he bleated.

"That's not on," Louise told the bitch. But the chastisement had had an effect and the ram followed his mother into the partitioned shed. Louise fastened the padlock.

At last Jason was free to inspect his new quarters. The flat over the old cow byres was dusty and he would have to work on it. Louise lent him a sleeping bag which he put on top of a mattress he had taken off one of the spare-room beds. The place needed cleaning. It needed decorating. It needed furnishing. But it was warm and dry and far more comfortable than the straw in the barn.

Even better it was his own. His home, to decorate as he chose, to live in by himself, without needing to worry about anyone else and above all, without needing to look after his father. He must find time to collect his clothes, which were in holdalls at the café.

He now had the kind of job he had always wanted. He liked Louise and the animals were fun. Before he fell asleep he surprised himself by wishing he could tell his gran. She would have been delighted.

He had a sudden memory of her, long ago, insisting that he knelt by his bed and pray aloud. Thank God for all his mercies, she always said. He felt guilty because that was a habit he had given up long ago. But tonight, he was almost inclined to do so. Luck had been a long time coming, but it had come, at last. Before he had time to put his decision into practice, he was asleep.

Four

L ittle pigs grow fast and as they grew they managed to develop voices that drowned every other sound on the farm. They squealed if they lost a teat. They squealed if they were pushed off a teat. Ceri, developing an appetite that increased daily, also squealed if Louise or Jason were late with her feed.

"What on earth does a large-scale pig unit sound like?" Jason asked, at the end of his third day.

"Probably nothing like this." Louise was grooming the dogs, who had been persuaded to stand on a small table. "For one thing, they probably all have the type of feeding that produces food when the pig pushes a button. So there's no need for them to wait, and food won't be late. I'm always late with everything these days. I feel like a donkey chasing its tail."

The next few days convinced Louise that she had indeed been fortunate. Jason was an enthusiast, and for the first time in his short life was doing something that he enjoyed whole-heartedly.

He had so much energy he could clean out sties and hen-houses more quickly even than Mervyn. He moved fast, yet remembered never to startle the animals, slowing when he saw any of them near him. The dogs trusted him: their instincts were always sound.

He learned quickly and soon took over many of her farm-yard chores. Louise laughed at his outraged shouts when he forgot to carry a piece of bread for Demon, and was thoroughly pecked because he had no food in his hand.

"He's a horror," Jason said, indignant at his treatment by such a small creature.

"We spoiled him," Louise said. "It was ridiculous. The duck wouldn't brood her eggs and Mervyn put them in the incubator. Only one hatched – Demon – and Mervyn brought the duckling indoors to keep him warm." She laughed at a sudden memory. "Would you believe, my idiot husband, who thinks he's as tough as nails, used to put him in the bath to practise swimming before letting him go out into the big wide world and venture on to the pond?"

She had a sudden vision of Mervyn walking across the yard, a minute Demon waddling behind him, followed by the two dogs and a much smaller Tarquin.

"I think Demon thought that Mervyn was his mother. He was a ridiculous little object. We got into the bad habit of rewarding him with titbits if he came willingly to be locked up at night, as he thought he was destined to live in the house forever. Somehow it escalated . . . and now we have a monster!"

"I'll remember to keep bits of bread in my pockets," Jason said. "Surprising how hard that beak is."

He became as anxious about Tarquin and the ewe as Louise herself, reminding her constantly of Mervyn, who had checked on them a dozen times a day.

He insisted that Louise gave up all the heavy work, and rested in the afternoon, promising to call her at once if there was something he couldn't handle. Her rests were seldom longer than an hour, but she did try to do as he suggested. Her ankles were beginning to swell by evening and the doctor had read her the riot act.

"You don't want to crack up and spend several weeks in hospital before the baby's born," he'd said. "I know there's a lot to do on the farm, especially with your husband away, but try and cut down your own input."

She in turn insisted that Jason took at least two half days off during the week and went to the village, using

31

the mountain bike that Mervyn had never had time to ride.

By the end of September she felt as if he had been there for ever, instead of just over three weeks. He came in one morning for his eleven o'clock break as she was marking the calendar.

"What's that for? Your birthday today?"

She shook her head.

"That's in June. I suddenly felt like keeping track. The baby's due around January fourth. And it's fifteen weeks since Mervyn vanished. It seems much longer, but it isn't really any time at all."

People missing in various war zones turned up after far longer than that, she thought, looking at the red ring round June 16th.

"And there's no news." Jason poured hot water on to instant coffee, and brought the cup across to Louise. "He's not a hostage . . . or I wouldn't think so. They'd have been in touch before now. Always want something, that sort do."

Louise sighed.

"I can't believe he's dead. I expect him to walk in, like the dogs do, every time I hear a car outside . . ."

Jason had been watching the dogs. Mott had given up and no longer reacted, but Fern, like Louise, was ever hopeful and always ran to the gate. He knew now that Fern had been Mervyn's and Mott attached to Louise. The dog was lying by her chair, and he shadowed her when she was working. Fern always lay by Mervyn's chair, as if her presence there might bring him home. She sometimes followed Jason, as if hoping he might lead her to her lost master.

"When the baby's born can you teach me how to herd the sheep with the dogs?" Jason asked. He had to fetch Louise whenever they needed moving, as neither dog obeyed him. He enjoyed watching her, listening to the shrill whistles, seeing the two collies working in harmony, bringing the sheep from one field to another, as the grass needed resting and time to grow again. The sheep were shifted, he discovered, every two weeks.

There were twelve fields, only six of which were occupied. Two were grazed by the cattle, and the others in rotation.

"I'm out of practice as far as trials go," she said. "Mervyn and I competed against one another. I've never beaten him yet. It's not the same as working the sheep on the hills. I've not had time."

"When do the rams go in with the ewes?" Jason asked. There were several rams in separate paddocks. Put together, they fought, Louise told him.

"Not till the end of November. We lamb late here, around the end of April and in May, when the weather's better. We'd have losses due to the cold otherwise, and we haven't yet got round to a proper lambing shed. Another thing on the list."

To Jason's amusement Belle and Tarquin did not need dogs to be shifted from one paddock to another. They were always near the house, and Louise only had to call them and they trotted after her, though Mott and Fern made sure they did not escape on the way.

He watched Louise's moods and if she felt sad, he told her silly jokes and made her laugh. He was observant, and soon noticed jobs that needed doing. He repaired fences, and coped with a backlog of work that Mervyn would have done, but which she had been unable to tackle.

"I wish we could do the hedges," Louise said, looking at the untidy summer growth. "We'll just have to pretend we're in Cornwall and let them grow into high lanes. When the baby's born I'll teach you to drive the tractor . . . but I don't think it'd be a good idea for me to drive it myself now."

Life seemed to have settled into a bearable routine.

The third week in October brought an end to a late summer, with high wind and heavy rain. Kane Merrit phoned to say that two of the sheep had escaped into the lane. He had them in one of his paddocks. He knew the marks on their backs: BM which stood for Bryn Mawr farm. Jason discovered a break in a fence at the far end of the farm near the river.

Louise took the dogs and brought the strays back and put

them in the top field while Jason collected his tools and went off, whistling. She went indoors to remove her wet clothing and make herself tea. There was an hour before they needed to lock up the ducks and the Suffolks.

Kane Merrit had decided that afternoon to add another kennel block to his property. He had divided the barns into indoor accommodation for the dogs, who were exercised in the paddocks. His passion for animals had grown over the years. He had longed, when young, to breed Jersey cows, having fallen in love with a herd of the beautiful animals that lived in the fields a mile away from his home. He had spent all his time there. He had no desire to work for someone else and realised, with reluctance, that owning his own herd was an impossible dream. Neither he nor his family could raise the necessary capital to buy the stock. Instead, he became a vet, and worked with many men's cattle and other animals.

He had been married once, but his wife could not bear the hours spent alone. When she left, taking their two sons with her, he filled his home with animals that nobody wanted.

He found the cottage one day just before he finally sold his practice. It was a small place, with convenient outbuildings, on the land of one of his major clients. He had always enjoyed making small pieces of furniture in the little spare time he had and now he built cages and kennels and an aviary, and found himself with a variety of creatures in need of homes, many due to injuries sustained on the roads.

The farm, half a mile from him, along a tortuous track, was the only building in sight, and he had no desire for company. He was horrified by the news of Mervyn's disappearance and felt he ought to go and console Louise, but had no idea how to do so. He wondered how she would fare when the child was born and thought of offering help around the time of the birth, but he was afraid she might resent his intrusion. She would have made her own arrangements.

He was anxious about the mare. He was sure she was overdue, but he had bought her from a man who had neglected her and who had not even known she was in foal. Only time had revealed that. Kane had paid little for her. Either that or the owner would be reported. It had taken weeks to restore her to full health.

She was kept in the field by the river, close to his cottage. Hopefully the foal would be born in the next few days.

Jason, busy with the fence, two fields away from the cottage, saw the mare move slowly and awkwardly, and was almost sure she was giving birth. He lifted his head as a helicopter flew over, very low, a much larger machine than usually came their way.

The mare, terrified by the noise and the sight of the monster in the sky, bolted towards the stream. She broke through the retaining fence, knocking down post and wire, which luckily did not trip her.

The foal slipped from her, rolled down the bank and into the water. Kane, hearing the flying hooves, raced out of the door, and ran towards her. He slipped, catching his foot in a trailing bramble and fell, awkwardly and heavily, his leg hitting an unseen rock. Pain knifed through him and, as he tried to stand, he knew the bone was broken, probably in two places. Angry with himself for his haste and lack of foresight, he swore comprehensively and furiously. The stream was shallow, but the foal could not yet stand and would drown.

For the first time since he had come to live in the hills Kane regretted his isolation. It was unlikely that anyone would be about. He would have to phone for help and that alone was going to be a major problem, as he could only crawl, and that with extreme difficulty. It would take hours to cover the distance to his cottage and then he would somehow have to stand to fit the key in the lock. It would be agonising.

Jason saw Kane fall, climbed the gate and ran, terrified, expecting to find a corpse. It was hard going over bramble and heather. Kane, far from dead, was furiously angry, and, knowing he was unjust, took out his wrath on his helper.

"Never mind me. The foal will drown."

Jason looked down at the broken leg which lay at an angle that worried him.

"You need help."

Kane cursed vigorously, sure he had met with an idiot who had no sense of priorities. He had not met Louise's new farmhand before.

"I'm not going to die if I don't get this seen to in the next hour or so. Get on with it, you imbecile, and don't just stand there. Leave me be. I might as well be here as in casualty on some damned trolley while they make up their minds how to slot me in. Get going, will you?"

Had he been fit it would have been a shout, but Jason still recognised the man's imperative need.

He raced to the river. The mare, standing bemused on the bank, looked down at her baby in the water. His small body was covered, but he had lifted his head clear of the stream. At least he was alive. He moved his head, his muzzle only just clear of the surface. Jason slid in faster than he had intended, cursing the mud and wondering if he and the foal could get out again. He was soaked to just below the knees. He managed to get his arms round the little animal, and push him on to the bank.

It took several minutes for Jason to struggle out of the water. He slipped back time and again as there was no purchase in the mud, but at last he managed to haul himself on to the wet grass.

The small body was limp. Jason took off his anorak and then his jersey and began to rub. The mare, as if recognising that he needed help, bent her head to lick. He stared down at the foal, sure he had died.

"Shake him. Make sure he's breathing," Kane yelled, impelled by fury at his own inability to come to the rescue.

Startled, Jason did as he was told, feeling that this was an impossible situation. The mare stared at him, her eyes astounded. He wondered if she would attack him for such rough treatment of her baby, but she was too exhausted to move.

Jason laid his charge on the ground. There was a sudden gasp and a sneeze.

"Bring him here."

That was less easy as the foal was heavy and Jason was afraid of tripping and injuring himself. That would mean trouble, as Louise was not likely to look for him here. The mare followed, anxious.

"Lie him down beside me. I can use my hands. Here, take my keys. Find me towels to rub him dry. This is no time for him to chill."

Kane was rubbing the soft hide. The foal, aware now of the world around him, was too weak to lift himself. He lay, unafraid of the ministering hands.

Jason, soaked and uncomfortable, ran to the cottage and opened the door. His presence produced a furore of barking, which startled him. In heaven's name, how many dogs were there? Although he knew time was precious he could not leave without notifying the ambulance services. The telephone stood on a small hall table. He dialled 999.

"Up there? You need a helicopter. You're sure his leg's broken?"

"I've never seen a leg at that angle before," Jason said, impatient to be off again. He tried to phone Louise, but she was busy putting the Suffolks in their night-time refuge and was out of earshot. She needed a mobile phone, Jason thought, not knowing that Louise had cancelled theirs, as the monthly payments were a drain on her finances.

Shock . . . keep the patient warm. He took the duvet off the narrow bed, rolled it up to make it easy to carry, and then hunted around for large towels.

He was an intruder and felt as if he were burgling. It seemed wrong to search through someone else's cupboards. The only towel in the little bathroom was far too small for the job. There were more in the airing cupboard. He grabbed an armful.

There was a fire blazing in the comfortable sitting room. So many books about animals and their needs and illnesses. Jason's eyes brightened. Maybe he could borrow some when the old man was home again. There was a fireguard against the wall, and he put that in front of the flames. One worry the less.

What on earth would the man have done if nobody had been near him?

He raced back, to be greeted by a curse.

"What took you so long? God in heaven, why did I have to do this now? Give me those towels. Take one yourself and rub; rub with all your strength and get him warm or we'll lose him."

Jason put the duvet over Kane in spite of his protestations. It did not need the shivering, or the half-controlled chattering teeth to tell him that the man was in a great deal of pain. It was a very cold day, a foretaste of winter. Hypothermia was a risk for both man and foal. The ground was damp but Jason dared not move the injured man. How long would the helicopter take? Also Louise was on her own and needed him.

The foal ought to be put inside. Was there a stable here? He had not seen one. Did the mare live outside in all weathers? Could he manage to walk her up to the farm while carrying the youngster? Louise had warm quarters big enough for both. Meanwhile, rub.

"Would you like a hot drink?" Lots of sugar for shock, his gran always said.

"No. You can ring the ambulance service now. This is a hospital job."

"I rang."

He tried to fight of the feelings of dismay. Somebody had to look after the menagerie, and maybe the invalid. He had a feeling it would be him and Louise. Hospitals did not keep people in for very long these days; and how would the man cope?

"They're sending a helicopter," he said, frowning as he looked down at Kane.

"The vet ought to see that foal. There's a stable behind the

38

cottage. It's part of the first barn, but has its own door. Straw's down ready to put Corrie in tonight. Can you get Russell . . . Mr Trent . . . here?'

"He's due at our place to see one of cows. She has mastitis. Said he'd be up around five. It's just after four."

Jason wished he knew some first aid. There might be something he could do to make the man more comfortable, but he dared not touch him.

"The kennels and barns are full of animals. God help them. I never bargained on this. They haven't been fed yet."

"We'll take care of everything." Jason knew he was rash and was not at all sure how they'd manage. Louise was becoming tired, and doing less than she had even two weeks before, though possibly that was because Jason willingly took over as many of her chores as he could.

"There are a lot of animals in need of attention. Ask Russell if he can help out," Kane said, well aware that he had landed this youngster with a major responsibility as well as an enormous problem. "You don't think of the difficulties till something crazy happens," he added. He tried to stop his teeth chattering, cursing his body for its misbehaviour. He could not remember the last time he had needed a doctor. Illness and he were total strangers.

Clouds veiled the tops of the mountains. The rain had stopped, but more threatened. The wind blowing across the heather made Jason uneasy. Suppose that it strengthened so that the helicopter couldn't put down? Or a mist covered the hills. But you didn't get mist with wind.

"Lead Corrie to the stable. You'll have to carry the foal. She'll follow. He's trying to stand but he's not made it yet. She can't stay here. She'll bolt when the helicopter comes, and probably injure herself. That would leave us in the soup."

Jason had never been so tired. His wet clothes clung to him and he began to shiver. The foal was an awkward burden and he had to put it down several times. Corrie stood patiently, watching this odd procedure.

The colt was heavy. The mare, placid and biddable, followed quietly, as if aware her baby was being taken to safety. The stable was dry and out of the wind. He added more straw, laying the foal where it was deep. With luck, the little animal would survive. He bolted the door on them, having made sure that the mare had hay in her net, and could reach it.

He went into the cottage to collect two sheets to lay out and make a marker for the helicopter as they might be hard to find.

Kane's small hold on his temper was rapidly leaving him. Even a hospital trolley in a warm corridor would be better than the cold ground and the wind that had an edge of frost in it. He swallowed, wanting to rant at the boy, but it was not his fault.

Jason paced the ground, unwilling to sit still, not knowing what to do or what to say, and worrying lest Louise thought he had walked out on her. It would soon be dark. How long before help came?

The waiting minutes seemed endless, but at last he heard the distant sound of the rescuers, and was thankful to surrender his patient to their far more professional care. Within an amazingly short time they were sky-borne again.

There was a crescendo of barking. He went back to the cottage, and opened the door of the first barn, to be almost deafened. It was divided into large pens in each of which was one of a number of dogs, all barking furiously. He counted heads. Fourteen of them, of all breeds and no breeds.

Dear heaven. What were they going to do with them? The second barn contained more than twenty cats, several with kittens, and at the far end, an aviary with a number of finches, as well as a mynah bird in a cage of his own, staring with angry eyes at this intruder. It must be long past feeding time. The noise was deafening.

Nobody had guessed the old man had a menagerie. They had heard distant barking, but never imagined it was caused by so many dogs.

40

Beyond the barns, well out of sight from the lane, were four small paddocks, where the animals must be exercised.

Another set of animals to care for. Dozens of them. Jason tried to fight of the feelings of dismay. He found a sack of dog biscuits and threw some into each compartment. There was also a sack of dry catfood. No time for feeding bowls. He threw handfuls to each occupant in the cat barn. The birds appeared to have seed in little bowls. What did mynahs eat? That would just have to go hungry till later. The vet would tell him, and hopefully they had something in the house that would do and he could bring down . . .

The sudden silence was a blessing. The food he had thrown to them seemed to have satisfied all the animals, but the mynah, indignant, began to beat his wings and shout.

"Hungry, hungry, hungry. Dogs hungry. Cats hungry. Damn bird hungry," he shouted. "Everything hungry. Be quiet, will you. Davie. Davie. Davie." It ended with two miaows, a bark, and the sound of a ringing telephone. Jason stared at it. It put its head on one side, and began to trill like a blackbird. A bird like that would drive him mad, Jason decided.

He went back into the cottage and looked about him, baffled. Meat? Eggs?

The refrigerator contained half a joint and eggs, butter and cheese. The old man would be in hospital for some time. Better take it all up to the farm and replace it when its rightful owner came home. It was a pity to let it go off.

There was a bowl of fruit on the kitchen table. Apples and bananas and oranges. Those too would go off. He fetched a carrier bag and loaded it, feeling as if he were stealing. None of that would keep.

After some thought he peeled two bananas, and took them and an apple and put them in the mynah's cage. The bird attacked one of the bananas greedily. Jason hoped he had not given it too much. Did birds get upset tummies? Suppose it was the wrong type of food and he killed it?

He stared at it unhappily, thinking how little he knew.

He had left work undone on the farm. The fence could not have waited, and he had had to leave other chores to make sure it was secure. There was a danger of more sheep being lost if it was not mended. Luckily he had finished that, though he would have to go back next day and collect his tools.

Louise would be frantic, wondering where he was. He dared not stop and feed Kane's charges properly now. He would have to come back later. His temporary measures had at least stopped the din.

He switched off the lights and locked up, thinking that it would be some time before the owner returned to his home. He started the climb back to the farm, wondering what Louise would have to say to him about such a long absence, and wondering too how she would greet the news of the many animals in the two barns.

There were times when life seemed impossible.

Five

Russell Trent looked down at the dog. It had been a long operation, as the lurcher's argument with a truck had caused immense damage. Brit was a cat chaser, and his owner had been unable to hold him as puss dived across the road. The cat ran free, but her pursuer was hit.

"Will he survive?"

Russell turned as his veterinary nurse spoke. She had been across to the house for sandwiches for both of them, as neither wished to leave the dog alone until he was well out of the anaesthetic and they were sure he was on the road to recovery.

Peta Hayes had worked for Russell for so long she was almost part of the family. He had inherited her when his father died. He hoped she would not ask to retire although she must be nearing sixty. Her work was her life. She lived in the flat above the surgery, waiting room and operating theatre. His father had bought the house next door and the two were connected by a long passage which separated work from home.

Kate, Russell's only daughter, said that Peta looked like a pug and that was why her grandfather had engaged her. He had owned a pug in his childhood and had loved the breed. Dark hair turning grey, snub-nosed and freckled, Peta's mere appearance gave confidence to anxious owners. She was invaluable when a long-loved pet had to be put to sleep for ever. Many remembered her kindness and sympathy and the long talk over a cup of coffee or tea in the little room she used as both office and sitting room.

43

"No internal injuries, which is a blessing. I don't know if
I've managed to put that front leg together again. I've never
seen anything so mangled. He's suffering major shock."

"I'll watch over him. You're due to go up to the Pritchards'
to see that cow."

"Louise would be well advised to get rid of that one."
Russell looked morose as he bit into his sandwich. "She well
deserves her name."

Trouble. She had been nothing but trouble since her
very difficult birth. He couldn't think why Louise kept
her. He looked out of the window at clouds building on
the mountains. He never tired of the view but today he
felt depressed and could not shake off a feeling of irritation.

"All quiet indoors?" he asked hopefully, and sighed when
he saw Peta's expression. Once he had enjoyed the weekends,
which were not so busy as weekdays, occasionally he even had
one completely free. Now he dreaded them.

"It could be worse, I suppose," Peta said. "Robin and Jock
aren't speaking which at least means they aren't shouting at
one another. They were both sitting at the table with sour
faces. Kate and your mother-in-law have had another row, so
Kate's in her bedroom, refusing to come down."

"And Roz? She's having to bear the brunt of all this. Is her
mother still bent on putting her house on the market?"

"She's done it. Roz says keep out of the way till this
evening. Robin's going out. So is Kate. Jock on his own isn't
too bad. And your ma-in-law has been invited to a meal with
her new crony, Mrs Dane."

"That's who gave Emma the idea of selling her house and
moving in with us and housekeeping for Roz so that she can
be free to work. What's worse, she has a buyer waiting, so it'll
be a quick sale. I wonder what other bright ideas she'll come
home with?"

Supplanting me and saving you my wages, Peta thought,
but didn't say it. Russell's mother-in-law had already made

one or two suggestions for improving their little hospital. She didn't mention that either.

Russell bent over the dog who was beginning to move restlessly.

"I'll wait till he's come round. He's not going to be very happy, poor fellow."

"I can stay with him all evening. I'll make myself some sandwiches and bring a book down. I've nothing to do to-night." She frowned. "I heard a worrying story in the village. There was a little group chatting in the post office."

"What was that?" Russell often wondered at the tales that were repeated, many without any foundation at all.

"That Louise has been married all these years without starting a family and isn't it odd that as soon as Mervyn is out of the way she becomes pregnant."

"That's wicked! And typical. There's always someone ready to dream up scandal. I hope she doesn't hear of it and that they don't start snubbing her. Life's bad enough for her as it is. I ought to go up more often but I'm so busy. Maybe it's as well she is keeping Trouble. I'm there professionally often enough, I suppose. Just think, Merv and I used to go fishing together." He sighed, pushing away a memory of a fast-flowing clear river, tree-lined green banks, trout rising, and a sharp pull on his rod. "Chance would be a fine thing. I wish there was something we could do to help Louise."

He bent to stroke the dog, who had lifted his head, and was trying to stand.

"There, there old fellow. Just settle." He frowned. "Did you say anything to the gossips?"

"I couldn't help myself. I pointed out that Mervyn dis-appeared on June sixteenth and the baby's due the first week in January. And that it's bad enough for Louise to be left like that without them making matters worse. I was so angry."

She flushed now at the thought of it. Russell grinned, visualising both her indignation and the discomfiture of those who bore the brunt of her fury. He kept his back turned to her. Peta could never bear injustice to man or beast. She might be very good with caring owners, but she flayed the careless and negligent with her tongue. People who left a dog in pain for days before deciding to come for treatment, and who then expected miracles, got short shrift from her.

"I'd better go up and see that cow," he said, half an hour later. "I like to call in on Louise anyway; then at least I can keep half an eye on her. Roz keeps meaning to go up too but life's been frantic since her father died."

"It's only six weeks," Peta said.

"That's why Emma should wait before plunging into action. She hasn't had time to settle again. Living with three teenagers isn't going to help. The children have all lost patience with her and she will keep criticising them. Kate's clothes and hairstyle, which I hate too but what can you do with a seventeen-year-old? Half the girls her age have already left school. Others are married. "

He stroked the dog gently as he tried to lift his head.

"She complains about Robin's selfishness with his computer so that Jock can't play games on it. Robin saved for it and bought it, for heaven's sake. Jock has to learn he can't have everything he wants and there's nothing to stop him saving for one of his own. Robin's afraid Jock'll erase things he needs. Jock's not competent enough yet, and he loses his temper if things don't go exactly as he wants." He sighed. "Emma believes in telling the truth and shaming the devil and telling people things for their own good. It wouldn't occur to her to tell a white lie for diplomacy's sake. She doesn't like Roz's hair style and disapproves of half the things she wears and says so. It doesn't make for peace in the home."

"Robin could be off to college next October," Peta reminded him.

"That's a year away. At this rate he might not even pass his A levels. Robin needs a room of his own and sharing with a fourteen-year-old isn't helping him at all. Kate has every reason to complain about sleeping in what is little more than a store room, while her grandmother occupies her room. All her clothes are in our wardrobe. She has to do her homework in the dining room and that causes more problems as people go in and out and disturb her."

He sighed again. Kate was far from easy to live with and she always went to pieces in examinations. With her A levels due next year she was even more temperamental.

He picked up his black bag.

"Much as I care for Emma, there isn't room here, and we can't move anywhere else. We'd never find another property as convenient and I can't face the upheaval and the rebuilding that would be necessary if we found a bigger house. Can't afford to keep this going as well as somewhere else. She doesn't seem to understand what problems she's causing us all."

"I feel guilty," Peta said. "Emma could have my flat and I'll find somewhere else to live."

Russell looked at her, shocked. The mere idea appalled him.

"Over my dead body. In any case, I need you here to special my very sick patients at night. I can't do without you. You know that."

He climbed into the Land Rover and started the engine. The thought of the years ahead with his mother-in-law creating havoc was almost more than he could bear. As he drove into the farm lane a possible solution occurred to him. If only it would work.

Louise was having a bad day. She had spent a restless night, the baby apparently having decided he would probably be a footballer when he entered the world, and was busy practising. Or maybe he was going to be a dancer. She couldn't get comfortable. At about two in the morning she gave up, switched on the light, and tried to read. Mott, delighted to see her awake, jumped on the bed, and tucked himself against her. She ought to push him off, but his warm body was comforting. Mervyn would have kittens, she thought, and half laughed as she imagined him coming in through the door and looking at her in horror.

A dog in the house was bad enough . A dog on the bed was unthinkable.

"You're not here," she said to his photograph. "So tough! I need company."

Fern preferred the floor. Maybe if Mervyn had been in the bed she would have come up too, if he had allowed it. She had a sudden vision of all four of them under the duvet, which made her laugh. He and Fern had had a bond which she did not share. Mott turned his head, beat his tail and looked up at her as if reading her thoughts and assuring her that he was her special companion. She stroked his soft fur.

Daily she hoped for news. When she was busy she could forget, but the darkening evenings gave her too much time indoors, and there was no one at all to share her loneliness. Jason was company, but he was in his own quarters at night, busy working on the flat, telling her excitedly each morning what he had done, taking her to see his improvements.

Her bad night had left her irritable and edgy. Today Jason had left the house at just after two to mend the fence, promising to be back by four. She had collected the two strays from Kane's paddock, but there had been no sign of the man himself. It was now almost six and there was no sign of Jason either. He had walked out and left her. He was not coming back. She should never have trusted him. Mature though he seemed, he was little more than a child, and was, in fact, just a teenager.

She had better get on with his chores. She would have to learn to be alone again. He couldn't possibly need all that time to mend a fence. There was no sign of him in any of the fields and it was growing dark. She suddenly felt totally alone. Jason had been company, as well as being essential to the farm's working. She could never manage on her own now. Only ten more weeks. Maybe within three months she'd be back to coping full time again. It was hard to imagine a live baby in the house.

Jason must come back. But she couldn't imagine what had

happened to him. Perhaps he had fallen and was hurt. Another hour and maybe she'd need to send for a search party. But if he'd just got fed up . . . there had been so much work to do. He hadn't been missing for long and the police would not be sympathetic if all he had done was to leave without a word to her. She wondered why her imagination was working overtime, and then realised that Mervyn too had left and not come back and she felt even more insecure. Suppose he had just decided that he was tired of farming and taken the opportunity of starting a new life somewhere else? No farm. No wife. No responsibilities. Other women had suffered that.

Don't be an idiot, she told herself firmly. He might leave me but he'd never leave Tarquin. He couldn't wait for each day to begin to greet his wonderful little ram. She needed to be busy so she fed the calves. Usually it amused her when they struggled against her, pulling on the teat of the mock bottle that Mervyn had fastened into the lowest part of the bucket, so that they could suck instead of trying to lap, which was always messy. Today she needed to hurry and they were uncooperative. If she had known Jason would not be back she'd have spent less time over her tea break.

Fortunately there were only two calves, as most of them stayed with their mothers. One little fellow was a twin and the other's mother, Trouble, had refused to accept him. Louise had tried salt and also honey, smearing it thickly on his head. It usually worked but all he received was a kick when he tried to go near his mother. The cow had mastitis, and Louise had not realised it at first. The rejected calf could have tried to suck on the sore teat. Trust Trouble.

Demon had already rounded up his harem and was quacking imperiously, demanding that she come and close the door and make them safe for the night. She brought food at this time. That was one of the jobs that Jason had taken over. Sighing, she plodded across the yard to do her duty, longing to rest. The walk to collect the two sheep had tired her, especially as it was uphill all the way home.

Mott and Fern took up their places, ensuring all the ducks and Demon were safely housed and locked in. They knew the routine so well she never had to command them. Mott always watched carefully until the padlock was on the latch. Louise sometimes thought that if she forgot he would try to do it for her. Once that was done, he relaxed, and led the way to the sheep paddock, again supervising the little group as they were led to their night-time quarters.

She was worried about Trouble. She did not like the cow, but hated seeing an animal in pain. Russell was very late. Louise prayed that he had not had an emergency call out. His brief presence was always a light in her day, now. She and Mervyn had rarely had time to socialise but Mervyn was godfather to Russell's daughter and Russell had promised to fulfil the same function for her son. Mervyn would have asked him, had he been here.

Jason, cold, wet and extremely uncomfortable, decided to change his clothes before he went into the kitchen. Better to reveal the unhappy truth gently. Louise, he guessed, would be annoyed with him for staying away so long.

Relief, to Louise's surprise, made her angry.

"Where the hell have you been? I've had to do most of your jobs. Is there any sign of Russell? How dare you leave me on my own so long?"

She was being unreasonable and she knew it. Jason went over to the Aga, and took the kettle, putting instant coffee into two mugs before he added the water.

"I got caught up," he said, feeling his explanation was inadequate. "I tried to ring. You must have been outside." He looked at her, anxiously. "Mr Merrit's mare bolted when the helicopter flew over and the foal fell into the stream when he was born. I had to go in to get him out. I was soaked and had to change before I came in . . . maybe I shouldn't have till I'd seen you but I was cold."

He looked anxiously at Louise, who was staring at him, startled by his story.

"And the old bloke in the cottage tried to reach him and fell and broke his leg. I had to send for the helicopter – I couldn't just leave him lying there, alone. It's a very bad break, the medics said."

Louise, wishing she had not been so thoughtless, could think of nothing to say. She ought to apologise, but if she did, she would burst into tears of relief and embarrass both of them. She felt irritated at herself. She had never been like this before. Pregnancy did odd things to women.

"Poor man. If his leg's broken he's going to be out of action for a long time. Does he have any help there?"

Jason put Kane's keys down on the table. The animals hadn't been fed, and he'd have to go back and do something about them. He frowned now, trying to work out how they'd manage.

"Not as far as I know. He'd have asked me to get in touch with someone, wouldn't he? He's got a whole load of rescued dogs and cats and birds and things," he said. "They need feeding and will need cleaning out tomorrow. We can't just leave them. I promised . . ."

Louise looked at him, trying to work out how they could cope. There was no question of leaving the animals untended. Maybe Russell would know of someone who could help. As it was she and Jason worked full stretch. How could they take on more animals? But they couldn't leave them uncared for, and who on earth would take them? No boarding kennels could cope with a sudden influx of so many dogs. Nor could any cattery take all those cats. And who took birds?

"We'll have to get up a couple of hours earlier. We can't shift them up here; there's nowhere to put them. It's going to take a huge chunk out of the day to go down twice to feed and clean them. And the dogs need some kind of exercising."

"It's only five minutes away in the Land Rover. We can bring the mare and foal up. She'll be on site and we can supervise her exercise more easily. Also notice more quickly if anything goes wrong with either of them. That water was very

51

cold. Do horses get pneumonia? They need stabling at night; and the foal needs the vet."

Louise sighed with relief when she heard a vehicle drive into the yard, to be greeted with a vociferous barking from Fern and Mott. Jason raised his voice above the din.

"I promised I'd take him to look at the foal after he's seen Trouble."

A knock had been followed by a head round the door.

"Sorry I'm late," Russell said. "A dog was run over. I had an emergency operation. Where's Jason taking me?"

"Kane Merrit broke his leg. Jason had to get him to hospital. The mare had her foal and it was born in the stream. Mr Merrit wanted you to look at both of them. There are dozens of animals there. We can't leave them."

"Kane? Poor old fellow. He'll be distraught. I'll see if I can find helpers," Russell said. "Roz is going past the hospital tonight. She's visiting a friend. She can drop a note in to tell him not to worry. We'll take care of everything for him."

Louise looked at him. A big man with shaggy brown hair turning grey, he towered over Jason who was just under six feet himself.

"Make me a coffee, Jason, and then we'll look at Trouble, and go on to the cottage. I take it Kane hadn't done his evening round?"

"No."

"I heard the animals yelling and wondered what was wrong. It's well past their feeding time. I'll come down as soon as I've seen that cow. She does live up to her name."

He accepted the mug of coffee, and sat himself in the big armchair that Louise never used. It was Mervyn's and she felt that if she occupied it herself she would be admitting that he was gone for ever.

"Roz and I have been meaning to come up and see you," Russell said. "But you know how it is . . . her own father died six weeks ago and we've had problems with her mother."

He hesitated, wondering if his idea was so good after all, and how Louise would take it.

"Look, you need help and you could be doing me a big favour. Neither of us can bear to think of you up here alone. Suppose you go into premature labour?"

"Do you think I haven't thought of it? But there just isn't the money to pay anyone to come and live in. It's all I can do to manage the mortgage repayments." Russell had put her own nightmare into words. "We had to re-mortgage a couple of years ago, when things were very tight."

"Roz's mother has decided to come and live with us and she's driving us both mad." He added two teaspoonfuls of sugar to his cup and took a bun from a plate on the table. "Sorry. Not had time to eat."

Louise felt apologetic.

"I don't get time to bake. Mervyn would be horrified if he saw me buying shop cakes and commercial bread. Jason goes down to the shops for me. He uses Mervyn's mountain bike." She smiled. "He adores it and it's never been so gleaming clean. He's very useful."

She fetched bread and butter and cheese and set it in front of Russell. He attacked the loaf with enthusiasm.

"Emma . . . that's Roz's Mum . . . has Kate's room. Kate is in Jock's tiny cell, and you can imagine how well that goes down with a seventeen-year-old. Jock and Robin are sharing. There's not much love lost between fourteen and almost nineteen. Rob's off to university, I hope, but that's not till October. He had to take his A levels again – hopefully he'll do some work this time."

He paused to cut a lump of cheese, and Louise, suddenly aware that she had been too busy and too worried about Jason's absence to eat that evening, cut herself a slice of bread and buttered it.

"Robin has a computer, and is working hard on it. Jock wants to play games on it. Robin has now put in a password so that Jock can't even begin to use it, and since my silly younger son has bought several computer games with his own money . . . well, you can imagine."

Louise, who had been an only child, was startled by this picture of family life.

"Also," Russell went on, "Emma seems to forget Roz is an adult and treats her like a little girl, doing things for her, butting in when we're talking with the children – and her views are even more out of date than ours."

He paused to cut more bread for the two of them, and was pleased to see colour return to Louise's cheeks as she ate and drank.

"I think we could solve problems for both of us. If Emma comes to lodge here, and pays the standard rates, she'll soon want to help with the farmwork and with you, and when the baby comes you have a ready-made sitter. She'll love to spoil you and there's more than enough work here to keep her busy and out of your hair."

He passed Louise a sandwich, which he had made while he was talking.

"She's a dear really and I'm very fond of her. But we don't have room for a permanent resident and she's put her house on the market. I can put it to her that you're in a very bad position here; and I'm sure she'd jump at the chance of being really needed. She's a trained veterinary nurse. Her husband was a vet too. I met Roz when I went there to see practice." He sighed. "I miss the old boy. He had so much experience and I could always rely on him if I was puzzled. I valued his advice after Dad died. He was a much better diagnostician than either of us. Had a flair for it."

He watched Louise eat. Her face was much too thin, with huge shadows under the eyes. She looked exhausted. He made her another sandwich and watched with satisfaction as she took it without thinking and began to eat it.

"And I've another favour to ask. Would you have Kate here as a lodger too? She wants to spread her wings and at the moment is talking of moving in with her boyfriend. At her age that's crazy. I think she just wants to get away from home. She wants to be a vet; and farming experience would be a benefit.''

"How will she get to school?'' Louise asked.

"No problem. She can walk down to the Keepgate and either Roz or I can pick her up and take her to the bus. If we're both busy, Peta would fetch her. And Robin can drive. It's not quite a mile from here, and it won't hurt her to have a daily walk. Do her good. I'd pay for her. Emma will be well off when she's sold her house. You'd have company and income.''

He stood up, careful not to hit his head on the beams. Mervyn had always had to duck too. Louise felt a stab of misery at the memory.

"Think about it. Emma could have the two big spare rooms and Kate the big attic room.'' He grinned. "I spent so much time here when Mervyn and I were both young. I suspect our parents weren't sure who belonged to who. Merv and I used to sit up there when we were sixth formers, and put the world to rights. It was his playroom and then his study. How little we knew and we thought we knew everything. Is it still empty?''

Kate nodded.

"Now let's look at Trouble.''

There was rain in the air and a wind rising. It would be a blustery night. Louise led the way across the yard, glad that the barns had all been wired for electricity.

Russell was still pondering his own problems as they walked across the farmyard.

"It would do Kate good to live with a baby. Discover it's not all cuddles and kisses and something to hug, but that it yells in the night and produces dirty nappies and has a constant need for attention. These teenagers don't have any sense at all.''

Louise was not sure that she wanted strangers around, but she knew that she could never manage on her own and there would be money coming in each week which would help with the mortgage, and maybe save borrowing so much all the time.

"Can I say we could try for a month with Kate?" she asked. "It might not work at all. I would be glad to have your mother-in-law here, if she'd come. I feel so alone . . . and I'm beginning to be afraid that Mervyn won't come home."

"He'll be back. These people never keep their hostages for long, and in any case this isn't really a hostage incident, is it?" Russell said, as they turned into the cowshed. He wasn't sure that he believed his own words. Men had been kept prisoner for several years, but he hoped Louise would not remember that. "Nobody's made any demands. They probably just don't know quite how to cope with the situation they've brought on themselves. It was the food they were after, and probably the truck."

He stopped, wondering if there was any consolation at all in his words. It was one hell of a thing, and how on earth did one cope? Better maybe to hold his tongue. He went over to the cow.

Trouble, who was feeling ill and far from troublesome, suffered her examination with more fortitude than Louise had expected.

"Mastitis, as you thought. Not too severe," Russell said, handing over the necessary remedies when they were back in the kitchen, and drinking yet another cup of coffee. "You know the ropes. Keep her calf off her, of course. But I don't need to tell you that."

Louise sighed. There was enough to do without having to put hot fomentations on Trouble, and strip out her milk. As soon as the cow felt better she would live up to her name. Jason would have a new lesson to learn. She dared not risk a kick in the stomach.

Russell, aware of the sigh but not of its reason, turned and looked at her, frowning.

"'I'm babbling. I don't know if I'm offering help, or imposing. We're both worried about your isolation. I haven't put this idea to Roz yet. I only thought of it on the way up here. I'm sure she'll agree. And once Emma knows your situation she won't be able to wait to get here, I'm sure of that."

He rubbed his chin thoughtfully.

"There's not nearly enough for her to do in our house. She's always been busy, and now she's lost. Roz can't stand her interfering with the cooking and household affairs that's she done herself for years. She's upset our Mrs Mop who comes for two hours daily, by criticising the way she works and trying to make her more efficient. You'll give her a goal in life, and a purpose, which she needs, badly."

More people around Louise would stop too much brooding, Russell thought.

"Kate might be an imposition, but she can be sensible and useful, and it would be a major benefit to have her here, learning about life. She's too protected at home. If she comes, don't mother her."

"That's one of the things that scares me," Louise said. "How do I know I'll be any good as a mother?"

"Scares us all," Russell said. "You can only fly by the seat of your pants and it changes all the time. I've been a parent for nearly nineteen years. You think you know the ropes and then find out the next child is so unlike the first that you're making all sorts of different mistakes. You can't win. There's only one thing certain; whatever you do will be wrong in their eyes. Think back to your own childhood."

That seemed as many years away as a teenager in the house. Louise had to live through baby days first and she was beginning to panic. An experienced mother and grandmother living with her would be a godsend. She just prayed they liked one another.

"I feel overwhelmed," she said. "Two hours ago I was terrified because I thought Jason had left me on my own. Now, I have the chance of three people around when I need them."

"Mervyn and I were close friends when we had less responsibilities. I feel it's something I can do for him," Russell said. "Also Emma can help Jason look after Kane's animals. She'll adore doing that and it'll keep her out of your hair while you get to know one another."

He wished he could say something consoling. A first pregnancy, especially at Louise's age, was difficult enough without this kind of appalling worry. She needed care and cosseting and that, he was sure, Emma would do with great expertise.

A few minutes later he was examining the foal which seemed little the worse for his experience. He agreed that it would be better next day to take him and his mother up to the farm. He'd come up with a horse box, which he could easily borrow.

"I'll call in on Kane and see how he is and also find out what needs doing here," he promised before he drove back to his own home.

Russell walked into a war. He had thought everyone but Jock was going out but instead they were all at home except Robin, Kate having precipitated a crisis.

She had packed herself a case and was waiting for her father to transport her to her boyfriend's house. She had had enough of sleeping in a room meant for a dwarf, of not having her own clothes in her own room when she needed them, and of being told what to do by her grandmother.

Emma, feeling to blame, had decided to stay in and help Roz persuade her daughter this was a bad idea. Uncharacteristically, the old lady had resorted to tears, and Roz was in the kitchen, making a meal which seemed to require a great deal of crashing of saucepans.

Russell poured himself a very small whisky with a great deal of soda. He would have liked to make it stronger but he was never sure that he would not be called out.

"You're not going anywhere till you've eaten," Roz said, banging a plate of sausage, mashed potatoes and carrots in front of her daughter. "Mother, for goodness sake come and have your meal. And if anyone says anything, I'm walking out and leaving the lot of you."

Russell did not need to be told that Roz was nearing the end of her patience. Sausage and mash was reserved for very bad days indeed, as he and the boys hated it.

Nobody dared speak. Roz, bringing her own plate in, sat down and began to eat as if she were biting her enemies. Kate made a mound of potatoes and took tiny portions from the edge of it as if afraid it might poison her. Jock, always hungry, ate ravenously. Emma, still sobbing occasionally, played with the food on her plate.

"Louise is in a very bad way," Russell said, not quite knowing how to broach his idea. "Nearly seven months pregnant with the whole responsibility of the farm on her shoulders and her only help a sixteen-year-old boy. Suppose she goes into labour over Christmas and help doesn't come in time? It's very isolated up there."

He chopped a sausage into three pieces and speared one of them.

"Jason's not a bad lad, but I wouldn't like to think he was the only midwife. The weather up there can be dreadful round the end of December and the beginning of January. They could easily be cut off with the phone lines dead and floods in the fields beneath them."

"Hasn't she any relatives to help?" Emma asked, her interest caught.

"None. And with her husband missing in Bosnia, not knowing whether he's alive or dead, she's alone all evening and night. She looks exhausted. She hasn't given up hoping that Mervyn's still alive, but it can't be easy."

"When's the baby due?" Emma asked.

"Early January."

"I could help out," Emma said. "Would she agree to that? I don't seem to be wanted here."

She blew her nose, making Roz look guiltily at her husband.

"The farmhouse is much bigger than this place," Russell said, anxious not to sound too eager. "There's a lovely big attic. I wondered if Kate would like to move in as a lodger. The money would help as farming's in such a bad way. You could do the room up as you wanted, and have far more space than in your own room here."

He demolished the last piece of sausage and cut himself a slice of bread. Emma passed the cheese dish.

"There's a new foal," he said, knowing that his daughter was crazy about horses and longed to ride, but there was nowhere near for her to learn. "And Kane's broken his leg, so that all his animals need attention. I promised we'd help but it would make more sense to have you on the spot than going up there every day."

"Could I do the room up just the way I want it?" Kate asked. Moving in to Roger's home had few attractions as his mother was nearly as bad as her gran.

"I'm sure Louise will let you decorate it as you wish," her father said. "They don't use it at all. You can furnish it as a bedsitter, and spend all your time up there if you want."

It sounded a much better proposition than a room in Roger's house. Gran being there too might be a drawback, but if she had her own room she could escape. Not much use trying to do so here, when she felt as if she were penned in a tiny cell and had no space at all for her own property.

"Will she agree?" Emma asked.

She had not visited Louise but she had seen the lane that led to the farm, and the house, just visible among the trees, when Roz had taken her in the car for an outing on her way to a call.

"Louise needs money badly. She's never said so, but she's sold nothing since Mervyn went away and the farm has no other income. They had very little capital and Mervyn spent their windfall from the dairy herd on their prize ram's mother." He frowned. "He discussed it with me before he bought. I encouraged him. I hope it's going to work out, but the ram won't be earning his keep for some time yet."

60

He looked at the slice of cheese he had just cut for himself as if wondering what it was.

"I'm sure she'll be happy to have you there. There'll be far too much for her to do when the baby arrives. There's no guarantee that Mervyn will ever come home." He tried to think of further attractions. "All the rooms are empty as she gave the furniture from them to Jason for his flat. Her mother-in-law had them as her own quarters in the few months before she died."

Emma paused, her fork halfway to her mouth. She could have her own furniture, a bedroom and a sitting room, and she'd be needed. When the sale of her old house was completed she'd be a rich woman if she didn't have to buy another home.

"When can we move in?" she asked.

Suddenly they were all planning.

That night, in bed, Roz was thoughtful.

"I hope it will work out," she said. "It seems a bit much to wish our problems on Louise."

"I'm hoping it will take Louise's mind off her own worries. She'll not have nearly so much time to be alone and brood. And she needs help, desperately," Russell said.

All the same, his conscience was not easy and it was a long time before he fell asleep.

Six

T hree weeks later, Louise found it hard to remember she had once been so alone. Russell, calling in the day after the move to see Trouble and check on the foal who seemed to have had no ill effects from his unusual birth, had a brief consultation with Louise and his mother-in-law.

"Kate wants to be on her own. Let her find out how," he told Emma. "She has to wake up without being called, do her own washing, and she wants to do her own catering. Time she grew up. Roz has always done the laundry for all of us, till you came and took over. Kate's in for a few shocks."

Problems did not materialise for the first week. At the end of it, Kate, putting out her school uniform for Monday morning, realised she had no clean underwear or blouses. She took the bundle of dirty clothes down to Emma, who directed her to the laundry room, which was an old scullery.

"Washing machine's there. You'll find the iron and ironing board in the cupboard," she said. Her granddaughter stared at her. This was a part of being self-sufficient that had not dawned on her, any more than had the need to shop and plan food or go hungry.

"Gran," she said hopefully.

"I've more than enough to do. You're on your own now."

There were more shocks to come, as Kate discovered on the third day, when she failed to wake in time to meet her father and catch the school bus. Nobody called her.

"Time she grew up," her father had said. Louise had been

62

tempted to knock on the door, but she had promised, and, after all, many girls the same age were living entirely on their own.

Kate had been determined to finish painting one wall and not gone to bed until nearly two, something her mother would never have allowed. She woke to hear Russell downstairs, asking if she were ill. Although she dressed hastily and ignored breakfast, and he drove her all the way, she was still late for school. On the way home she bought a small alarm clock.

The walk each morning was another chore she had not considered. It was almost a mile to the Keepgate, which was at the far end of the lane that led past all the farm fields, and was where the post was delivered. On cold mornings, or in rain, the walk was a penance. Her father had warned that he would only wait ten minutes. If she were later than that she had to walk another mile to the bus stop because her school bus would have gone. The normal bus dropped her half a mile from school instead of taking her into the grounds.

Inevitably, she did miss the school bus and by the time Kate had slept twice through her alarm and was again late for her first lesson, she was having second thoughts about being independent. It was much harder than she had realised. Only now did she appreciate what had to be done to keep a place clean and tidy – nobody else was going to do her room for her.

The first weeks were not easy for any of them, but by the end of the fourth, they had worked out their roles, and Louise was relaxing, enjoying the presence of other people around her all the time. It was a relief not to have to worry about the animals, should she be taken ill suddenly. Emma, delighted to have someone who needed her, and a purpose in life, was anxious to make sure Louise did not overtire herself. Louise, who had no desire whatever to stop caring for her animals, found she had to fight to avoid being coddled.

She was, however, glad to hand over the twice daily trip to Kane's kennels. Driving was becoming increasingly difficult, as her tummy was now too close to the steering wheel for comfort, and if she put the seat further back, she could not reach the pedals. Emma had her own car.

Kate, after a few more days of problems, due to sleeping through the alarm, decided to share the daily care of Kane's animals. This ensured a knock on the door to wake her up. It also had an unexpected result as Emma decided that one good turn merited another and when it was raining heavily drove her to the Keepgate after breakfast, which she now shared with her grandmother and Louise and which Louise prepared while they were at the cottage.

Freedom, Kate was discovering, had unexpected snags. She had thought she would decide just how she lived but other people still seemed to decide things for her. There was no way her pride would allow her to neglect her involvement with Kane's animals, nor could she avoid the need for clean clothes for school. But not even Louise was sympathetic, looking at her in astonishment, when she complained that there was too much to do.

"Try my life," Louise said, as she went out to feed the squealing piglets, noisier than ever now they were being weaned and dependent on her and not their mother for most of their food. She couldn't understand how Kate could sleep through the early morning din they made. She was up at five. Kate slept until six thirty.

The mynah, which had been brought up to their kitchen as he needed warmth, was a nuisance, squealing like the little pigs, barking like the dogs, or shouting people's names. He also imitated the telephone bell. Jason took him over to his own flat, which was also heated by an Aga. There he could make as much noise in the empty rooms as he liked by day and be covered at night.

"I promise I'll rest when I'm tired," Louise told Emma a number of times in the first few weeks. She felt the older woman was clucking around her like an over-protective hen with ducklings instead of chicks, refusing to let them near the water. "In any case, I need to keep busy. Then I don't have time to have panics about Mervyn."

There was still no news and, as the weeks passed, it was difficult to remain hopeful. The lorry, its drivers and its load had vanished as if they had never been. The rescue operation to that area had been suspended, but that was no consolation at all.

Emma, recently widowed herself, understood how Louise was feeling. They worked out a method of living together. Emma took over the shopping. She persuaded Louise to have her hair cut short again, as she complained it took so long to dry when she washed it. The curly cap of dark hair suited her far better. Emma also accepted, at last, that Louise would rest if she felt tired, and meanwhile could cope easily with those chores she wanted to do. Nobody else was going to let Tarquin and Belle out each morning. That was a pleasure Louise refused to give up.

Kate, excited by her new independence and her huge attic room, was busy planning and decorating, in spite of discovering some of the not so pleasant commitments that she had now taken on. Her grandmother, to her surprise, offered to provide the cash for furniture and improvements.

She was learning fast. She had, one morning in her first week at the farm, unwisely complained to Jason about having so much to do as well as her A level homework.

"Grow up, little girl," he said, infuriating her. "No one forced you to leave home."

"How's freedom?" Russell asked his daughter one morning on the way to the school bus stop.

"I hadn't realised how much responsibility there is in living on your own," Kate said.

Her father smiled.

"Your granddad always said nobody's really free; we're all fettered – by society, by laws, by the need to survive and keep ourselves healthy and fed and clean. Even animals have to conform to the last part of that. Those that are careless, or don't learn, or neglect themselves, die. Even so, cherish what you have."

Food cost more than she expected and she had not considered the need for cleaning materials, or shoe polish, or the other hundred and one small necessary items that competent housewives took for granted. Coffee couldn't cost all that, surely? She did not have to buy milk as Louise let her share the goats' milk.

Jason, at first resentful, realised he was no longer the only one responsible if Louise started labour unexpectedly, and he relaxed. Emma enjoyed his company and he discovered she had a sense of humour all her own and could make him laugh.

Russell borrowed a horse box and brought mother and son to the farm. Louise hoped Kane would let them stay there when he returned. She'd gladly keep them for nothing, just for the pleasure of their company. The mare settled.

Kate had no real responsibilities for any of the animals. She began to wish she had something of her own. One Saturday afternoon, the mare came to her when she returned from visiting her parents and greeted her with a whinny. She always patted Corrie, as she came by, but had been too busy trying to sort out her new way of life to do anything more.

"Can I groom Corrie for you?" she asked Louise.

The mare adored attention. She stood while her mane and tail were brushed and Kate found an unexpected pleasure in watching the gleam that developed as she worked. The foal stood near, but was wary of most people, though he allowed Jason to pet him. Jason had been the first human to touch him. Kate determined that he would trust her too.

He delighted all of them. He had terrible panics and galloped round screaming if his mother was out of sight for a second.

"Awful life, being a foal," Jason said, and was rewarded with laughter.

Emma soon became part of another morning ritual. Every

day, at precisely nine o'clock there came a rat-tat-tat on the door. The first time she had answered the summons she had stared in amazement, as did Demon, the big drake, who had expected to see Louise, and who hissed at this strange woman.

"He wants his morning toast," Louise said, laughing, as she brought the last piece over to him. Emma had wondered why she had prepared more than they needed. He snatched it.

"Manners," Louise said, and was rewarded by a glinting glare from his small dark eyes.

"It's no use forgetting. He hammers on the door with his beak until he gets his own way. He's the bossiest bird I've ever met," Louise said.

After that both Emma, and Kate at weekends, made sure there was always a spare piece left. The hammering went on until he was rewarded.

Trouble was able to open gates, and let herself and the rest of the herd out. Given the chance she did, if nobody remembered to put on the chain and padlock. Kate was a frequent offender, but the day she was sent out alone to bring the animals back cured her of forgetfulness.

Kane had broken his leg very badly, necessitating an operation. He would be in hospital for some weeks. Emma took time, every few days, to call on the invalid and report on his charges.

"I'm Russell's mother-in-law," she said on her first visit, by way of greeting. Russell treated all Kane's animals, and was probably the nearest thing to a friend that the retired vet had.

He looked at her with irritation. He did not feel like making conversation with someone he had never met before. He could not imagine why she was there. Russell had called in briefly to tell him that there was no need to worry about his animals.

"Did Russell ask you to call?"

"Yes and no. Jason, the boy who helped you when you had your accident, is helping Louise and me to care for your

67

charges. I know Russell told you that there was no need to worry. I just wanted to report that they're all doing well."

Bedbound, his leg raised in the air, Kane was far from happy, but was relieved to find that his refugees were in good hands.

"They'd all been badly treated before they came to me," he said. "How did they take to you?"

"They were too hungry to care by the time we were able to feed them," Emma said, putting down a small basket of fruit on the bedside table. "From all of us."

"I let some of them run together in the paddock," Kane said. "Need to be sure which get on and which don't. The big fellow, who's a Heinz 57 of nearly all the guarding breeds, is very nasty with other dogs."

Emma, who was hiding a bitten finger inside a pair of gloves, did not comment that he was also likely to be nasty with people. She and Jason had christened him the Black Devil. Luckily Kane had put him in a big kennel with an outside run and it was possible to entice him into one part and shut the door on him while the other part was cleaned. Unaware, on their first day, of his tendencies, she had put her hand inside the gate to take out his food bowl, and been bitten. He allowed no intruders on his territory.

"He'd only been with me for two weeks," Kane said. "An abuse case. There's a prosecution pending. I'm hoping to change his attitude, but it'll take time."

Emma left, feeling sorry for the man. He was prickly and awkward, and, she suspected, had probably had as much to endure as some of his dogs during his life.

Visiting him was unrewarding, but Emma persisted, feeling she ought to report on her charges. Also on occasion she needed advice for one or the other of them. One small terrier had gummy eyes, and she wondered if this was normal or an infection

"Sammie. As long as the discharge is clear he's OK. Just one of those things," Kane said. "Bathe them. He's a sweetie and won't make a fuss."

The details of minor problems comforted him, as he was then sure nothing was being hidden from him. He discovered, after a few days, somewhat to his own surprise, that he looked forward to Emma's visits and news of his own world.

"Kane'll be coming back just before Christmas," she reported one day early in November as she began to dish up the evening meal. "He's decided to go to a convalescent home for a week or so, till he's mobile. They have physiotherapy facilities there, and it would be difficult to get from his home to the hospital without calling on someone else to drive him. He'll still need help, he'll be on crutches."

She served curry and rice, and sat herself down at the table. One of the cats, a big tabby, which usually lived outside, had crept in and was lying on the hearthrug, one eye on anyone who might be about to evict her. Her kittens were due and she had her mind on the warm cupboard beneath the hot-water tank in Kate's room. It was warm there and she often followed the girl upstairs and spent time with her.

Kate now joined them for the evening meal, taking her turn at making it. Independence was not quite so exciting, she discovered, when she had to shop for her own food, and plan and budget. A diet of toast and ready meals had soon palled, and was too expensive. Her father was giving her an allowance.

"Your rent, your food, your clothes, a little leeway for presents for birthdays and Christmas, and anything else you need," he said, setting her up with her own bank account. "And don't go into the red, as I won't pay. You're on your own now."

He agreed, after a fervent plea at the end of two weeks during which she did her own cooking, to give her more money so that she could add her board to the rent of her room, and change her mind later if she wished.

Jason, always ravenously hungry, rarely shared meal times. He preferred sandwiches and a flask and took little time off at lunchtime. When persuaded to join them for a proper meal he seemed anxious to escape the three women in the house. Not even Louise realised that he was anxious about the farm, and with Kane's animals to care for as well, was worried about the responsibility.

"Saturday tomorrow," Emma said, one morning at the end of November. She glanced across at Louise. She disliked early winter and this year it was bleaker than usual, with incessant rain which depressed all of them.

Louise felt clumsy, and tired so easily that she wondered how on earth she would have managed if she had been on her own. She hoped, desperately, that the baby would not be late. She could not find a chair that was comfortable and bed had become a penance, her nights, interrupted, often spent sitting in the kitchen with the door of the Aga open to give light and life. Walking far too slowly and finding balance difficult at times, she felt as if she was waddling like the ducks.

She had not heard Emma's remark.

"Louise. Wake up! Time we went into town and found some clothes for that infant. Haven't you made any preparations at all?" Emma intended to persist with her plan. "I've been nosy and looked round. Where's he going to sleep? In your room? And what's he sleeping in? A drawer from your chest?"

"I've not had time to think," Louise said. The baby did not seem a reality. She could not imagine him as a presence in the house, needing food and comfort, crying for attention. "I suppose I thought it could all be done right at the last minute. I don't even know what I ought to be buying."

There were occasions when Louise felt that Emma was forcing her into action. She did not like to confess that she was so superstitious that she was afraid of providing for the baby before he was actually there. She would have a house full of clothes and equipment for him, and he might be born dead.

The long nights brought dreams and worries that threatened to overwhelm her. She was sure by now that Mervyn must be dead. The official who reported to her at intervals had little comfort to give. They were doing all they could. It was a very difficult area, and nobody knew who was responsible for the hijacking. No one had asked for a ransom. No group had owned up to having the two men.

Emma was aware of much of this through night-time conversations. But at least the last antenatal check had assured both of them that all was well. Louise was glad to have someone with her when she went to the hospital and not to have to drive herself.

The next morning was misty, and Emma hesitated before starting out. They were soon in lanes where the damp hedges held rainbow images in the drops and the bare trees made dark patterns against a soft blue sky. Snow had dusted the hilltops, and softened the stark contours of the high places.

Unexpectedly, Louise enjoyed the shopping expedition. It was an escape from the endless chores. Emma, concentrating on being positive and cheerful, was at times weary with her own efforts, but the day was doing them both good and they were almost light-hearted.

Louise had had no one to shop with for years, as she and Mervyn never left the farm together for such expeditions. She had forgotten how it felt to comment over items in the shop windows, to laugh at some of the more hideous objects on display, to marvel over tiny garments that were well beyond her price range and put them aside, reluctantly, wishing she could afford to buy lavishly for once.

Emma, seeing a beautiful little model of a foal, bought it to put away for Kate's Christmas present. That, she thought, was something else that had to be planned. Louise would want to spend the time in her own home because with the baby only two weeks away, she would be uncomfortable anywhere else. Not that she would be comfortable there either, she thought. She wondered if perhaps the scan had missed something and there were two babies there and not one. That would sort them all out.

"Backache?" she asked, as Louise stopped and leaned

briefly against the edge of a doorway before entering the shop. "You need a rest."

I need it to be January and the baby born, Louise thought, but did not say so. Her feet ached and her ankles were now always swollen at night, though not enough, the doctor had said, to worry about at the moment. She had thought Emma was being over-careful when she suggested that in a week or so, Louise would find the drive to the town and the shopping far too exhausting. As it was, she longed for the day to be over so that she could take off her shoes and lie flat. Shopping seemed much more tiring than farm work.

The stores catering for mothers-to-be did have chairs on which she could rest. She had already decided that the money from her two lodgers would go towards the baby's layette, but she had had no idea just how much she would need.

"Don't buy those. Buy wool. I'm a fast knitter and I love making baby clothes," Emma said, putting aside several tiny jackets. "And you want old-fashioned nappies. You'll spend a fortune if you use disposables, and they'd take up half the car when I go shopping."

Finding those proved much more difficult than either of them had imagined but at last they tracked down a shop which promised to order a supply.

"They looked at me as if I'd asked for something ante-diluvian," Louise said as they walked out of the shop.

"They probably thought it." Emma was pondering the list in her hand. "You don't need a bath for the baby. You can line the wash basin with a towel and bath him in that. It's daft to spend unnecessary money."

She insisted on stopping for lunch. The pub that they chose had an extensive menu, and Emma decided on a treat; smoked salmon and scrambled eggs for both of them, and insisted on paying.

Kate and Jason could cope by themselves until four that afternoon, so there was no need to hurry back. It was an unusually bright day for the time of year. A huge globe of sun was low in the windscreen and Emma drove with care. At the start of the lane she stopped, and they both looked out in pity. A Jack Russell lay at the side of the road, his small body bleeding, his back legs obviously broken.

"Hit by a car," Emma said. "They didn't stop to help him and I bet they won't report it. He's still alive. We can't leave him. Though I doubt if he'll survive till we get home, and it's too far to go back to Russell. I wonder where he's come from?"

"Maybe dumped," Louise said, as Emma climbed back into the car and put the dog, wrapped in her jacket, down on the back seat. The day's shopping was in the boot.

"He was too weak to do more than snarl at me," Emma said. "Often when they're in pain they bite."

They turned a bend in the lane, passing the overgrown fields of the abandoned farm that lay below Bryn Mawr. They both stared. Russell's Land Rover stood beside Roz's smaller runabout. A police car was parked beside them.

Twelve mangled sheep lay dead in front of the barn and both Roz and Russell were busy stitching injuries. Torn bodies and bloodied fleeces shocked both women. Louise gave a cry of misery, and Emma took her hand.

"Oh, my God," she said.

Fern, with a ragged bite on her face, and a badly torn ear, lay in the yard. Mott, apparently uninjured, was lying exhausted by Kate, who, her face swollen with tears, was helping her mother.

Jason came up the lane, carrying a small dog in his arms. He was covered in blood. He walked over to Russell.

"She's beginning to whelp. First pup's jammed and dead. And she's a gash down her middle. I'd guess she tried to jump barbed wire. She's one of the most timid of all Kane's dogs."

"We'll have to take her home and operate," Russell said, after examining her. "Not a lot I can do for her now. She needs sedating." He handed her to his wife and turned back to the injured sheep.

73

Louise couldn't believe her eyes. She didn't want to. She glanced at the field where the rest of the huddled flock stood apathetic, not bothering to graze.

"In heaven's name, what happened?" she asked. She knelt beside one of the victims, stroking the fleece. Tarquin, her treasure. He couldn't be dead. He moved his head, but he was so badly injured that she was sure he wouldn't survive.

She was swept by a feeling of rage so strong that it frightened her. Russell put out a hand to help her up.

"He was our future," she said, her lips trembling. "Our beautiful boy . . ." She couldn't say any more.

"He's not been bitten in any vital parts," Russell said. "He's badly shocked, and he's badly hurt, but there's a chance. Don't give up yet. I'll do everything I can to save him."

The two policemen were making notes. The older man looked at her.

"It's tough," he said. "We'll do our best to get them. We'll need to talk to you, but it can wait . . . you've had a bad shock."

"Hope she doesn't go into labour," he said to his companion, as they waited. "She's enough on her plate." A thin rain added to everyone's misery and snow was building on the cloudy mountain tops.

"Some maniacs let out all Kane's animals," Jason said, so furious that he could barely speak. "They've left home-made posters and painted messages on the barns. 'Animals need to be free.' It was easy as no one is ever there for most of the day now. Dogs, cats, ferrets – the birds. The dogs got in among the sheep. I'd like to kill the brutes who let them out."

"I know who they are," Kate said. "It's a group at school. How are we going to get Kane's animals back? How will they survive?"

Louise wanted to scream. She stared at her sheep, startled by the rage that possessed her. Tarquin, her most precious possession, the climax of all their hopes, was lying there with

74

Russell working on him. Russell would need to take him down to the surgery. Belle was also bitten, but not badly. Ten more of the ewes which had been due to lamb in March now lay dead.

"Belle kicked out at them. You should have seen her," Jason said.

"Many of the other ewes may lose their lambs." Russell glanced up at Louise. She was leaning against the paddock fence, looking dazed. She'd lost a fortune and her future. Tarquin was irreplaceable. He couldn't possibly survive.

"There were three dogs in the field," Jason said. "We chased them off. I didn't realise at the time they were Kane's dogs. It was well past feeding time when I went down and saw what had happened there. I was late as I had to cope here."

My fault, Louise thought. I shouldn't have gone shopping.

Jason looked at her anxiously.

"We discovered this first about two this afternoon. There was no further damage to Kane's place except for the broken locks on the barns. They just opened all the doors and let everything free. I don't suppose we'll ever find the ferrets."

"Where are the dogs now? Will they come back and do more damage in the night? How many were there?" Louise felt frantic. "What possessed the idiots to let the dogs out? I'd like to kill them."

Jason lifted Tarquin gently, carried him over to Russell's Land Rover and laid him on the floor between the seats, and then continued speaking. Roz had already driven off with the whelping bitch.

"It was weird. I went down to the kennels when Russell came – I'd recognised the dogs by then. I didn't see how they could have got out and was afraid I'd left the doors unlatched, or something equally careless. I had to make sure."

He held one of the ewes as Louise washed the blood from her fleece.

"Most of the animals had just come back when it was quiet again and were lying in their beds, pretty scared, with the

75

doors open. They wanted to be safe and that's the only home they know."

Louise had never felt such anger in her life. If only she could lay her hands on the monsters who had done this. Jason was still talking.

"There are still two missing. The Black Devil – and that's worrying – and a little Jack Russell. The Devil was here. The other's not much more than a pup. A nice little dog, but he's one that would scare easily and run from strangers."

"The Jack Russell's probably the dog in my car," Emma said, feeling guilty because she had completely forgotten him. "He was run over."

Russell went over to the car and picked up the little animal.

"Only one answer to that," he said and in a couple of minutes another pathetic corpse had joined those that lay in the yard.

Emma, who was afraid that the shock might bring the baby too soon, ignored Louise's protests and made her sit and rest. She brought out soup, hot sweet tea, hot-water bottles and a rug, all of which Louise refused, though after some argument she did go inside to drink the soup. "I'm OK," she said. "I need to be out there. They're my sheep."

Pregnant women were supposed to keep away from sheep but it was no use telling Louise that. Especially now. In any case she had been with them all the time, so what difference would it make? Emma did not realise her own confused thoughts were also due to shock.

The two policemen decided to come back next morning.

Russell phoned a friend who had a six-man practice sixteen miles away to come over and help. He needed to get back to the surgery with Tarquin. The newcomer brought an assistant and a nurse with him. Louise, as soon as she had finished her soup, came out again to help bathe the injuries. Emma gave up trying to make her rest, and she and Jason helped too.

It was two more hours before the clearing up was finished.

Another four sheep had to be destroyed and sixteen needed stitches.

"I can't tell how many will survive. Too much shock," Jim Harrison, Russell's colleague, said. Jason closed the barn door on the invalids. They should at least be safe and quiet there. Emma and Jason produced tea and sandwiches for everyone.

"The mare and foal? Are they all right?" Louise asked, suddenly aware that she had not seen either of them. Were they both dead too? She was emotionally exhausted and dropped wearily into the big armchair which was now the only one that was comfortable.

Jason handed her a plate containing three ham sandwiches and a couple of small buns. There would be no evening meal.

"The mare's fine, and so's her son. I put them in the stable as soon as I heard the din. The dogs were too busy with the sheep to notice them. I couldn't think how to get the dogs out of the sheep field," he said. "I thought Fern and Mott might do it for me. They did . . . but Fern met the Black Devil. Mott helped her see him off. I don't know where he's gone. He did much of the damage. He's big."

At that moment the phone rang. Louise, who was nearest to it, answered.

"Thanks. No, we've suffered too." She listened for a moment. "Good." She rang off.

"Gareth from Ty Coch. The Black Devil and two companions he must have collected on the way have been among his sheep. He's shot all three. The other two are village dogs, not Kane's. He wondered if we were OK. He saw other dogs in the distance heading away from the farm towards us. He's lost twelve sheep and a number of chickens. He was out this afternoon and his barn was broken into. He keeps barn hens. He also has a bull. Pity they didn't let him out, but maybe even such lunatics have a bit of sense. Titan's a devil."

"We've lost all but two of the ducks," Jason said. Louise nodded. Demon was among the victims. He would never march up and bang on the kitchen door for food again.

She could not take her mind off the ram.

"Tarquin," she said, her voice forlorn.

"Is he insured?" Emma asked. "They'll pay his vet bills. Russell's sure he has a chance."

Russell had not said that, but she was not going to repeat his words: not a lot of hope; have to pray for a miracle.

"He's the only one that was, but not for his true value. We can't claim for the lambs he never produced."

Kate had gone back with her father to sit beside the injured ram in the car, and make sure he did not bounce around too much in the rutted lane. Russell rang just before midnight. No one had felt like bed.

"He's holding his own," he said. "The main problem is shock, but he's a sturdy youngster. I've stitched him up and he's full of Rescue Remedy. Peta's watching him and he's being kept warm. If he's still alive in the morning, we can hope for recovery. Kate's staying here tonight. She's going to take turns with Peta to sit with him. There's still hope."

"You mean that?" Louise asked.

"I mean it." Russell hesitated. "I've been thinking and I'm pretty sure I can get the culprits' parents to pay my bill. Rest, and try not to worry. At least the dogs won't be back. They're all safely locked up again, and Bob Strang's sleeping in Kane's cottage tonight."

Bob Strang, a powerful man well over six foot six in height, was brother to the local policeman. Their father was English, their mother Welsh. Bob had been manager of a small local factory that had been forced to close. Unable to find other employment, he had set up as a superior odd job man, ready to help anywhere that he was needed. He had a natural authority and often stopped arguments. His presence made those intending mayhem think twice, and he was given free drinks at the Penrhyn Arms on Saturday nights, just to keep him around.

It was some consolation to Louise to know that he would be

sleeping in the cottage, and could be reached by phone. He also had been at school with Russell and Mervyn, and had come up to the farm on several occasions to fix things she could not manage, but he was always in demand, and Louise only called him in when the need was imperative. She lay awake listening for the sounds of milling sheep and barking dogs. She could not sleep and soon after two she went downstairs. Emma, equally wakeful, joined her and made tea for both of them, bringing out the remainder of the sandwiches.

"Poor baby," Louise said. "He's not coming into much of a world, is he? I feel like selling up, but I doubt if I could even find a buyer or start somewhere else. Nobody in their senses is going to buy it as a going concern and if I sold the house, what happens to the land? It'll all go wild like the fields below us on the old Thomas farm. I can't do anything till Mervyn comes home. He wouldn't want to sell, anyway."

"I didn't realise those fields were part of a farm," Emma said, stirring sugar into her tea. She sighed. "I ought to diet. I've put on weight since coming here and I've only been here a few weeks."

"It seems much longer than that," Louise said. "It's hard to remember when you weren't here, and Kate and Jason. It's all that baking you do and all those dumpling stews and pies and pasties."

"You can keep stews and casseroles simmering for ever, but dumplings are fattening and so is pastry. And the outdoor work makes me hungry so I can't win." Emma bit into a sandwich.

She pushed the plate across the table for a second time. Louise took a sandwich and discovered that she was indeed hungry.

"I envy Kate," she said. "In fact at times I hate poor Kate. She's slim and pretty and races around, and she sleeps at night. I feel like a wallowing hippo." She sipped her tea and added more sugar. "I suppose I ought not to, but I feel in need of something sweet."

79

Emma fetched a sponge cake and cut into it.

"Then eat this. I've been thinking about Christmas. You ought not to be travelling around, so suppose we ask Russell and Roz and the boys here on Christmas Day for lunch? What do you usually do?"

"Have a blow out in the evening when all the chores are done. We've always been on our own and not felt much like celebrating; it's just another day. I don't even put any decorations up though I do stand the cards on the various bits of furniture. We don't get that many. There's never time to keep up with friends."

And we give each other presents, Louise thought. No need to shop for Mervyn this year and agonise over what to buy. Last year he had bought her a lovely model ram to celebrate Tarquin's advent. It was on the sitting-room mantelpiece. She could not bear to look at it. Would he still be alive tomorrow?

"Bed," Emma said, and chivvied her upstairs and tucked her in as if she were still a little girl. I'm thirty-three, Louise thought, but was comforted. At least when she started in labour she would not be alone in the house, relying on Jason.

Mott, they had discovered, had a deep puncture bite on his leg. His paw bandaged, he had, with immense persistence, limped upstairs after her, and now tried to climb on to the bed. She helped him up and cuddled him against her. He put his head on her shoulder and licked her cheek.

Fern was too badly injured to come upstairs with them. She lay in her bed in the kitchen, and had only given a feeble wag of her tail when Louise had gone over to her before going up to bed herself. Emma had given her a drink of glucose and water through a syringe, but she had refused food and shown no desire to move.

"Oh, God," Louise said, looking up at the curved arc of new moon that shone in through her window. "If only Mervyn had known about our son. Please let him come back."

Sleep came at last but was haunted by dreams of dogs that chased sheep and tore out their throats. She tried to run and save Tarquin, who vanished suddenly and then turned into Russell saying, just before she woke, "I operated on the little bitch. All her lambs were dead."

The absurdity of the sentence stayed with her throughout the next dreadful day while they tidied up and assessed the damage, and made a list for the police. Russell arrived with Kate just after nine. He wanted to check the survivors. Tarquin was still alive, but it would be a few days before he was entirely happy about him. That did not help at all. Another thought struck her. Suppose he was crippled? Or had become sterile?

"Dad's got an idea," Kate said when they met for the evening meal. Everyone had been busy all day with the injured animals.

"What idea?" Louise asked, wearily pushing her hair back from her forehead. She had been feeding Fern every hour with glucose and water, but the bitch showed no sign of improvement. Mott nosed her unhappily, and then limped over to Louise, holding his injured paw in the air. He leaned against her, needing comfort.

Kate seemed to have forgotten that she had spoken.

Nobody had much appetite that evening.

Seven

K ate could not sleep. Her mind was filled with images from the day before. She had helped Peta with the little bitch after her father had operated. All the pups were dead, and the bitch was very weak. She and Peta had spent much of Saturday night awake looking after the dog and Tarquin.

"I'm too angry to sleep," Peta said. "It's such a waste. I wish we could punish the idiots who let the dogs out."

The animal hospital had been converted from the big kitchen of the old house. The bitch was in a large cage, and Tarquin lay on a rug on the floor in a recess by the Aga. There was a campbed already set up and Peta brought down a reclining garden chair for Kate. She anointed Tarquin's forehead every hour with Rescue Remedy.

"Tomorrow I'll give him glucose and water and arnica tablets," she said. "He's not going to die on us."

Kate couldn't bear to see the ram lying so still, his body a patchwork of stitches. Louise would miss him terribly in the morning, and there would be another big gap – no Demon to make them laugh.

Time and again during the night she had gone over to the ram to make sure he was still breathing. It was such a fragile breath, barely raising his chest. Once Peta had held a mirror to his lips. By morning he had opened his eyes, but showed no sign of wanting to move.

Kate had gone in search of Robin. Her elder brother sometimes had very good advice.

He had looked at her, frowning. "I don't think you have a

choice," he said, when she told him what was worrying her. "You'll never be easy with yourself if you keep quiet but you won't be popular in some quarters."

She knew that. It was difficult not to worry. Monday was going to be one of the worst days of her life. In some ways even worse than yesterday. There was still time to back out. Then she thought of Tarquin and the little bitch and the dead sheep, and knew that was impossible. On Sunday morning she went back to the farm with her father and spent the rest of the day helping Louise and Jason tend the injured animals.

Kate's thoughts were in turmoil. It was no use trying to sleep and she was hungry. She had not been able to eat, but now her body rebelled. She crept downstairs. not wanting to wake the others. She opened the door to see Louise and Emma sitting on either side of the kitchen table, both drinking tea. The fat brown pot which Emma insisted on using, putting the teabags in that instead of in the cups, stood on the top of the Aga.

"Tarquin behaved more like a dog than a sheep," Louise said, her voice seeming to come from a great distance, "he always ran to greet me." She laughed, and Kate wondered how laughter could sound unhappy. "Mind, I always had a goodie for him. He was a greedy . . ." the voice died away.

Kate walked into the room.

"Can I join in?" she asked. "I can't sleep either. I'm sure Tarquin's going to be OK," she said, accepting the cup her grandmother handed to her. "Peta's a wonderful nurse. She can perform miracles."

"Suppose he's crippled," Louise said. "He was very badly mauled. I've never seen any animal recover after damage like that."

"Peta helped Dad stitch him. She said nothing vital has been hurt. The dogs didn't get at any organs. And he's strong and very fit, Dad says, and he reckons there's more than a fifty-fifty chance now, as he was still alive this morning. Shock's the worst danger."

Emma refrained from pointing out that Kate was telling them both things they already knew. She was, Emma realised, intent on reassuring Louise and she had a sudden urge to hug her, which she restrained, knowing it would not be well received.

There was not much of the night left when they all went back to bed. Louise gave Fern a drink of glucose and water with Rescue Remedy in it. Russell had brought a large supply for her. All the injured animals needed it.

Kate was still worried. She went over and over in her mind the conversation she had had with her father, who had listened with interest to her suggestion.

"Are you sure you want to do this?" he had asked. "I can keep you out of it. There's no need at all for anyone to know you're involved here."

"I'm sure," she had said, although she felt afraid. She had written down six names, all of their owners in her form, the lower sixth. Robin was in the upper sixth and Jock in the fourth form. Even if she did not stand beside her father, the culprits would know she had informed on them.

When she went downstairs on Monday morning Louise was already up.

"I want to check the sheep in the barn," she said, putting on the thick fleece-lined anorak that belonged to Mervyn. It made her feel that he was close to her, thinking of her.

"I'll come with you," Kate said, feeling a further worry. What would Louise do if more of the sheep had died in the night?

Jason, taking hay to Corrie, met them outside the barn.

"Don't go in," he said. "I'll clear up. Two of the ewes died in the night and three more have lost their lambs. We need Russell."

"I want to see for myself." Louise opened the door and switched on the light. Four of the ewes were standing, watching her with apathetic eyes. If only they kept their lambs; she was going to lose so many. Three were lying still, barely able to lift their heads, evidence of the night's abortions beside them in the straw. Two would never move again. Both had been badly torn and Russell had held out little hope, although he had stitched the wounds.

"You can't do anything, Louise," Kate said, taking the older woman by the arm and forcing her to turn away and leave the barn. Louise felt helpless. How would she tell Mervyn if Tarquin died? And how would she cope if Mervyn never came home?

Kate wanted to comfort her by putting an arm around her, but felt too shy to do so. Louise might resent such familiarity. Her own resolve hardened. When she was a vet she too would be qualified to try to alleviate some of the harm done to animals like these. She was still not used to death but even Peta cried with the owners when a dog was put to sleep, or a cat; so what if she never did grow used to it? Maybe good vets and doctors never did; they just hid their feelings successfully.

She had wanted to be a vet since she was a small girl, but for some reason in the last few months, had wondered if she ought to strike out in some other field, to assert her own identity. She sighed, wishing she could understand her own feelings, which often seemed, these days, to be thoroughly confused. A neigh interrupted her thoughts.

"Corrie's calling us," she said.

Daylight was still a long way away. The small patch of grass growing among the cobbles was crisp under their feet. They opened the half door of the stable and were greeted by the push of a warm nose, and an eager snatch at the carrot that Kate had remembered to bring with her. Her daily visit to the mare was one of the highlights of her life.

The foal peeped at them from behind his mother. He was growing bolder but as yet was wary if there was more than one person near him. He was unbelievably dainty with his smooth dark coat and tiny mane and rocking-horse tail. He now knew Kate, who spent a great deal of time watching and talking to him. She adored the little colt and understood how Louise felt about Tarquin. He allowed her to touch him but he had not yet granted that favour to Louise. Jason had always been able to handle him.

"Thank God Jason put him inside so the dogs couldn't get him." Louise said. He probably owed his life to that. He would have had no chance, though the mare might well have been able to lash out and injure them. If only Jason could have reached Tarquin as well.

Louise let Belle out. It seemed so quiet without Tarquin shoving and butting and pushing against her, eager for caresses. He would race wildly round the paddock, as if the pent-up energy of the night had to be released in those first minutes.

Corrie was nosing Kate's pocket, hoping to find another carrot.

"The foal needs a name," she said, wanting to distract Louise. "Do you think Mr Merrit would let us choose it? I'd like to call him Lucky Chance. Chance for short. It was only by chance he was saved from drowning. If Jason hadn't seen Mr Merrit fall, he'd be dead."

"It was also probably only by chance he was saved from the dogs. If Jason hadn't put him in . . . We can call him what we like," Louise said. "If Mr Merrit wants a different name, then he can have two."

Russell, arriving very early to check his patients, looked in the barn and came out with a grim face. He examined Fern and then Mott and gave both dogs injections.

"Tarquin's in better shape than the little bitch this morning," he said, accepting coffee from Emma. "Though that's not saying a lot. But every day gives hope."

His expression lightened when he looked through the window and saw Corrie and Chance in the paddock, the foal bucking and jumping, delighted to be alive.

86

"It's good to know they weren't harmed," he said.

He walked outside with Louise. The sheep in the fields were wary and unsettled, reluctant to graze, galloping to the far end of each field whenever any vehicle or person approached. He watched them, frowning. How many lambs would die before birth? They had been hounded from one end of the field to the other, the dogs rioting and enjoying their freedom.

Bob Strang had came up from Kane's house. He grinned at Kate, who was his goddaughter.

"Hi, BFG," she said.

"Greetings, Tich."

Some of the tension drained away at the familiar exchange. She had christened him when she was five and he had looked even more enormous than he actually was, towering above every adult she had ever met. He seemed the personification of Roald Dahl's Big Friendly Giant. He had never married, and found pleasure in his brother's children and those of his friends. He was everybody's favourite uncle.

"He's like Bill the Lizard," Emma had once said, speaking of him to Louise and Jason, and had to remind her audience that Bill was a character in *Alice in Wonderland* who could be relied on to do every job he was asked, whatever it was. "Bill'll do it," everyone said at once.

Kate was dreading their visit to her school.

"I've had a word with the head," Russell said. He looked at his daughter. "There's still time to back out."

"Those who aren't involved will listen to me," Kate said. "I'm one of them. I saw what happened. And I've things I want to say."

Even so, she wished the journey was longer, and was reluctant to leave the sanctuary of the Land Rover. Bob squeezed her hand.

"Chin up, girl," he said, and she marched determinedly after him into the school hall, where they were expected. Her father had spent some time with the headmaster the day before.

87

It was the first time that Kate realised that James Arnold her headmaster was not a tall man, yet as he stood beside Bob he seemed the bigger of the two. He was angry and at his most formidable.

"You are quite sure you want to do this, Kate?" he asked. Her father had already told him the names of those pupils she thought were involved.

"Yes. They wanted me to join them last term. I wouldn't. It's stupid. And now see what's happened." She thought of Tarquin and felt near to tears, but that would never do. She had a role to play and she intended to do it to the best of her ability.

The headmaster was in his familiar position at his desk on the stage. Assembly was over and the rest of the school had been dismissed, only the two sixth forms remaining, as the headmaster did not think that what was to follow was suitable for the younger children. But the sixth formers were near adults, soon to be on their own in the world, and it was time they appreciated their responsibilities. There were three teachers present: the deputy head, Kate's form mistress, and the upper-sixth form master.

She looked down at her classmates, feeling small beside the three men. She searched their faces and saw Robin, who put his thumb up.

"I regret to say that something very serious has happened and that is why you are being called to this meeting." James Arnold settled his gown around him. "I am going to ask Mr Trent, who is our local veterinary surgeon, to take over for me. You all know his daughter, Kate."

She looked up at her father. Russell stared down at his audience, his face grim.

"On Saturday," he said, "a group of misguided enthusiasts went to a cottage on the hill and released a number of animals, among them cats and dogs. Three of those dogs got into a sheepfield."

Bob, who added photography to his many skills, had taken pictures of the ram, and of some of the injured sheep and enlarged all of them. He held up the photographs, one by one and then passed them down to the front row for the students to look at and circulate among the others. There was shocked silence.

"In releasing those dogs, you released death," Russell said. "You released them to inflict terrible injuries. Among them, injuries to this ram . . ." He held up a photograph of Tarquin. "He's one of the most valuable in this part of the country. He is at the moment in my hospital with over five hundred stitches in him. I don't know if he'll survive. The dogs dealt death to a number of ewes, while others are badly injured and have lost their lambs. Death to chickens and to ducks. What in God's name did you think you were doing?"

"I suppose you think it's right to keep animals confined and use them for research?" said a voice from the back of the hall. "They wanted their freedom. They all ran off as soon as we opened their cages."

"What research? Those animals were all rescued from cruel homes. Many of them have been the subject of court cases. Do you know where they are now you've gone and their homes are free of noisy humans? All except the sheep killers, which are now dead themselves, having been shot, went straight back to the kennels. They were found there in their own beds, waiting to be fed."

Miss Carling, Kate's form mistress, had been gazing at the photographs of the dead sheep as if she were mesmerised. She stood up, her voice shaking. Someone at the back was sobbing.

"You have no right to bring these pictures in here and traumatise the children. They'll have nightmares for weeks. How were they to know what the dogs would do?"

Kate was suddenly so angry that she lost her fears.

"They're traumatised? What about me? I was there on the farm, helping to drive off the dogs; helping my dad and mum

89

clear up the carnage. So was Jason, who all of you know. He's younger than some of you. He only left school last year. He had to get the dogs out of the sheep field and he had to watch the sheep being torn apart." She took a deep breath. She was so angry she had forgotten her fear. "He had to listen to them crying in pain, terrified; he had to bring the ewes out, bleeding, torn, some with their throats gashed, others with their guts hanging out. I helped bathe their wounds. I listened to their cries. Those sheep have feelings too." She took a deep breath.

"They're the source of the farm income. Many of them have lost their lambs and that means a big loss to Mrs Pritchard. Some of them were pets: there was a drake that used to knock on the kitchen door every morning, wanting bread."

She picked up her school bag and opened it, taking out, not books, but the clothes she had been wearing on Saturday still stiff with blood. She held them up, so angry that she was shaking.

"Jason had to send the farm dogs in to chase off the intruders. They're both badly hurt. You'll have nightmares, just looking at pictures of the dead animals? Good. I hope they never leave you. What sort of dreams do you think we have? Or their owner, who's struggling to keep a dying farm on its feet, whose husband is missing, perhaps dead – nobody knows – and she's expecting her first baby just after Christmas." She was aware of astounded faces. "What have you done to her? This ram is her future . . . if he survives, and there's a big chance he won't. He was to father some of the best lambs in this part of the country. His father cost £38,000. He was worth at least £10,000. Probably a lot more."

"She'll be insured," said a sullen voice from the back.

"That makes up for the loss of a valuable life? That makes up for not seeing him run to greet us every morning, or play in the fields in the sun? That makes up for not seeing his lambs in the spring?"

Kate surprised not only herself but all those who heard her.

"He'll have produced some lambs," said the same voice. Kate tried to see who was speaking, but since no one stood up, it was difficult to pinpoint them. She could only detect that the speaker was male.

"He hasn't. He wasn't old enough at the start of this breeding season – he's not even a year old yet. If he dies he's lost for ever and so is his progeny."

She was exhausted. Miss Carling was staring at her as if she had never seen her before, a small muscle by her eye twitching.

The headmaster stepped back to his desk as Russell moved away.

"The vet bills alone add up to well over two thousand pounds, and that's something I do not intend the farmer to pay," he said. "The parents of those who are guilty will be contacted and expected to share the bill. There were sheep killed on another farm and that farmer has complained to the police who will be here this morning to interview you. I am ashamed that anything like this should have been instigated by pupils of this school."

"Animals have rights," said another voice, though it did not sound quite so convinced.

"Those rescued dogs and cats had the right to live in peace, not be loosed into a frightening world and hounded by lunatics," Kate said, her voice rising in anger. "The sheep have a right to live in safety, not be tortured by dogs. Tarquin has the right to live, as did the ducks and chickens. Think about it, all of you."

Bob, who had been listening, amazed at Kate's speeches, stepped forward and put his hand on her shoulder.

"If any of you have any human feelings, you'll think about what my goddaughter said. She knows the sheep that died. She knows how the farmer feels. She saw how every dog and most of the cats crept back to the only homes they knew, the only places where they were well treated, as soon as the marauders had gone."

91

"All except three," Russell said. "One of those, a little Jack Russell, was killed by a car as he bolted from you. He was terrified of people, having been badly used and rescued by Mr Merrit. Another, a big dog, collected two local dogs running free. They ended on another farm and all have been shot." He paused, staring angrily at those who had interrupted him. "A little bitch, about to whelp, jumped barbed wire in her panic. She was too heavy to clear the fence, and wire ripped her. I had to remove all the pups, and part of her insides and I have no idea whether she will survive. She's only a little dog. No pedigree. Her ex-owners are due to be prosecuted for cruelty. The next dog I get in in the same state as she was when she was first brought to me six weeks ago I'll bring to school and show you what Mr Merrit really does. Also the barn where the dogs and cats you let loose were housed needs a new padlock. Breaking and entering is a criminal offence."

He looked down at them from the stage.

"Those who were guilty disgust me. What did you get out of it? Pleasure? A kick at thinking how generous you were being to release helpless animals into a wild environment, presumably to hunt and feed themselves when they are used to a warm shelter at night and food being given them?"

Bob collected the photographs. Kate, uneasy again now that her anger had died, went down to join her classmates, wondering what reception she would get.

Her form captain, Mike Holt, stood up.

"I wasn't involved, sir," he said. "And I appreciate what has been said. I think Kate did a great job. I don't think I could have coped and I'm sure that goes for most of the other members of my class. I do want to disassociate most of us from this. And to say that if there's anything we can do to make amends – though I don't see what – we'll try."

Everyone was silent as Russell and Bob went out of the hall. The vet turned to look at his daughter but she was surrounded by a small group of classmates, talking eagerly.

"I hope that's settled them," he said. He sighed. "It's not

helped Louise. Emma's very worried about her. It's bad enough not knowing if Mervyn is alive or dead. If Tarquin dies it may possibly be the last straw. I wish to God there was something we could do for her . . . life is so bloody unfair."

Eight

K ate was more than an hour late home and Emma was
just beginning to worry when an unfamiliar car drew
into the yard and parked. She went out to meet them.

"This is Mike Holt, our form captain, and his mum," Kate
said, introducing her two companions. Sandra Holt, who was
small and dark with a cap of close cropped hair and dark eyes
topped by high arched brows, climbed out of the Mercedes.
Her son, already taller than his mother, had inherited her
facial bone structure and her eyes. Flared eyebrows, lifted at
the outer edges, gave him a quizzical expression.

Louise, at the window, looking at the woman's slim legs in
tight designer jeans and the belted leather jacket, felt larger
than ever. The visitor reached inside the boot of the car and
produced an enormous bunch of mixed flowers. An elderly
golden retriever regarded Emma thoughtfully from the back
seat of the car. Both Kate and Mike held several very large
carrier bags.

Louise returned to her big armchair; she did not feel at such
a disadvantage when sitting. The dogs were at her feet, both
reluctant to move more than necessary. Mott lifted his head
and gave a token bark, but was not feeling well enough to do
more than signal his warning. Fern couldn't be bothered. She
hurt abominably. She had not moved all day, which worried
everyone. She accepted the glucose and water that was syr-
inged into her mouth, but there was not even a token wag of
her tail.

The kitchen seemed full of people. Mike was as big as Jason

94

and Kate was almost as tall. They radiated energy. Kate sat astride the bench by the pine table, and Mike hovered, unable to decide where to stand.

"Do please sit down," Louise said. She felt overpowered by their presence, and was not at all sure that she could cope with them. She could not imagine what they wanted, unless it were to apologise.

"Mike told me, at lunchtime, what had happened," Sandra said. "This won't make up for it. Nothing can. But the parents of those who weren't involved clubbed together for these for you. Not only Mike's form, but all the school."

Kate shook the contents of the carrier bags out on to the table and Louise stared in disbelief. There appeared to be a mountain of tiny clothes – bibs, little jackets, two babygrows, several slightly larger romper suits – and a cuddly teddy bear, baby soap and baby powder, cot blankets and pram covers, and small embroidered pillow cases.

"Kate says you're expecting a little boy. I went round to all the mums I knew to ask them to show that they were as shocked as I was by what happened." Sandra smiled at Louise. "Kate and I had a ball, with more money to spend than I expected. It's years since I bought baby clothes, and they're so much nicer now even than when Mike was tiny."

Mike looked as if he would like to run from the room.

Louise sat speechless. Emma made coffee for everyone, and began to chatter, to give her time to recover.

"I don't know how to thank you," she said at last.

"Don't. We owe you. And don't worry about the vet's bill. The parents of the children involved have agreed to help pay it. They were as shocked as the rest of us when they heard what their sons and daughters had been doing. The police went to see them all."

A lot had happened since the morning, Kate thought. Sandra had overwhelmed her. She had arrived at the school after lunch with Mike and had asked for Kate to have the afternoon off, to help her. She had been extremely angry and had needed to make amends even though her own son had not been the cause of the trouble. The headmaster, saddened by the behaviour of his pupils, was only too ready to agree to Kate's absence and to add his own very generous contribution to what Sandra named her impromptu baby shower. A visit to the staff room brought a further unbelievable amount of money and Robin and Mike had collected from their forms. Sandra had then taken Kate to call on the mothers house by house.

"We can't make it up to you; but we can show that we care," Sandra said.

Emma brought out scones and buns, and jam and butter and cream. Kate took some of the little clothes over to Louise and put them in her lap.

"Aren't they cute? One of the girls in my form has a baby brother born just over two years ago. Her mum's offered you a high chair and a carrycot. She doesn't need them any more and says they're in good condition and she'd be glad to let them go to a good home."

"Sounds more like a dog," Jason commented, having come into the room just before this speech. He nodded to Mike, who he knew from his own schooldays. Emma, watching them, was reminded of two dogs circling, tails stiff, eyes wary, ready to growl and attack. Was Kate the problem? she wondered, but Kate herself seemed unaware of either of them. She was much more interested in looking at the results of their afternoon's shopping, anxiously showing the things to Louise, who, she hoped, would feel better as a result.

"Some of us want to help with the dogs and cats," Mike said. "How many are there?"

"Not as many as there were," Jason said, his face grim. "All the dogs except for the one injured and the two dead have come back – that's about fifteen. Most of the cats appeared at feeding time, though a few of those are still missing and so are the ferrets. They'll probably survive quite well on vermin and the cats will manage. They shouldn't cause problems; they'll

96

go for mice and rats and maybe hang around the farmyards. Always room for them in the barns."

"What has to be done each day? What could we do to help? There are six of us, with Kate." Mike, like his mother, needed to do something tangible.

"It would free you, Gran," Kate said.

Jason thought, trying to make a list of everything that he took for granted. He, Emma, Kate and now Bob had worked out their own routine.

"The cages and pens have to be cleaned thoroughly and disinfected. We put clean newspaper down on the floors. Each animal needs to be checked to make sure it's well; invalids given their medicine; the friendly ones need their little bit of a cuddle and fuss. The dogs have to be exercised, one at a time, as I don't know which get on with which, and don't want to find out the hard way."

He paused to take a pasty from a plate on the table. Their evening meal would be late and he was always ravenous. Hollow legs, his gran used to say and he hoped Emma wouldn't do the same. It made him feel greedy.

"The cats have litter trays which have to be emptied, cleaned thoroughly and refilled. They all have to be fed and then the bowls washed. Water bowls need washing and refilling. Blankets need washing once a week or more if there's a problem dog that isn't house-trained."

He looked at Mike, who was as elegantly dressed as his mother, summing him up as a spoiled brat, still at home, never having to do a hand's turn. He used to pass Mike's home on his way back from school: a black and white timbered house that seemed a mansion to Jason, standing in an immaculate garden, the Mercedes and the Porsche often in the paved courtyard.

"It's a very mucky job," he said, hoping to discourage Mike.

"It must take hours," Sandra said.

"Around two hours morning and evening." Jason took a

scone and spread butter, jam and cream lavishly. "Bob does a lot of the walking during the day. It would certainly be useful if there were more of us. It would free Emma to help Louise." He was trying to be fair but he didn't want strangers around.

"Before school tomorrow." Mike sounded positive. "Those of us that don't do a paper round can come up. Mum can drop us off and afterwards we can join Kate at the Keepgate, if her dad doesn't mind giving us all a lift to the school bus stop."

"It sounds too good to be true," Emma said. "Jason can always ring me from the cottage if you let him down. It's a big commitment, and how many of you are used to such early starts to the day?"

"If Jason can do it, we can," Mike said.

Jason looked at Emma and raised his eyebrows.

"Seeing is believing," he said, when Kate had gone out to the yard to say goodbye to Mike and his mother and to pet Sultan, the golden retriever, who took it as his right. Jason was not convinced. "They'll start off with the best of intentions and within a week they'll all be gone again." He slammed his empty mug on the table, his eyes angry.

"Mike's OK," Kate said, coming back into the kitchen. "If he says he'll do something, he does it."

Emma began to fold the clothes.

Jason looked at them, suddenly realising that within less than two months, Louise's baby would be a reality.

"Is it really going to be that small?"

"Babies are, stupid." Kate began to lay the table. "We've been having talks on fitness from school. How what we eat and drink can affect our children, even years later."

"Nasty to think that lots of kids are only half healthy because their mums smoke or drank or drugged," Jason said.

He brought a small table and set it in front of Louise, who found hard chairs very difficult to sit on.

Emma had made a quick meal with a pie from the freezer, a salad and jacket potatoes, which were always being popped into the Aga oven, and could be taken out and re-heated if things went wrong. Jason, coming in cold and hungry, could help himself, add cheese and pickles, and fill the gaps.

Louise glanced down at the two dogs. Mott was recovering enough to look hopefully at her as she ate.

Kate took up the syringe and went over to Fern, who gave a faint twitch of her tail. She was becoming used to having liquid dripped into her mouth and now swallowed without having to have her throat stroked.

Jason went off to his rooms. Kate, who had homework to do, decided to leave it till later and sit with her grandmother and Louise. She was reluctant to admit that being on her own was lonely.

She bit into an apple.

"Dad suggested I go home for Christmas. Can you manage if I do? I can come up here each day to groom Corrie. Chance let me brush him this morning. I wish they were mine."

"You're all coming up here for Christmas dinner, anyway," Emma said. "And Bob and Kane if he's home. You can help me with the cake and puddings and mince pies."

Kate finished the apple and tossed the core into the Aga.

"Jason'll have you for that," Emma said. "It's compost."

"One little core?"

There was a knock at the door.

Emma opened it and stared at a man who was a stranger to her. He came in on her invitation, taking off his cap to reveal grizzled hair. Jason followed him in, shaking rain off his jacket.

"I'm Dai Griffiths from Carreg Mawr," the visitor said. "Is Mrs Pritchard in?"

"I'm here," Louise called, wondering what the farmer wanted. He lived about three miles away, down in the valley, a small quiet man, who acknowledged her with only a nod if they passed one another.

"I heard from Russell when he came to calve a cow yesterday. I was lucky," he said, accepting the chair that Emma pointed out to him. "The dogs didn't get to me. Brought you two in-lamb ewes and one of my ram lambs. Nothing like your lad, but you'll be down in stock and I've had a good year. Lots of twins and triplets last spring."

He took the cup of coffee that Emma handed to him but refused one of her little buns.

"Just eaten, thanks, but they look good. If you need help with the sheep when the baby comes . . . that's my phone number." He handed her a grubby envelope on which it was written.

He looked at Louise.

"You'll be missing your man. Not knowing . . . that's always bad. Do you get news? Is the government doing anything to find him?"

"The Foreign Office people do seem to be trying . . . but what can they do? They sent detectives over as well, but there aren't any clues. They've just vanished. Nobody admits to having even seen the lorry arrive or the men who must have ambushed it. There aren't any leads and no one has the least idea who was responsible. It's desolate country apparently, very remote with people hiding in the hills. The people around are scared and won't talk, even if they do know anything. They can't tell me how he's likely to be living; or if he's ill, who'll find a doctor for him. Is he well treated, or tortured and half starved?"

All her night-time fears were surfacing. She had not voiced them aloud before, even to Emma, but now she felt they must be said or they would reduce her permanently to a dark pit of misery which would overwhelm her. She needed strength for the baby. It was better to express her thoughts than to keep them hidden.

"I sometimes wish they'd bring me news that he's dead . . . I could settle then. Now . . . I hope, and then despair, and it's like living on a roller coaster."

Kate looked at Louise in dismay. It was the first time she had been faced with the reality of Mervyn's disappearance. She was relieved to hear the sound of her father's Land

Rover. Nobody knew what to say. What comfort could they offer?

Russell, coming into the kitchen, overheard the last few words. He bent over Fern, and then brought out his syringe and injected her.

"She's going to take time to recover; she's still in shock, but she's definitely on the mend," he said. Mott had walked stiffly over to nose the vet as he knelt. "We'll give you a prick too," Russell said, and Mott sat, knowing the drill and not minding it. "They've both got puncture wounds and those are the ones that cause trouble. This should prevent it, but keep an eye on them."

Outside the wind rose and shook the trees. Rain drummed against the window panes. Kate, looking through the window, saw the lights of the village spread below her. Once she had been down there, and, looking up, seen the gold patches that shone on the side of the hill, and wondered how it felt to live there.

"Mr Griffiths has brought me two ewes and a young ram," Louise said, as Russell accepted the mug of coffee Emma had poured for him, and took a pasty from the plate that Jason offered. "And the parents from Kate's school have produced a mountain of baby clothes, enough for quins, I should think."

"Guilty consciences," Russell said.

"Time I was getting back. Maybe you'd help me unload the trailer?" Dai turned to Jason. The kitchen door was almost wrenched from his grasp as he opened it. Heads down, they went into the yard, thankful for the security lights that came on as soon as they entered their beam.

"Come up and see my room, Dad," Kate said. "I've finished decorating it at last."

Louise sighed as they went out and tried to settle herself more comfortably. Chairs and her bed seemed to have become instruments of torture.

"No one came near me when Mervyn disappeared," she

said. "Now the whole world seems to be making a way to our door."

"No one knew how to handle that." Emma added wood to the opened Aga and poked it into a blaze. "This is manageable and the school parents are trying to make amends. Mr Griffiths knows that if he'd lost sheep the way you did, Mervyn would have brought him a few replacements. A friend of mine lost her whole kennels in a fire, and a number of dogs died. She was inundated with puppies for the next year."

The kitchen door suddenly slammed open. Jason fought to close it, and came into the room, his colour high and his hair on end.

"You need a haircut, my lad," Emma said, and he grinned at her.

He took a banana from the bowl and peeled it, throwing the skin into the compost bucket. He had plans to take over Louise's kitchen garden next year, and every scrap that could be converted went into his bin.

"We're branching out," he said. "The ewes and the ram are Jacobs. The ewes are patched but the ram is more like a Dalmatian. Spotted all over. He's been hand reared and he'll be a pest: he looks in pockets, and apparently comes to the farmhouse for food handouts. Follows you like a dog. Have to watch when Tarquin comes back. Doubt if he'll like competition."

"Who wants the wool?" Louise asked. She was not familiar with the breed. Most of theirs were Welsh mountain sheep that thrived on the rough grazing and were winter hardy. The lambs were great explorers, finding the smallest gaps and getting through.

"Mr Griffiths says that home spinners like it; they don't dye it. There's a big demand."

"Where did you put them? Not with our sheep? They'd not get on. And none of our rams will tolerate a new one." Louise was suddenly anxious. Jason was not farm bred.

"I'm not daft." Jason wished Louise would trust him more,

and not tell him things he already knew. "If it weren't so windy I'd take you out to see them. The ewes are in the dog shed. You never use it now. It's big enough for the two of them and I put down plenty of straw. The ram's in the old stable. It's a bit run down, but it's weather proof. He seems placid enough." He grinned at her. "I'm not so green as I'm cabbage-looking, as my old gran used to say."

Louise often wondered if half the things he attributed to his grandmother were in fact true.

The ringing phone startled them.

"Russell's needed," Emma said, after she had answered it. "There's a horse in trouble at the Derwent farm. Someone let off a firework and scared it and it jumped barbed wire. Very nasty gash. Roz says he'll know where it is."

"He will," Russell said, coming back into the kitchen. "I wish they'd stick to one night for fireworks. I'm for ever clearing up the damage the idiots do by letting them off in stupid places, for days before and after the fifth." He was reluctant to leave the big friendly kitchen. "I thought that might be for me. It's been too quiet all day. Couldn't last. Kate is actually going to get her homework done, and she asked me to say goodnight for her. She seems to be settling. She's made a good job of her room."

An hour later, just as they were wondering about bed, Kate came down the stairs, racing into the room.

"Spice has had her kittens in the airing cupboard," she said. "Six of them: one ginger, one grey, three tabby and one almost black and white. She's a bit hissy and spitty. Don't think we'd better move her, do you?"

"She'll only take them back," Louise said. "She always does if we try to move her to her own bed, but she usually chooses the bathroom airing cupboard. The attic's always been empty before, and the door shut."

Kate sounded rueful.

"I'm going to be short of clean clothes – I hadn't put them

103

away, and she's on top of them. They'll need another wash. She'd better have a litter box up there and she'll want some food too, won't she?"

"No peace for the wicked," Jason said, as he went out into the storm. He returned a few minutes later with a large seed box and a carrier bag full of peat. He lined the box with aluminium foil and added the litter.

"I'll pinch a couple of proper litter boxes from Mr Merrit tomorrow," he said. "He has a vast store of them. Don't think he'll mind, it's all in a good cause. Do you know six people who want kittens?"

"I'll ask at school," Kate said. "Can I keep the black and white one? He'd be company up there at night."

She picked up the litter box and a plate of cat food that Emma produced, together with a small carton of milk and a bowl.

"I don't see why not," Louise said. She manoeuvred herself out of her chair and over to the radio, and switched it on.

". . . reports have just come in from that area. Two bodies were found today. Both men had been shot. We hope to have further details in our later bulletin." The announcer's dispassionate voice continued. "They have not yet been identified." There was a pause as Emma and Louise stared at one another. The voice went on. "Three people, a man and two women, were killed when a car went out of control on the M25 . . ."

Louise switched off the set, and stood, white-faced, looking at Emma.

"Where?" she asked, but was sure she knew the answer.

Nine

Sleep had become an enemy to be dreaded, rather than a friend to be wooed. The words beat in Louise's mind: two bodies were found . . . The room was so silent, except for the sound of her own breathing. Mervyn smiled at her from their wedding photograph.

Dear God, please.

She switched on the light and took a book from the little pile on her bedside table, but the words made no sense. She read and re-read the same page three times and was just about to get out of bed and go downstairs, where at least she'd have the company of the dogs, when the phone startled her by ringing.

She stared at it, afraid to lift it. Would the Foreign Office phone at this time of night? It was nearly one o'clock. Hours before the day began. Imagination took over.

"Mrs Pritchard, we are so dreadfully sorry to have to tell you . . ."

The summons continued.

She picked up the receiver.

"Louise, I saw your light. It's all right . . . they were in Africa, not Europe. I rang the BBC. You can go to sleep now." Jason. She began to calm down. She breathed deeply. She could not tell him how much the ringing bell had frightened her.

She could not find any words at all. She felt as if she had a fluttering bird inside her chest, trying to get out. Just to add to her discomfort the baby gave a sudden powerful kick, as if to tell her to still her thudding heart and let him rest.

"Louise, you're OK?"

"I am now," she said, finding her voice at last. "Thank you, Jason, I wouldn't have thought of that. It's a relief to know."

"No problem. Goodnight."

"Goodnight," she said, and put the phone down. She stared at it, her mind totally blank.

"Louise?" Emma tapped at the door.

"Come in."

Emma opened the door and walked in.

"What's happened? I heard the phone. Who was it? At this time of night."

"Jason. He saw my light, guessed I was worrying, and rang the BBC. Those men were in Africa, not Bosnia. It wasn't Mervyn."

She began to get out of bed.

Emma sighed with relief.

"Thank God for that. Why don't you stay there? I'll bring up drinks and sit with you."

"I'd rather come downstairs for a bit. I was scared when the phone rang . . . I thought it was the Foreign Office . . . I won't settle . . ."

"So did I," Emma said. "Jason should have thought . . ."

"He'd be so anxious to tell me that it would never cross his mind that I'd think it was bad news from the government. Don't say anything tomorrow, Emma. It is good news, in one way, and he does try so hard. I don't want to upset him when he meant to put my mind at rest. It was thoughtful."

It was better to think about Jason than to worry about Mervyn.

"I keep on thinking he'll up and leave. It's not as if he gets a decent wage. He says it's OK because he gets his flat rent free and full board, but I still feel I'm imposing on him."

"Once upon a time apprentices paid for their training They didn't get a wage," Emma said, as they walked down the stairs. Louise gripped the handrail, terrified of falling. She felt

106

unbalanced. "College isn't free and you're having to teach him everything."

"Things change," Louise said.

Fern looked up at them when they came into the kitchen, and very slowly, managed to get to her feet. She staggered to the door and looked back appealingly. Her eyes were now focused.

"She wants to go out," Emma said "That's a good sign. I'll put your anorak over my night things and go with her. She looks as if she'll collapse any minute."

She fetched the anorak, put it on and then walked briskly to the door to open it for the collie bitch. Mott had followed Louise downstairs and was sitting by her chair. He considered the darkness and decided to stay indoors.

Emma followed the little bitch, afraid she might lie down and get cold. She was very unsteady on her legs. The place was suddenly unfamiliar, shadows hiding the corners, light spilling across the yard. The village was dark except for the few strategically placed street lamps that shone at the various small crossroads. A cottage window, far below, gleamed brightly.

She too had been unable to sleep, worrying lest Mervyn was one of the men whose bodies had been found. In spite of her fears, she felt content for the first time since her husband had died, feeling that Louise could not do without her. They worked well together and the night-time confidences had forged a friendship that would, she was sure, endure. If only Mervyn were alive . . . his son needed a father.

It would be good to have a baby in the house, occupying all of them. Her grandchildren would, all too soon, leave home to make their own way and parents and grandparents would then be considered either interfering or redundant. That was already beginning. She had been lonely when she lived with Russell and Roz, feeling she had no part in their lives and was in the way. At times she felt they did not appreciate what an enormous gap had been left in her own life or that she had no idea how to fill it. Here, she had a role to play, and hoped that, even if Mervyn returned, she might be able to stay on. She could take over so much for Louise in the house and with the baby and free her for outside work, which she knew the farmer's wife preferred.

The wind had died to a faint breeze that stirred the branches of the trees that sheltered the farmhouse and caused the leaves to whisper incessantly. An owl cried and was answered and far away, a dog barked. Corrie stamped restlessly in her stall, aware of Emma's presence at a time when the yard should be quiet. There was a scuffling noise from darkness that seemed more intense beyond the area of light that flooded the cobbles near the house.

Mott, having changed his mind about going outside, joined Fern, nosing her and then the ground, before running to the wall and cocking his leg. Light shone on their black and white coats. Listening, he heard another dog bark in the distance, and his head went up, his ears pricked. He gave a token reply, but he did not yet feel well enough to bother with the messages on the wind. Far down the field beside the house a fox ran silently, the rat in his mouth dangling. He helped the cats keep the vermin under control, though few appreciated his efforts. He was not among the sheep and Mott ignored him, although he caught his scent.

Fern, her duty completed, staggered over to Emma, who picked her up in her arms and carried her indoors. Mott followed. It was a relief to Emma to come out of the frosty air. Pyjama legs were no protection against the chilly wind, she thought as she closed the door. She must buy a full-length, much warmer, dressing gown. Babies cried in the night and Louise would need rest.

"Try Fern with some chicken soup," she said, as she closed the door.

Louise had made coffee, knowing it was absurd and would keep her awake, but that was preferable to the dreams she had been having. The soup was one of Emma's favourite standbys.

Thick with onions and other vegetables, it was a wonderful warmer when coming in from the cold. There was always a large bowl in the refrigerator.

Emma spooned a quantity into a soup plate to heat in the microwave. Mott sat, eager, his ears pricked, always alert when food was prepared. Even Fern looked interested and, when Louise bent to stroke her, thumped her tail gently against the floor.

Louise poured some soup into Fern's bowl and put it in front of the collie. Mott, intrigued by food at this time of night, put his tongue in, and stole a quick mouthful. Fern, now hungry, growled. Emma called him, and gave him his own share.

She turned on the radio. They were greeted with a raucous cacophony of sound that Louise decided was meant to be singing. There were only about ten words in the whole song. Emma made a face.

"To quote Kate: yuk. I feel like a dinosaur at times. Outdated and unable to understand the modern world. I was nearly forty when Roz was born. She was very much a surprise baby. We'd not intended to have another . . . I'm glad she came, though."

She sipped her coffee.

Mott was gobbling noisily. Fern smelled the broth suspiciously, tasted it, and then swallowed. A moment later, she began to lap more eagerly.

"They say chicken soup has antibiotic properties," Emma said, "though I don't think it's nearly as good as beef tea. Would you like some?"

"Beef tea?" Louise was beginning to feel as if she might sleep if she went back to bed.

"Chicken broth. I just fancy a snack, and it smells good."

"Why not? I never can eat much at a time these days. There doesn't seem to be room but I'm always hungry." She took a deep breath, and moved awkwardly over to the table where Emma had set two places for the dishes she had just filled. She sat, sideways on. "I can't even get near the table now, and as for driving . . . I don't know what I'd have done if you hadn't come here. Another seven weeks if I'm lucky. I do so hope he won't be late."

"Roz was two weeks late," Emma said. "I don't know why as the other two were early. You never can tell. My sister's first was three weeks late."

Louise eased herself out of her chair.

"I keep discovering new places that ache, and I've got swollen ankles and heartburn."

She left Emma to wash up and went back to bed. She woke to find Jason standing beside her, carrying a portable table on a stand. She glanced at her clock. Ten thirty. She couldn't believe it.

"Merciful heavens . . . why didn't anyone wake me?"

"Emma said to let you sleep. And you're to have breakfast in bed." He grinned at her. "So, ma'am, no arguments. I'll go down for your tray."

She looked at the table, which he had swivelled across the bed.

"Where did that come from?"

"It was my gran's. Russell picked it up from my dad's house. His neighbour had the key."

"Where's your father?"

"In hospital. Cirrhosis of the liver, which is no surprise."

"Have you been to see him?"

"No. And I'm not going. I'll get that tray."

He went downstairs, and Louise got out of bed, feeling in need of a wash and a comb through her hair. She had not had breakfast in bed since she was a small girl and ill, and was not at all sure she wanted it, but it would be a shame to disappoint them.

Emma had cooked scrambled eggs. She had added thin slices of toast, cut into triangles, butter in a silver dish, and marmalade in a little bowl. She had found the china that was only used on state occasions and there had been very few of

110

those. The tiny cornflowers spilled across cups, saucers and plates. The butter dish had been a wedding present and was never used. Emma must have polished it. It glinted in the light.

There were two cups of coffee. Jason took his and walked across to sit on the big window-seat. He looked around him appreciatively.

"Lovely room. When I win the lottery I'll have a big house, with lots of space so everyone can get away from everyone else. Reckon the world would be a better place if everyone had room around them, instead of being stuffed so close they get on one another's nerves all the time." He took a sip of coffee. "Emma says I'm to stay and make sure you eat."

"Did Mike and his friends come?" Louise asked, buttering a slice of toast. She was surprised to find that she was hungry and Emma's tempting tray made eating a pleasure.

"Yeah."

"And?"

"Mike gets up my nose. He's an organiser, and bossy with it. He had everything planned before they even arrived. Steve to empty the litter boxes and refill them. Kate and me to see to the animals and take them their food. A girl called Mollie who has ten thumbs and three left feet washed the bowls, and dropped most of them a dozen times. Lucky they're metal."

He jumped up and walked round the room, looking at the pictures on the walls. Mervyn's side of the room had three seascapes. Louise had chosen mountain scenery, and a placid lake on which a fisherman angled for ever. It always hung crooked. Jason straightened it. He seemed unable to be still for more than a few minutes at a time and Louise envied him his energy.

"There was a red-headed boy who's new to the school since I left. He did the water bowls, emptied them, washed them and refilled them. Mike prepared the feeds. That's not easy as they all have different things. Mr Merrit has a card on each kennel door with how much and what."

"It sounds efficient." Louise spread marmalade on the last

111

piece of toast and poured more coffee for herself and Jason.
Emma had given them cream instead of milk.

"It was . . . but he could have asked me, couldn't he,
instead of wading in and dictating? If he's ever prime minister
he'll be a proper little Cromwell."

"I expect he meant well," Louise said, as she finished the
last mouthful of toast.

"Oh, aye."

"What does that mean?"

"Nothing." He walked over to pick up the tray. "It means I
wish I'd been born into a family that could afford to go skiing
every year, and buy me designer clothes, and had a mum who
cared for me . . . and a dad with a Mercedes . . . and a big
posh house with a real garden. Doesn't make me very nice,
does it?"

"Do you like living here?" Louise asked, not sure how to
answer that particular question. Life dished out a miserable
portion to some people, she thought.

"First time I've been happy in my life," he said. "I like
feeling needed. I wasn't happy looking after Gran but I felt
necessary . . . I guess this morning Mike made me feel it
wouldn't matter if I weren't there at all. They could cope."

"Who took the food into the dogs and cats?" Louise asked.

"Kate and me. They know us. Strangers scare them."

"So you were the most important part of the whole exercise.
Without you, the animals might have been terrified all over
again by people they'd never seen before."

He grinned at her, suddenly light-hearted.

"You're happy with what I do?"

"We couldn't cope without you," Louise said. "I'm always
scared you'll get fed up, and look for work with a real salary
and some prospects."

"I've got my keep and live rent free. Gran left me her house
and furniture and a few hundred pounds. She had her insurance for her funeral so she could be buried decent. There
was quite a bit over, and more when her things were sold. One

or two nice things, my gran had. Didn't realise till old Joe
Hicks in the antique shop came to see me and bought them.
He used to visit Gran and always admired her Staffordshire
dogs and one or two bowls she had. Gave me a fair price too. I
don't need much money. I don't go in for designer clothes and
Nikes. Not like some."

"You've got your head screwed on too well for that,"
Louise said.

He took the tray and walked over to the door, then
hesitated.

"Can I ask a favour . . . say no if you want. Only . . ."

"Only what?"

"Can I have one of the kittens to live with me? I've always
wanted a cat. We did have one once, a cute little thing but
Gran was allergic."

"Of course you can have one. It never matters how many cats
there are on the farm. I haven't seen them yet. Have you?"

"You'll see them. Spice decided that they needed to be on
the hearthrug today and she's brought them all down. One at
a time. Very determined is Spice. Good job you won't have to
carry your baby in your mouth. It must be tricky."

Louise laughed.

"It would look most odd, even if it were possible. I'd
probably get arrested. Or have it taken into care."

He turned back a second time.

"There's a cute little grey one. They don't look much yet, do
they, but in a week or so they'll be pretty things."

Jason left her and she dressed, wishing it didn't take so long.
She went downstairs. There was no one in the kitchen.

Mott was out, probably with Jason, but Fern lay on the rug,
the kittens, still blind, crawling against her, and the cat
cuddled up to her, as if trying to comfort her. Louise suddenly
wondered if Spice had indeed had that in mind when she
brought them down. Fern was busy soaking the two nearest to
her with her tongue. She thumped her tail when her mistress
came into the room.

Jason put his head round the door.

"Come and see the Jacobs," he said.

He led the way to the paddock where Corrie and the foal were usually put to stretch their legs during the day. Corrie, her head over the stable door, called to Louise, who paused to pet her.

"I thought Corrie could go out after lunch. Give these the chance of some fresh air and grass." He leaned on the white gate. "Lovely, aren't they?"

The two ewes, one a mottled dark brown and black and the other patched with white, were in lamb. Dai lambed early, being down in the valley. They'd have to be kept indoors after Christmas, Louise thought. February could be a very cruel month. Hand tame, they came to the gate to have their heads rubbed. The ram, his horns as yet only half grown, turned to look at her with suspicious eyes, and then began to feed again. Jason had put down turnips for them, as the grass was winter sparse.

"I'll put them inside early, I think," he said, viewing the clouds building on the hilltops. "Going to rain, and rain heavily. Let Corrie and the little one stretch their legs before the downpour."

They both turned as Russell opened the outer gate and drove his Land Rover into the yard.

"Came to check on Fern," he said, "and to cadge a coffee. Been to see a horse over at Ty Newydd. Poor brute had navicular, and there wasn't anything I could do for him. It's gone too far. We've been trying to help him for weeks, but he was in too much pain. I didn't think they'd want me to stay on after I'd put him out of it for good . . . they were very upset. I hate my job at times."

He walked into the kitchen and then laughed.

"Fern appears to have had kittens. I take it that Kate's protégé has brought them down?"

"She seems to have left Fern as babysitter." Louise looked down at the tangle of different coloured furs on the hearthrug.

"It's doing her good. She really is perking up. I'd think that by tomorrow she'll be almost herself again. None of those bites is infected."

Fern licked his hand when he finished examining her. Russell, whatever he did to her, remained one of her favourite people. Outside the door, Spice yowled to come in and, as soon as it was opened, marched over to her kittens and spread herself so that they could feed. She checked each head as if afraid one or more might have vanished in her absence. Her purr drowned the ticking grandmother clock.

Russell glanced at it. Mervyn had inherited it from his own great-grandmother. It might be worth a fortune and help with the finances, but he did not like to suggest that to Louise.

"Tarquin is eating and up on his legs, though he's very sore indeed, poor fellow. I'd like to have him under my eyes for the rest of the week, to make sure there's no infection. Then maybe he can come home."

"He's going to be all right? Really all right?" Louise was unable to believe it.

"Let's say there's an eighty per cent chance now instead of fifty-fifty," Russell said. "You know as well as I do that there can be unexpected snags and he was very badly torn."

It was wonderful news.

"I hope Emma and Kate are proving a benefit and not a penance," Russell said. He was looking out of the window at Emma who was at the far side of the yard, talking to Jason.

"Anything but. Kate's good company, and spends quite a lot of time with us, and Emma's wonderful. Spoiling me rotten, and believe me, Russell, I can do with it. I feel cosseted and cared for, and she's great company. I can't imagine how I coped without any of them. Jason's doing well, too."

"His father died this morning. I don't know whether to tell him or leave it to the hospital. It's probably a benefit . . . the man was a menace in more ways than one. Harry dreaded a call out to him. He was either comatose or aggressive, and he was always falling and injuring himself."

Harry Pardoe was the village doctor.

"Harry sent you a message: don't come down to the surgery any more. He doesn't want you jolting over that bumpy lane. He'll come up."

Louise was thinking about Jason's father.

"Jason said he was ill and that he didn't intend to see him. He did at least know he was in hospital. Maybe his next-door neighbour will get in touch. He lived in a council house, didn't he? So Jason won't have to worry about getting rid of that."

Russell nodded, walked to the window and looked out at the lowering sky.

"I don't like that. It could snow." He took the pasty that Louise offered him.

"Eating on the wing again," he said apologetically. "I spent more time with the horse than I should have done and there are several other calls to make. There's enough work for three of us but not enough money. And with farming in the doldrums, it takes a long time for bills to get paid."

"The parents are definitely paying for the work you did here on the sheep, aren't they?" It would be a colossal bill and Louise was worried.

"That's already been settled and I didn't come cheap. I thought it a good idea to ram the lesson home and make sure that the young idiots don't do anything like it again. They see everything in black and white, don't see consequences, and don't have much sense."

"How's the bitch that was cut on the wire?"

"Not at all well. I'm still not sure she'll live. I had to spay her, which didn't help as she was in shock already. The pups were all dead so she has nothing to comfort her for her pain. Peta's decided to keep her. She's nursing her full time and has her upstairs with her at night. I'm hoping a bit of TLC will make all the difference. She's taken to Peta. Kane's pleased to have her find a good home."

He glanced at the clock.

"I'll never get through today." He nodded at his mother-in-

116

law who came in as he went out. She picked up the ringing phone.

"It's for Jason. I'll find him. I think he's cleaning out the pigs."

Jason ran in when he was called, picked up the phone and listened, frowning. He put the phone down and said, "My dad's dead. I suppose I have to make arrangements about burying him."

"I'm sorry," Louise said.

"Don't be. He's better off where he is now than lying dead drunk every night, and seeing snakes and toads and little green men. He never had a life."

"I'll drive you to the hospital," Russell said, having come back into the kitchen when the phone rang in case it was another call for him. "Want some help with the details?"

Jason nodded and followed the vet out to the Land Rover.

"I'm not free of him, even now," he said. "Still things to do for him. Just a blood tie. We hated one another. He resented me. Ruined his life, he said, as he'd never have married my mum else. I never had a dad, just a spoiled brat who never grew up and never took any responsibility. Never kept a job for more than a few weeks and lucky not to land in jail at times."

"Freedom," Russell said, remembering his conversation with Kate. "You cherish the idea, but no one's entirely free to do as they choose."

"I bet Mervyn cherishes the idea of freedom if he's alive," Jason said.

Russell sighed.

"That's beginning to seem unlikely. You'd think someone would know about him and his companion, and get in touch . . . it's difficult to imagine what has happened. It's such a wild part of the world now. The fighting never seems to stop."

He looked up at the mountains, unusually black against a pale-blue sky.

"If I were free, I'd go fishing. Now that is a thought to cherish."

Halfway down the lane that led to the Keepsakes gate he braked.

"There's Kate. What on earth is she doing here at this time of day?"

Kate, walking towards them dragging her feet, looked as if the world around her had collapsed.

"Kate!" Her father stared at her. Her face was bruised and swollen with the aftermath of tears. Her coat looked as if it had been slashed with scissors over and over again. "My God, love. What on earth's happened?"

Ten

K ate looked at her father, her eyes quite blank.
 "I want to go home," she said,
"I'll ring your mother and tell her you're coming. Jump in."
He picked up his mobile phone.

"No. My home. At the farm."

Russell looked at her, wondering why the statement hurt so much.

"Jump in anyway. I can easily turn round and take you back. I won't be able to stay . . . I've calls to make."

Kate climbed into the back of the Land Rover, ignoring Jason. She was shivering, her damaged coat unequal to keeping out the cold. She was not sure how she had got there, having run away from a situation that had become increasingly unbearable.

Jason glanced at Russell, who shook his head. Kate would tell them when she felt able. Worry flared in both of them.

When they reached the farm, she jumped out of the Land Rover and opened the gate so that her father could turn.

"I could come in for a few minutes," Russell said, "and you could tell me what happened."

"Not now. No need for you to come in. I'll be all right. Thanks, Dad."

She walked away from him.

"Should I stay?" Jason asked.

"No. We'll find out in due course. You have things to sort out and I have a job to do. Damn it," he said furiously as he accelerated away from the gate, tyres screaming, "once your children grow up all you can do is be a spectator. You can't suffer for them . . . you can't even bloody well help . . ."

Jason stared at him. It was a viewpoint that he had never considered – he couldn't imagine his father caring what happened to him. Gran had, though. He longed for her, achingly and suddenly. She had been the only mother he had ever known and she had been a good one at that. They'd had their rows, but lots of fun until that damned stroke. Life wasn't fair. Even then she'd managed to make light of her disability and laugh about it.

He looked out of the window at the passing scene, not wanting to think of the task that lay ahead at the end of the journey. Russell drove with a set face, wishing he could take the law into his own hands and teach the young thugs a much needed lesson. He wondered what they had done to his daughter.

Kate, watching them go, took a deep breath, knowing she would have to face more questions. She felt confused and frightened, sure that her tormentors had worse in store for her.

Both Emma and Louise stared as she came into the room, shedding the ruined jacket.

"Don't ask," she said. "I want a shower . . . and some peace. I'll tell you later."

"I'll make a hot lunch," Emma said, as Kate vanished through the doorway.

She picked up the jacket, which her granddaughter had flung on the settee. Kate had loved that jacket. It was a soft golden colour, warmly padded. It was ruined beyond repair.

The pockets felt stiff. Emma frowned. She took out a number of cards, cut to the same size, with writing in neat capitals and crudely drawn pictures on them. All the little figures were caricatures of Kate. They were far from flattering, but Emma had to admit that they were clever. Someone was misusing a considerable talent. There were six of them. And the pictures were very nasty.

KATE TRENT IS A GRASS.
TELL TALE WAS MADE TO CARE,
TELL TALE WAS HUNG,
TELL TALE WAS PUT IN A POT AND BOILED
  TILL SHE WAS DONE.
SUPPOSE YOU THINK YOU'RE CLEVER?
YOU'LL BE SORRY.

There was Kate with her head peering out of a witch's cauldron. Kate suspended by the neck with her tongue hanging out. Kate being whipped with a cat o'nine tails. Kate suspended over a bath, her head immersed, her heels held by two demons. Kate being held by the heels from a bridge, the river and rocks far below.

Emma felt sick.

She spread them on the table.

"I suppose it's those creatures who released the animals at Kane's cottage."

Louise looked at the cards, and stared at Emma, appalled.

"No wonder Kate ran away. She must have been terrified."

She had not seen Kate come back into the room.

"I was, but I shouldn't have run away," she said. "Suddenly it got to me. They'd written 'Kate Trent is a grass' in all the lavatories. I kept finding the cards: in my coat pockets, in every book I opened. And wherever I went two of them followed me, walking behind me, not saying anything, not doing anything, just staring at me."

"Why didn't you tell one of the staff? Or the head?"

"How could they stop them? How can anyone stop them? They were just there . . . not saying anything. Just looking. And grinning."

"What happened to your face? Did they touch you?"

"No. I was running and fell. Honestly. There's a little stone wall along the path outside the school, and I tripped and hit that with my cheek. I went to get my coat at break, as it was so cold outside . . . and found it like that. That was when I ran. I was trying to catch the bus, only I missed it. I was afraid they'd start on me. I loved that coat . . ."

Emma had heated chicken soup. She put the plates on the table. Food always helped. She cut a thick chunk from a new baked loaf, the inside still hot.

Kate sat and looked at her food.

"I should have known something like this would happen. They're furious with me for telling on them. They're all being punished. Their allowances are stopped to help pay the vet's bill and they don't see why I shouldn't be punished too. I didn't have to tell."

Emma looked at her, wishing there was something she could do, but this was Kate's problem. Nobody else could help.

"Eat up, love. It'll warm you."

Louise eased herself back in her chair. She too was wondering how to help Kate.

"How would you feel if you hadn't told, but had known who was responsible?" she asked.

"It would have bothered me all the time. I'm so angry . . . if they could see Tarquin . . . and the little bitch. Peta's called her Susie. She'd been badly treated before she came to the kennels and now she's lost her puppies. She was so badly torn that dad had to put about a hundred stitches in her."

"If Peta saves her she'll have a good life in future," Emma said. "Your father says she's going to keep her."

"I wish I could leave school and start college now," Kate said. "But there's no way I can get to vet school without A levels . . . and no way I can take them till next year . . ."

"You still want to be a vet? Even after Saturday?" her grandmother asked.

"More than ever. I did help, but think how much more I could have done if I'd been qualified . . . anyone could have done what I did."

"Anyone wouldn't have done," Louise said. "Half the girls in your school would have run a mile in horror and been unable to face up to the need to clean those awful injuries. I'm used to coping with sick and injured animals, but that was worse than anything I've ever met before. Your mother said you and Jason did wonders."

"I called in to see Tarquin on the way to school. He's beginning to move, but he must be so sore." Kate began to eat. "I'm not sorry I told on them. I didn't have a choice."

"Who are they? How many were there?"

"Six of them. They formed their own group, a sort of animal rights organisation. Five of them are just daft, but Damon, he's the ringleader . . . he scares me. He's crazy. He's not really interested in the needs of animals . . . he just likes to cause trouble. He stole a car and went joyriding when he was only fourteen. The teachers hate him and he's nearly been suspended several times, but he's always got away with it."

"Why does he do it?" Emma asked.

"No one really knows. Jason said he was awful in play-school; they were there together. He broke the other children's toys, and was a bully, right from the start. He's bigger than the other boys. He has two sisters, who are very nice girls. His mother always stands up for him . . . I don't know anything about his father."

Kate put down her spoon, having finished only half her soup

"He wants revenge on me. He's probably sure that no one would have found out who was responsible if I hadn't told. I don't suppose he'll go away. Would they put him into some sort of secure accommodation for letting the dogs out?"

"He didn't know they'd attack the sheep." Emma was trying to be fair. "I suppose they imagined the dogs would just wander around, and maybe be taken in by people. They knew nobody would be there as Kane's in hospital. An easy target."

Emma went over to the Aga to make coffee for all of them.

"You have to show them they can't get to you," she said. "Run away and they'll feel they've won. It'll give them power.

123

If you don't take any notice . . . they won't dare touch you."
She wondered if that were in fact true. You read such things,
but this wasn't the work of children but of perverted adults.

Adding sugar to Kate's mug, before passing it to her, she
thought it likely that Russell would go to see the headmaster.

"You're dreaming, Gran. I don't take sugar. Jason does."
Kate stood up. "I'll go back. I've only missed the last lesson and
the lunch hour. I can say I came home to get a warm coat."

"Take the ruined one back with you," Louise said. "Take it
into the classroom. Let everyone see it. Does Mike know
what's been happening?"

"He tried to persuade me not to come home. Said he'd drive
me. I ran away from him too and got the next bus, and then a
lift to the Keepgate from the postman."

"Didn't he say anything about your coat?"

"He looked at it, and raised his eyebrows. I told him some
idiots had been jealous and cut it up and I wanted to go home
for another. I don't suppose he believed me; I looked a mess
anyway. But he didn't ask any more. Just told me about his
new niece. She was born two days ago and they've called her
Alys."

Some of the colour had come back into her face. The
bruised cheek was darkening and she had the beginning of
a black eye.

She took an apple from the bowl on the dresser and slipped
it into her pocket.

"I'll eat it on my way down," she said.

"I'll drive you. It'll be the end of the afternoon before you
get to school if you wait for the bus," Emma said, and then
turned her head as the kitchen door opened to reveal both
Jason and Mike.

"Thanks. Saved me a walk," Jason said and vanished.
There was work to do.

"I told Mum what happened," Mike said. "She drove me
up. We saw Jason on the way. You OK? I was worried. So
were the others. Steve saw Damon slash your coat but he's

124

scared to tell. Damon's dad's sold his moped and makes him keep to a curfew. The money for the bike paid their part of the vet's bill. He's gunning for you . . . really mad. But we'll watch out for you. We'll be there, in future."

"You can't be there all the time," Kate said. "I'll come back with you for afternoon lessons. I shouldn't have run away, but they got to me. We'll just make it." She put on a thick fleece-lined anorak and picked up the ruined jacket. "I'll be OK. I just needed time . . . it threw me."

Emma wanted to hold her back, and watched her go, suddenly afraid.

Kate, fastening her seatbelt, gave a rueful grin.

"I'll be telling more tales, I suppose. I'm not keeping this dark." She looked at the coat. "There's no way anyone can say it was accidental damage. It cost more than I could afford. I loved that coat. Oh, well."

"Where was it?"

"On my peg, of course."

She said nothing more until they reached the school gates.

"Take care, Kate," Mike's mother said. "Don't let them win." She looked at the coat, which Kate had picked up from the back seat. She gasped. "I didn't realise it was that bad. What are you going to do?"

"I haven't a clue," Kate said. "I don't intend to retaliate, or try and play them at their own game."

"Your face is bruised. Did they do that?"

"She fell against the little wall round the playground," Mike said. He looked at Kate consideringly. "That's quite a shiner. You know, if we don't say how you did it, we could worry them. Each one might think one of the others was responsible and I don't think they would have resorted to physical attack. Not even Damon."

"It's an idea," Kate said, as she followed him through the gates.

*   *   *

125

Louise and Emma spent a worried afternoon, their thoughts with Kate. Jason, feeling in need of violent action, chopped wood until the pile grew high and his arm ached.

The people at the hospital had been kind and helped him with all the funeral arrangements. He had no intention of attending. He felt grateful to Russell who had offered to lend him the money to cover the expenses. It would take much of what he had inherited from his gran but he supposed his father's property would fetch some money. It was a council house, so no joy from that. There might be a small savings account. He didn't know. Death left muddles. Not everyone was as organised as his gran.

He went across to his flat, needing to be alone, and come to terms with yet another loss in his immediate family. There was no one left now. No uncles or aunts or cousins. He had hated his father, but his going left an unexpected emptiness.

There was an envelope on the mat with his name on it. Inside was a note from Louise, and a cheque.

"This is to help with the expenses," she had written. "You've earned it and if the farm picks up I'll pay the balance, so that you have a proper wage. You'll need it. It's the only way I can say thank you. I couldn't have managed without you."

Louise had given him £20 for each week he had worked on the farm. He felt a sudden lump in his throat. Maybe he did have people who cared after all. When he next went to the village he'd buy her a pot plant.

Kate arrived home, an hour late, in a strange car, by which time both Louise and Emma were worrying. She brought her driver in, a tall thin woman with the most glorious auburn hair that Emma had ever seen. It framed a weary face which was not improved by dark-framed glasses, but which broke into an unusually appealing smile when she was introduced.

"This is our biology teacher," Kate said. "Mrs Hunt. She has a suggestion to make."

126

"I've several," the visitor said. "First of all, I grew up on a farm in Derbyshire. Sadly, it was a tenanted farm and my parents have now retired. When I was at school we had a lot of trouble with children from the new housing estate."

She smiled her thanks as Emma offered her a mug of coffee and plate of cakes.

"Then my mother had an idea. She went to see the head-master at my school and suggested that the school adopted the farm. Every child could have an animal as its own, come and see it, name it, and help protect it from vandals. Small parties came round from each class, to choose their animals. It escalated and we did projects: on the amount of land that could be put under potatoes, rape, barley, corn; on the milk quotas for the cows; on the kinds of milking parlour that were available. It worked like magic. The children protected the farm, warned off any child that was bent on mayhem, and became fascinated by what went on." She took another cake. "Since then the idea's caught on. There's a Food and Farming Education Service with more than 800 farms which children can visit. I can get fact sheets about beef and cereal farming, and the health and well-being of the animals. Even fish farming and plant breeding. We've talked about it in the staff room, and the head thought if you'd agree, you'd be an ideal place to start us."

She looked across at Louise.

"We wouldn't be interfering, and we'd only visit when you told us we might; we don't want to be in the way or cause problems. We want to save those from developing. Modern children have so little to do with animals. I've been surprised how much Mike's little band are learning already about the way a kennels and cattery is run."

"We had lots of ideas," Kate said. "The girls doing needle-work asked if they could make baby clothes for you; you'll need loads as babies grow so fast. The woodwork master suggested that his classes might do farm repairs; he's sure you need fences and walls mending."

127

"I couldn't repay you," Louise said. "It seems an awful imposition."

"It's not. It would give a lot of children a purpose in life. They drift so aimlessly, without any real interests. Maybe when the baby's born and you have more time, you could tell the children about running a farm and all it involves; give them lessons here. And . . ." she hesitated . . . "this is real cheek. The council sold off our playing fields some years ago and we have no football or hockey pitches. Is there perhaps a field here? We'd pay, of course."

Louise frowned, with visions of noisy children yelling encouragement to their teams and hordes of parents leaving their cars outside in the lane.

Jason, who had come in and was listening quietly, looked at her.

"What about that field by the Keepgate?" he said. "It's a bit of a pest, being so far away from the rest of our land. There's plenty of parking space and it's a good distance from the rest of the farm. We'd not notice the noise from here."

Mervyn had bought the field beyond the Keepgate just before the owner died. It had been part of the now derelict farm. They had intended to buy two more fields, but no one knew how to complete the purchase. If only the son would come home and tidy up matters, Louise thought, but perhaps he couldn't afford the fare. Australia was a long way away.

"Can we think about it?" she asked. It could be a good idea, but she did not, at the moment, feel like making big decisions. Christmas lay ahead. Her first without Mervyn. She dreaded it. She had no desire to celebrate, though both Emma and Kate were making plans. She drifted into a daydream, with Mervyn home.

"Come back, Louise," Kate said, laughing at her. "This could be important."

"I'm sorry. Pregnancy is addling my wits," Louise said, feeling guilty. "I find it more and more difficult to concentrate."

"It's one of the hazards of the condition," Mrs Hunt said. "I remember how dismayed I was to find I seemed to be unable to do anything well when I had my three. Don't worry. You'll recover. We all do."

"How old are your children?" Louise asked, wondering how on earth anyone with a family could also work outside the home.

"Older than Kate, all of them. To get back to my idea, it would, I think, solve Kate's problems. If we could start talking about it in school now, you'd would have plenty of helpers over the holidays. I don't think that gang would strike again but they do have it in for Kate, and, quite frankly, we don't know how to deal with them. If they're excluded from school they might cause far more trouble than if we keep them."

Louise was not sure that she wanted children round the farm. They would need supervision and could easily hurt themselves by interfering with the machinery, or making some unexpected move towards a frightened animal that might kick or bite.

"I know you need to think it over. There wouldn't be a mass of children descending on you, and there won't be young children either. The sixth form suggested perhaps two or three at a time at most could come up and help with necessary chores; cleaning things out. Some of the girls are horse mad and read nothing but pony books. It would be wonderful for them to help look after real horses. The younger children would only come as part of a lesson in school time and it would be made very plain just how they should behave. It would be tremendously good for them." Mrs Hunt gave a brilliant smile. "Even though they live near farms, half the children don't realise that meat is grown up here, or that eggs don't start in cardboard boxes or milk in cartons. They just don't associate the food they eat with being grown and cropped and then marketed. I think there would be far less trouble if they did learn about animals from the animal itself."

"What about insurance?" Jason asked. He had been listening intently and was not at all sure that he liked the idea of children running free around cattle and machinery.

"You probably have that already, don't you?" Mrs Hunt asked. "It might put up the premium a little, but you must be covered against people being injured on your premises."

Louise had recently renewed the insurance, but she had not looked at the policy.

"It's quite an idea," she said. "But insurance is one thing I must check."

"I could bring up one or two of my friends during the holidays without a problem, couldn't I?" Kate asked. "You wouldn't need to alter the insurance for that."

"And perhaps I could visit with one or two children too? I'll have plenty of time over Christmas." Sheila Hunt looked as if she would like to move in.

She left soon after, refusing the offer of a meal.

Kate, who had suddenly decided to knit for Louise's baby, picked up the needles.

"Mrs Hunt's husband died last year. Very suddenly. He had a heart attack." Louise stroked Fern who had broken all the rules and crept on to the sofa beside her putting her head on her mistress's knee. She ached and she hurt and she wanted sympathy. There was no room for Mott. He sighed deeply and put his head on Louise's foot.

Kate cast on for the second sleeve.

"I wonder what I'll be doing in ten years' time," she said. "Just think. I'll be nearly as old as you are now and you'll be over forty!"

There seemed no answer to that.

Eleven

B ob Strang, who now came up to the farm nearly every
day once the rescued animals had been fed to see if he
could help, walked into Jason's flat one lunchtime. "The pigs
don't get any quieter," he observed, looking out of the
window as Emma and Louise, armed with food for the
screaming weaners, crossed the yard. He had to raise his
voice as the mynah bird was helping them scream. "I've an
idea. There's room for Ceri and her offspring in the big sty
beyond the second barn at the cottage. Kane was intending to
put more kennels there, but that's on the back burner now.
And I'll take the mynah off your hands."

"Davie?"

"His name's actually Tito," Bob said, grinning. "Davie was
a visitor, and you know how quickly that bird picks things
up."

"Picks things up. I'm getting as nutty as the rest of them.
Maaa. Maaa. Maaa."

"Oh, for heaven's sake," Bob said, and covered the cage.

"I bet he sits there sulking," Jason said, producing some
pasties that Emma had made for him. "I'd be glad to be free of
him. He makes more work than he's worth."

"I'm moving in with Kane permanently." Bob, who could
never bear to be idle, poured boiling water on to the coffee
powder in two mugs. "Going into partnership. I can work as
well from his place as mine, and he can take on more animals
if I'm there to help."

"Seems like a good idea for both of you," Jason said.

"I'll have more room than I do now, and no rent to pay. Just half of all the bills. And rooms with a view instead of looking out on to the street."

He walked to the window. The high mountain tops were softened by snow. Above them a blue sky was mottled by thin cloud, and the slopes were patched with sheep.

"No news of Mervyn, I suppose?"

"Nothing that I've heard. I think Louise is beginning to believe he's dead but she doesn't want to admit it."

"The first Christmas alone is always hard," Bob said. "Next year she'll have the baby. That'll help. She'll be well occupied."

"She is now. Emma keeps telling her to rest, but she won't. Especially now Tarquin's home. He looks like a patchwork quilt, with parts of his fleece shaved."

"Russell did a good job of stitching him. Looks like he'll be as good as new in a week or so. Once an animal recovers it forgets fast, I suspect. Though he may well be very wary now of strange dogs."

The young ram had come back two days before. Russell had kept him until the stitches could be removed knowing that Louise had too many invalids to care for and would not hand them all over to Emma.

"Kane isn't due back until Christmas Eve." Bob picked up the mynah's cage. "I persuaded him to go into the convalescent home, to be looked after once he's out of hospital. Once he's back at the cottage he'll insist on helping with the animals, even on crutches."

They went down the steps together.

Tarquin was in a paddock by himself. He and Belle nosed one another through the wire mesh that separated them. Louise was afraid that movement might pull his wounds apart. The long scars showed angrily against the white skin, and he looked decidedly moth-eaten. There were no bites on his head. Most of the damage was on his shoulders and legs and on his left side, which had been ripped. He came to the gate and stood enjoying having his ears rubbed. The piglets, recently fed, were blissfully silent.

"I do miss Demon," Louise said, as Bob came up to her. "Silly, isn't it? The ducks miss him too. But oddly, they know when it's time to be put in for the night and have been waiting at the door without needing Mott to herd them in. I'll buy more after Christmas. We need more hens too. There aren't enough eggs for the four of us now. Most of the survivors have stopped laying since the dogs came."

"Are you mating Ceri again?" Bob asked.

"I'll wait till summer. The baby will be six months old then and I'll have worked out my routine. It's going to make a difference."

"I'm taking the mynah. He's driving Jason up the wall."

"I never realised how noisy a bird could be," Louise said. "He never stops making some kind of sound."

"He'll have a whole new vocabulary for Kane when he comes home." Bob looked at the ram, considering. "He's making a brilliant recovery. Russell's very pleased with him." He paused, wondering if Louise would object to his next suggestion. "I can take Ceri and the piglets off your hands if you like. There's a good big sty at the cottage. Kane suggested it. We can look after her for a few weeks, and it'll be a deal quieter when the baby comes if they're not here. You'll only hear them when the wind's blowing this way and it doesn't do that often."

"Can you really manage them? It seems like an imposition," Louise said.

So few weeks to go now until the baby's birth, and she was forced to admit that she could no longer cope with everything she wanted to do.

The ram, feeling better, butted at her hand. She delved in her pocket and gave him a tiny piece of bread crust.

"Tarquin has a fan club," she said. "There are several children who come when they can to see how he's progressed." She laughed. "He knows his name and acts to the gallery. I do so wish Mervyn could see him now."

Bob put an arm round her shoulder and hugged her briefly, but said nothing. Words could not help.

She stroked the ram's head and turned to walk back across the yard.

"I'd be grateful if you can really manage Ceri and her brood. It would give us a great deal more free time during the day without the weaners to feed. We're having to supplement the grass for the sheep now and I ought to bring them close to home. They're forecasting snow on the hills."

"I can do that. Mott'll work for me, won't he? I use the same whistles as Mervyn."

Louise looked up at him.

"Have you time?"

"I'm going into partnership with Kane," he said. "I'm not taking on any outside jobs except for emergencies when people can't get someone else in."

During the last few days of term Kate had cause to bless Mike's organising capabilities. Together they reviewed her lessons, and where she had to go during the day. Many periods were shared with others of his group, and he made sure that she always had at least two people with her, even when she went to the cloakroom.

As she began to feel more secure, and her tormentors discovered their tactics were not having any effect, Kate's bodyguards became almost a joke. Mike insisted that they protected her right up to the end of term, and either he or his mother drove her home, so that she did not need to use the school bus. She was safe in the mornings as the kennel gang, as they had now named themselves, were with her.

The days were peaceful but she was thankful when the final bell announced their freedom from school until after Christmas.

Louise had decided to accept the school's offer of adoption and to allow them the use of the Keepgate field. There was a promise of help during the school holidays and the first groups of children would come in the New Year. Sheila Hunt had sent for the information packs and reported that interest in "their farm" was high, especially with Tarquin as a major attraction. They knew there would be no lambs in the spring, but Louise had promised they could bottle feed any orphans. The children wanted to know if Tarquin would father lambs the following spring.

"I could use a farm visit as promise for good behaviour," Sheila Hunt said.

Two days before Christmas, Louise came downstairs very slowly, holding on to the banisters and wondering if she would ever get up to her bedroom again. She did not feel festive: Mervyn haunted her dreams, and the imminent birth was suddenly terrifying. If only he were with her.

Kate, however, celebrating her first Christmas in her own home, was excited and so was Emma who had been hiding presents and hurrying around with carrier bags and wrapping paper. Louise had to pretend an interest she did not have.

Emma was in the kitchen, flushed from the heat of the oven, her arms covered in flour. Kate and Jason were down at Kane's cottage, feeding the animals. Much to Jason's surprise, the school team still turned up daily, although the holidays had begun. Kane was due to leave the convalescent home the following day, and had been invited, with Bob, to share their Christmas lunch. Kate's family were coming too. Emma, who had always loved family Christmases, was delighted to have a large number of people to cater for again.

Jason was enjoying himself too. He had never been part of a family celebration before. Just him and Gran, and his dad had never bothered.

It was a new departure for Louise too. She and Mervyn had never had anyone with whom to share the whole day.

Jason had brought his cassette player and some tapes of Christmas carols into the kitchen.

Kate had gathered enormous bunches of berried holly from a tree in her parents' garden, and had borrowed vases which she spread around the house. Some of the others' excitement began to infect Louise.

Hunting through cupboards, she found the decorations that she and Mervyn had put up together only the year before. There was a tiny nativity scene that had been in the family since he was a small boy and though battered and chipped, it could not be thrown away. She looked at the baby in the cradle and at Mary in a faded blue cloak, sitting beside him. She found paints and a paint brush and revived the dull colours. Ox and ass, sheep, a rather odd-shaped goat and a donkey watched the child.

Mike had decided that every day after the dogs and cats had been fed, exercised and cleaned out, he and his helpers would come up and help on the farm. "If it's OK with you," he said to Louise. "Holidays are a bore, especially in winter. We'll all be glad to be useful, and our mums will be glad to have us out of their way."

"Let's see how it goes," Louise said. "Just one thing. Whatever you do here, Jason is in charge. Understood? Clear everything with him and find out from him what you can do and what it might not be wise to do. Farming's a considerable skill; it doesn't just happen. Jason's farm manager here in my husband's absence, until I can take over again after the baby's born."

"Understood," Mike said. Jason, who had just come in and was standing in the background, slipped out of the room, wondering if Mike would actually be able to work under somebody else's instructions. Louise couldn't have given him a better Christmas present although she was unaware that he had overheard. He treasured her words, repeating them in his mind throughout the day.

Emma, busy rolling out pastry for what appeared to be hundreds of mince pies, looked up as Mike went out.

"Hope that works," she said. "Our two young men are considerable characters, and stubbornness is one trait they both share. Jason's envious of Mike's background. It makes him more conscious of his own, which doesn't help. Mike doesn't think before he speaks and isn't very sensitive to other peoples' feelings." And Kate is an added complication there, she thought, but didn't say it aloud.

Louise moved Spice, who was occupying her chair. The kittens were all on the rug. The farmyard was too dangerous for them, and now, when people were busy, the little family was shut in the big scullery, which was a store room for wellingtons and coats. No chance then of tiny animals escaping and being lost or forgotten, or trodden on, or stealing food.

"It doesn't feel like Christmas, in spite of everything." Louise settled herself in Mervyn's chair. She needed Emma's help to get out of it.

"Next year there'll be a baby in the house," Emma said. "That's always wonderful. I adore their eyes when they see the Christmas lights for the first time. They're enormous and full of awe. A miracle just for them."

She rolled the pastry and began to cut it into shapes, putting each piece deftly into the bun tin, filling them with mincemeat and putting the tops on. There were mince pies cooling on every flat surface.

Louise was eating buttered toast.

"I think everyone had better give me indigestion tablets for Christmas," she said. "I can get heartburn just by talking, let alone eating."

"Just a few more days," Emma said. "Think ahead. By the end of February Ceredig'll be nearly two months old and this'll be a faint memory."

Ceredig Mervyn Pritchard. It was hard to visualise him as a real presence in her home. If only his father could see him.

Kate bounced into the kitchen through the back door, carrying a bag full of parcels.

"Secrets," she said. "Don't spy. I do love Christmas."

She raced out, and clattered up the stairs two at a time.

"I used to do that," Louise said. Had she had as much

energy and enthusiasm as Kate at that age? It was hard to remember. Life had a way of hitting you too hard, she thought as she tried to find a more comfortable position in the chair. Both she and Mervyn had shared it in the early days of their marriage, now it seemed too small and she couldn't imagine how they had fitted in.

"I waddle like an overweight elephant and feel I'm about as attractive as a warthog. I wonder if he warthogs think she warthogs are beautiful?"

Emma laughed as she put another batch of mince pies in to cook.

"They must do. And also think their babies are the most wonderful and handsome things in the world. Do you think a hundred mince pies will be enough? I bet Mike and his gang will turn up for elevenses if nothing else on Christmas Day. He was asking if there were any jobs we don't do then, and what had to be done. Kane'll be home, but won't be up to coping. He's lucky to have Bob. Isn't it odd how good things can come out of bad? If he hadn't broken his leg . . . if Jason hadn't been there . . ."

The sharp rap on the kitchen door startled them. Emma opened it. Mike stood there, grim faced, holding a smaller boy by the collar.

"This is Paul Berry. He came up the lane into the yard," Mike said. "I don't know what he's up to. He's one of Damon's lot and was in on the kennel raid."

Mike, always elegant, even when working, was frowning.

"I was only coming to bring something for Kate, and I wanted to see Tarquin. I've heard so much about him," Paul said. "Look, I didn't want to go with them in the first place and I feel awful about it. Ever since Kate brought the pictures of the sheep to school . . . I didn't know what the dogs would do . . . Damon can be very nasty if you don't do what he wants. I won't be having anything to do with him any more. My mum and dad are furious with me for being so silly as to believe him. I just wanted to tell Kate I was sorry. Mrs Hunt thought it would be a good idea. I made her these."

He held out two solid beautifully shaped bookends, the wood polished until it gleamed.

"OK, Mike," Louise said. "I think Paul's made his point, don't you? He can stay until Kate comes down. I doubt if he has any evil designs on Emma and me."

With a reluctant look, Mike left.

"Think you could manage a mince pie?" Emma asked. "I'll tell Kate you're here. Look after Louise for me and see she doesn't start dancing."

Paul looked at her in astonishment and both she and Louise laughed. He took the proffered mince pie and sat on the stool that Emma pulled out from under the table. He was a solid chunky boy with blonde hair parted in the middle, cut to just below his ears. Brown eyes and dark lashes contrasted with his fair skin.

Emma left the room, anxious to fetch Kate.

"How old are you, Paul?" Louise asked, wondering what on earth she could talk about to her unexpected visitor.

"Sixteen."

"Do you want to work with wood? Those are beautiful."

"My dad designs and makes furniture. Craftsman work. He taught me. I think I'll probably go into business with him. But I'm not flavour of the month at the moment," he added ruefully. "Dad and Mum are mad at me, and say unless I break off with Damon's gang they'll take me away from school altogether, and send me somewhere else. I'd like to get some A levels and maybe go to college. Only it's going to be difficult to ignore Damon. He'll take it out on me if I don't do what he says."

"Why did you go with them?"

"I didn't know what they intended. I thought we'd take the animals and find them new homes. And Damon was so sure that Mr Merrit was a vivisectionist and the dogs and cats were being tortured for the sake of making things like cosmetics or researching the effects of smoking. He persuaded us all that Mr Merrit was the devil himself, a sadistic fiend who enjoyed inflicting pain. I hate animals being hurt. That's why it was so awful seeing what had happened to your poor sheep. I could have killed Damon then."

Kate came into the room, eyebrows raised.

"Paul? What are you doing here?"

"I brought you these. I felt rotten about Damon's lot and what they did to you. Mrs Hunt suggested I came. I'm not having anything to do with him any more."

"And that's going to make life pretty awful for you too, isn't it?" Kate said. "I reckon we'll both have problems next term."

She picked up the bookends and ran her hands over the gleaming wood.

"These are lovely. Thank you. Would you like to come up and see my room? I've just finished decorating it for Christmas."

She took a mince pie from the tray on which they were cooling and walked out of the door, eating it as she went. Mott scavenged behind her, licking up crumbs. Paul followed her, still looking anxious.

"Who on earth said schooldays are the best days of your life?" Louise asked. "I don't see how their problems are going to be settled."

She looked thoughtfully at the mince pies.

"They look gorgeous. I'm sure I'll suffer, but I can't resist at least one." She bit into it, savouring the pastry and the filling. "Emma . . . I can't thank you enough. You've done so much for me."

"You've been my lifeline," Emma said. "Much as I love Roz and Russell, I was in the way there, and though they tried not to make it obvious, the children did. I did wonder when I first came here . . . but somehow there seemed to be a slot waiting for me. I hope I can stay on . . . I can do so much for you when the baby's born, and you'll have an on site sitter in.

140

Probably two as Kate will help out." She hesitated. "Would you like me to come with you when you go to the hospital? I can hold your hand and talk to you and wipe your fevered brow."

"Would you?" Louise knew at that moment that she would never see her husband again. She had to get used to being on her own, and with Emma living in the house, that problem would be considerably eased.

"Of course. It's always scary the first time. Even though you've seen calves and lambs and pups and kittens being born frequently, it's different when it's you. Husbands and relatives weren't allowed in the room when my children were born . . . it was very lonely."

There was a sudden roar from the sky and a scream of engines as three jet planes flew over, lower than any of them had ever seen before. For a moment Louise thought they would hit the chimneys. The sound hung on the air and then they were gone, leaving chaos behind them. Sheep ran in the fields and there were squeals from the stable, and a drumming of hooves. Mott barked and Fern fled, hiding behind the settee. Spice gathered her kittens round her and washed them frantically, as if sure that would eliminate fear.

Kate and Paul rushed down the stairs.

Emma raced to the kitchen door and opened it and Louise followed her, wishing she could hurry. Mike and Jason were pelting for the stable, where the foal was telling everyone he was terrified.

"Bloody idiots. What the hell were they doing, flying as low as that?" Jason said as he opened the top of the stable door. Corrie had panicked at the noise and as she kicked out, had caught her foal on the side of his head. Blood poured over his face.

Mike ran to the house to phone for Russell.

"Leave it to me," Paul said, astounding them all by taking charge of the situation. He walked to the stable door and began to talk very softly, a slow monotonous chant that gradually soothed the mare. She stood sweating, the wild look in her eyes beginning to soften. He went into the stable, put a head collar on Corrie, and led her out, handing her over to Kate.

"Just talk to her and stroke her. Keep on talking. Make her forget," he said.

"Her foal's windy, and not too sure of people," Jason said.

"Not to worry. Just go away, all of you. Leave him with me."

Half an hour later, Paul led the foal out into the yard. Russell was waiting in the house, aware that his sudden entry might cause further problems. There had been calls for him from all down the valley.

"Huw Ty Croes's bull was in the yard," he said, over the inevitable mug of coffee. "He went berserk. Luckily there were four of them about, and Huw's three sons are pretty spry. They got him back into his pen with pitchforks. Some damage to machinery and also to Llew, the bull, but nothing too disastrous. He'll be my next call."

He glanced out of the window.

"That boy. Paul Berry. He's the grandson of Dai the Plas Coch Stud. Usually spends all his holidays there. The old man uses Monty Robert's methods – the horse wizard. Let him help with the horses if he's coming up here. You couldn't do better."

He went out to look at the foal, who jibbed when he saw him.

"Keep talking to him, son. I'll sedate him. Then I can have a good look and see what's happened. Hopefully it looks worse than it is."

As soon as the injection took effect Russell bathed away the blood. There was a triangular flap of skin torn away at the side of his face.

"I'll stitch that back. He only needs a local. Then I'll cover it with acriflavine . . . I know it's old fashioned, but believe me, it works."

He went back into the kitchen, once he was sure his patient was comfortable, to wash his hands, and then absent-mindedly took a mince pie from the table.

"Never can resist them," he said, "especially Emma's. That foal should be OK now. Better leave the wound open to the fresh air. Keep an eye on it. I've given him an injection of antibiotics. Just watch him when he's put back with his mother . . . or rather, watch her." He frowned. "I hope to God those planes don't come back. I'm going to ring up and complain. Maybe they'd like to pay some of the vet bills." He took a second mince pie. "Not that there's a hope in hell of that, but it's worth a try and might make them think. That foal's going to be plane shy. Watch him. Trouble is you can't tell when the damned things are coming. There are days when I hate progress. Does more harm than good sometimes. I'll be lucky to see my bed tonight."

"I hope the baby's not plane shy," Louise said, when she and Emma were alone again. "I jumped out of my skin and he's stopped kicking ever since."

"He might react to your shock," Emma said. "I doubt if he'd hear the noise."

"I wasn't shocked," Louise said, indignant, "just startled."

She sat, fondling Jason's kitten, which had decided it needed a human lap.

"Time for you to wrap up some of those presents you've bought the youngsters," Emma said, trying to think of something that Louise could do without too much difficulty. "Do you want me to help you?"

"I'll do them at bedtime. Then I won't have to climb the stairs twice. Meanwhile I want to look at Chance." She struggled out of the chair and Emma came to give her a hand and help her to her feet. "It would be nice to have a few uneventful days so that we can all settle down and enjoy some quiet."

There were voices in the yard as Kate and Mike's gang worked. A wheelbarrow squeaked loudly, and Paul came into the kitchen, the open door revealing Mike pushing one of the girls, who was giggling, across the yard towards the stable. Corrie and the foal were in the paddock.

"He'll be OK now," Paul said. "I'm used to horses. My granddad owns a stud for Welsh Cobs."

"Russell told us." Louise had a feeling that she knew more than that and she suddenly remembered. "Your grandmother's Aliena Dare, isn't she?"

He nodded. "The horses belong to Mr Merrit, don't they? Would you like one of her paintings of a foal to give him for Christmas?" He looked up at Louise, his expression anxious.

"I couldn't afford it," Louise said, wishing it were possible. Aliena was the best horse painter living. Her pictures started at well over a thousand pounds each.

"I've my own collection," Paul said. "Gran does me one every birthday and Christmas. She won't mind if I give one to you . . . she and Grandpa are mad at me too and they won't let me go there this Christmas holiday. I need to be punished, they said." He looked almost tearful. "Please, my parents would be glad and so would Gran. We did a lot of harm that night, and Mr Kane has been very upset indeed."

"How do you know that?" Emma asked.

"My mum's a nurse. She's been looking after him."

Paul looked longingly at the mince pies and grinned when Emma offered him the plate.

"Take three," she said. "I can always make more and I know you boys."

"Mum says if Mr Kane could have got out of bed and laid into us all with a horsewhip he would have done. She said he was ready to do murder. I don't think he'd be very civil if he comes across Damon."

"I'm sure he'd love a picture of a foal, especially an Aliena Dare," Louise said. "But it must come from you, not from me. Then he'll know how sorry you are. OK?" she asked, seeing his doubtful expression.

He thought for a moment and then smiled.

"OK," he said. "I wish . . ." but he didn't voice his wish. For all that, Louise knew that he was wishing none of it had happened.

"We all make mistakes, Paul," she said. "Yours was only to stand by your friends and believe something that wasn't true and that was hardly your fault, was it? Maybe you've learned a valuable lesson."

He stared at her, and then walked over, hugged her and kissed her cheek.

"Thanks," he said as he went out into the yard.

Late that evening Emma began to pack the cooled mince pies into tins.

"I'll freeze some of them, then I can be sure there will be enough," she said. "We seem to have had inroads made on them already. What a day. I'll do some more tomorrow. Only two nights and one day to go . . . I hope it's going to be a really good peaceful Christmas."

You can say that again, Louise thought, as she climbed the stairs, feeling as if she were ascending a mountain. There had always been mishaps, when Mervyn was home, but somehow they hadn't seemed so bad then. Now she was responsible for everything. Though she talked of selling the farm, she knew she could never do so. Not unless circumstances quite beyond her control forced her to.

It was her home and she loved it. Even if Mervyn didn't come back, there were memories of him and anyway, it belonged to his son. She couldn't deny him his birthright. If Mervyn had died, there would have been enough insurance to take care of everything. She either had to prove he was dead or wait for so many years before she could claim the money . . . and that was when trouble might surface, because there definitely was not enough money coming in now.

She put the thought resolutely out of her mind and finished wrapping the little gifts she had asked Emma to buy to give to the youngsters. Kate had been commissioned to buy Louise's gift to her grandmother.

She felt a sense of achievement as she looked at the small pile of gaily ribboned and tagged parcels. This year without Mervyn was so different. And so lonely in spite of a house full of people.

It would be different again, after Christmas. It was hard to imagine a baby in the house.

Tarquin was nearly full grown and far more handsome than she had ever imagined. If only she could show him next year . . . he'd soon make a champion.

She had not mentioned their thirteenth wedding anniversary the month before to Emma and Kate. It had been a lonely day, and had been hard to blot out memories which now made her sad. Mervyn watched her from the photograph. She picked it up to look at it. If only he were here.

"You're going to have a son soon," she told him. "You'd have been so proud."

Mott, hearing her voice, was sure she was speaking to him as no one else was in the room. His tail thumped hard on the ground.

Twelve

Anne Berry glanced at her watch. Another hour before she could go home. She was in charge, by day, of the little convalescent home into which Kane Merrit had gone when the hospital had decided he was fit for release. He knew he would not be able to cope at home for some weeks but he hated his enforced inaction.

Anne and her husband had been furious with Paul when they had found out what he'd been up to at Kane Merrit's cottage. But when he had realised that they had to pay a proportion of the enormous vet's bill he had taken all his savings out of his post office account and given them to his father.

"Are you accepting it?" Anne had asked after her son had gone to bed.

"I think he'd be upset if we don't," John Berry had said.

The next day Paul had visited Kane Merrit who, fore-warned by his mother and impressed by the boy's courage in facing a man he had so wronged, had accepted the apology.

"It's very hard to accept that my own son was involved," she had said to Kane that night, going in to thank him for the way he had treated Paul.

"We can't choose our children's companions," Kane had said, with memories of his own. "My son spent much of his time with the son of one of the most notorious poachers and envied his family because most of the children apparently had beds in the garden shed, there not being room for them in the house." He looked back with regret. He had enjoyed his young family. "I never see him now, but friends tell me he is a very sober accountant, with a young family of his own. Don't worry about Paul. I suspect he's had a very severe shock."

Anne looked out of her office window at the ever-changing hills. The tops were hidden in thick cloud and there would be more snow on them tomorrow. Today the slopes were sombre and winter bleak. She loved them when the sun shone and the wind chased cloud patterns across the ground.

Time for her last round before handing over to the night staff. She preferred working in this small private home to the hospital because she could keep to daytime hours and be at home for Paul and her husband every evening. Those without families shared the night shifts. She had moved only a week before Kane had arrived there.

He was her last call. Anne helped him into bed and plumped the pillows behind him.

He sighed. "I hate being dependent."

"You'll be home in a few more days."

"Emma's been busy. Louise has invited us up to Bryn Mawr. Roz and Russell and the boys will be there. I don't like parties, but we needn't stay long. I'll want to get back and rest. Bob says the school kids have promised to come in although it's Christmas. I never thought they'd last."

He was sorry when she went, he liked Anne. He settled to his book, but could not concentrate. He was glad when the night nurse brought Russell in. He had special visiting privileges, due to his unpredictable work.

"Roz sent a couple of magazines," the vet said, sitting in the armchair by the curtained window. "She thought you'd probably had your fill of grapes. The *Field* and *Country Life*. Maybe not your style but something to fill the time. It hangs, doesn't it?"

"I'm not used to being idle. How's Susie?"

"She's settled in with Peta as if she'd been there all her life. She's a dear little dog. Quite a character and very bright – not always to our advantage. She discovered how to open the refrigerator and stole a whole joint that Peta intended to last several days to save her cooking. It didn't upset her, luckily, but she wasn't too popular."

Kane laughed.

"I thought she had possibilities during the time I had her. She ought to have been terrified of people after the treatment she had but she still trusted them. I'd thought of taking her into the house. I miss my old fellow. Though maybe it is as well he died before I did this. He would have fretted terribly. I had him from eight weeks old and he'd never been kennelled. A great gun dog. Don't know that I'd have the patience or energy to teach another."

Trojan, a black Labrador, had been one of Russell's favourite patients.

"He did well. Few of them live to fifteen. But I've a feeling his place is filled," Russell said. "The police picked up an old dog, wandering loose – no collar and someone said he'd been pushed out of a car. He's around eleven, and has arthritis badly. His owners wouldn't pay the vet's bills or pay for him to be put down, is my guess. I offered him to Bob. He's in the cottage as there wasn't a spare kennel."

"Is he in pain?"

"I've been treating him and he's responding. He's a bit stiff when he gets up after a rest but I'd think he's good for several more years. He needs medication, and feeding up and somebody to care about him. He's a dear old fellow. Grateful and co-operative and adores being petted. I hate people at times."

"Breed?"

"Black Labrador. Pedigree. Same as your old fellow. Well bred. He's well trained too; been used for shooting, I'd think. Done his job and now thrown away."

Kane, somewhat to the physiotherapist's surprise, proved an ideal patient. He was soon able to move quite fast along the corridors and join those who had meals in the little dining room. Every small achievement cheered him, so that by the time his day of release came, he was almost as excited as a small boy waiting to be taken to the circus. Bob had bought a little present for Anne and had wrapped it up. He gave it to her with a slightly embarrassed smile.

"A sort of thank you," he said. "Not very adequate."

She opened the parcel in her office, discovering a Cairngorm paperweight, that she stood proudly on her desk, the coloured swirls in the glass catching the light. It would remind her of a very odd period of her life, she thought, hoping that Paul would now settle down, and cease to be a problem.

He refused to speak about school and spent most of the days either at his computer or up at the farm, where he spent a great deal of time with the foal. Chance ran to him, and he spent hours talking softly to him, teaching the little animal to trust him.

Kane was driven home by a Red Cross volunteer in an ambulance taxi. Tired from the journey, especially the last part over the potholed lane, he sank into his armchair by his own fire, and surprised himself by his pleasure at being in familiar surroundings.

He looked up as an elderly black Labrador padded into the room, walked across, sniffed him thoroughly and then sat, his head on Kane's knee, looking at him with pleading eyes. Bob, who had been walking him and another of the dogs when Kane arrived, followed him in.

"I've named him Don. We were both lonely. I don't know if you allow dogs indoors; but he's clean and well mannered, and I couldn't resist him. He's missed out on affection all his life and he craves it."

Kane stroked the dog's chest and was rewarded by a lick across the hand and a black body that appeared to try to melt into him, pushing against him, yearning for attention.

"I reckon we've a house dog," he said. "Maybe we can give him something he's never had before."

Don, apparently knowing he had been accepted, gave a deep sigh and settled on the rug, his head on Kane's shoe.

By the next morning the invalid felt well enough to visit his charges. The team had not yet arrived. His voice was greeted by a furore of barking, and one dog after another jumped at the wire, eager for petting. Don was the only newcomer. The others had known him before he went into hospital and responded to his voice. Kate and Jason, coming down to start the feeding, were astounded by the din which usually did not begin until their arrival. They were relieved to find its cause, and greeted Kane with smiles.

"Happy Christmas," Kate said.

Kane perched on a stool and watched Mike and his team work.

"Very efficient," he said.

"We can continue to come till you're mobile again," Mike said. "Or longer, if you like."

"They would make a difference," Kane admitted, as the two men relaxed and drank coffee a couple of hours later.

"You won't be doing much for a while," Bob said, getting up to answer a knock at the door. Kane looked up in astonishment as Anne Berry and her son were ushered into the room. Paul was carrying a brightly wrapped parcel, which he took over to Kane.

"Happy Christmas," he said. "I hope you like it."

Kane, astounded, unwrapped the parcel and sat and looked at the contents, unable to believe his eyes. The foal that bucked across the field was so alive that he almost expected it to leap out of the picture. He looked at the signature and then looked again.

"An Aliena Dare! I've always wished I could afford one of her pictures."

"She's my gran. It's from us all . . ."

Paul wanted to ask if he was forgiven but had not the courage. Kane looked at him from under massive eyebrows.

"It'll have pride of place over the mantelpiece," he said. "Another task for Bob. He'll put it up for me. Something I can look at every day. Thank your grandmother. I'll treasure it. I forgot she was married to Dai Plas Coch."

Bob made two more mugs of coffee. Kate had brought a tin of mince pies down with her, as a gift from Emma. Russell, calling in to collect the two men for their Christmas lunch, found an impromptu party just finishing, as the team had been invited in when they had finished. They presented Kane and Bob with their own gift: they had put their money together to buy an expensive bottle of wine.

Kate had collected the morning's eggs, which she had put in a basket lined with scarlet paper and topped with holly, as a present for Kane. He sat back and listened to the teasing. Russell, persuaded to stop and share their small festivity, told Kane about the foal's accident.

"He'll recover quickly," the vet said, "but I suspect it's left its mark and he's going to panic whenever he hears a plane. We'll need to make sure he has room to run. Louise is putting him in a much bigger stall on his own at night now. The woodwork master at school brought some of the boys down and they've renovated one of the older stables that's been out of use for some years."

"Mervyn's grandfather bred Shires," Kane said, remembered the handsome heavy horses. They had gone long ago to help pay death duties. "Louise has been keeping the mare and foal for nothing. I must make that good. I'll offer her full livery fees for the pair of them. Do you think that will be OK? I think she could manage to keep them."

"Kate and Paul do most of the work. They adore them. I'm sure she'll be glad to have them and the money for their keep. I know things are tough," Russell said, as the team and the Berrys gathered their outdoor clothes and prepared to leave. It would help Louise with her cash flow problems.

"In six months you'll be as good as new," Russell said, while admiring the picture of the foal. He'd have loved one too. "You need more physiotherapy to get those muscles in working order again, but a broken leg isn't a sentence of immobility for ever. Just a temporary blip and a nuisance."

Kane, manoeuvring himself through the door, down the step and then into the Land Rover, gave a long sigh. He wondered how long it would be before he could walk like other people. He felt singularly disadvantaged and far older than his years. Also, the crutches hurt to use. He gave an involuntary prayer to the sky to keep frost and snow away. Another fall would be a disaster.

Listening outside the farm kitchen door to the laughter from inside, he wondered if he had been insane to take up their offer and come to lunch. He hated parties. Bob opened the door and he followed, Russell bringing up the rear.

There were shouts of "Happy Christmas!" Kane stood, uncertain, among so many people he didn't know, and Louise came across to him. He looked at her. She had dark rings under her eyes and moved with extreme difficulty. He thought that she looked in imminent danger of giving birth during the celebrations. Unexpectedly, he grinned.

"And I was feeling sorry for myself," he said. "How many more days?"

"About ten. I think I'll survive, though at times I wonder. Look, if you come to the window you can see Corrie and Chance. They're out in the paddock."

"Chance?"

"Kate named him Lucky Chance because he was lucky to be alive . . . If Jason hadn't been there . . ."

Kane was saved from a reply by the sound of a car being driven into the yard and a knock at the door. Turning, he was surprised to see Anne Berry again, this time flanked by her husband as well as her son.

"We wanted to bring our Christmas presents personally," Anne said. "Paul has a tremendous feeling of guilt, and we hope this will help his apologies."

Her husband vanished outside again and returned carrying two large parcels. Louise stared at him, and then opened the biggest, which proved to contain a modern version of a

153

Victorian rocking cot, the red-brown mahogany highly polished. It was fully equipped with mattress, sheets, blankets, a quilted cover in a variety of pastel shades and a pillow with a matching embroidered case.

"It's beautiful," Louise said. "An heirloom. Did you make it? Paul said that's your profession."

"Yes, and my wife made the bedding for you," John said.

Paul proffered his own parcel, which was also outsize. Opened, it revealed a painted wooden horse wearing a little red saddle, with a red bridle and reins. His mane and tail were black. He was anchored to a small platform on wheels, with a handle to push it.

"I made it," he said. "Dad made one like it for me when I was little, and I loved it. Dad suggested I gave him to you, but I didn't want to part with it. He sits in my room as a mascot now."

"Paul always called his Orse," Anne said, laughing. "He had the greatest difficulty saying his aitches."

"Mum!" Paul said, his face suddenly fiery red.

"I used to call grasshoppers galobbers," Louise said. "It became a family word."

By now Emma had to resort to the deep freeze for mince pies. Louise sat, listening, but unable to make the effort to join in. Momentarily, she remembered last Christmas and Mervyn toasting Belle.

"To our future and her lamb. May he bring us fortune," he had said.

For a moment, he was as vivid as if he were in the room, looking at her, holding the glass of wine, that right eyebrow raised as he laughed at her. Next year, their small son would be joining in the celebrations, but she was now sure that Mervyn would not be there. The solemn man from the Foreign Office, who had called on her two weeks before, had been unable to offer much comfort.

"While there's no news, there is hope," he had said, as he left the farm.

Hope. Was it now a fool's dream? Was it time to face reality?

No, she decided. She would go on hoping. There was still a chance, even if a very slim one. Miracles did happen.

Kane, opposite her, his leg on a stool, was equally silent.

"When you were small, did you make bargains with God?" Louise asked him, wanting to draw him into the conversation, and unable to think of anything to say.

He looked at her, guessing what was in her mind.

"Please God, if you don't let my rabbit die, I'll be a good boy," he said. "Is that what you mean?" Louise nodded. "I think we all did it. God doesn't always listen, though."

"He did with Tarquin and with Chance. Would you like to see them close to? Can you manage to walk that far?"

"I can if you can." He grinned at her. "We'll look a pretty pair. Luckily it's not frosty. Neither of us can risk a fall. Lead on, MacDuff."

Russell gave her a hand to help her out of the chair.

"Need me?" he asked.

"I can look after the lady. Anyone comes near to hurt her and I swing a mean crutch," Kane said. "It's not my arms that are out of action."

They both laughed when they came to the paddocks. Belle and Tarquin had giant bows attached to collars of tinsel. Louise had bread in her pocket and gave them both a piece as they came to the gate. Tarquin nosed them through the bars.

"He's the handsomest ram I've ever seen," Kane said. "Are you going to show him? You'll need to get him known, if you want to make the best of him."

"I can't see there ever being time." Louise scratched the black poll. "I'll have to see. I'm coasting at the moment from day to day. Each one is an achievement. Mervyn would have loved him." She leaned against the gate, turning to look at the farmhouse. "Life never turns out the way you hope, does it?"

"It can turn out better," Kane said. "You never know what the next year will bring. I often find that something that

155

seemed terrible at the time brings benefits afterwards. Look at the kennel raid. You have far more help now than you could ever have expected . . . so have I. It's changed our lives already. There could be further changes waiting."

"I do appreciate that," Louise said.

"Nobody but a fool would expect you to forget Mervyn so soon."

"Meanwhile life goes on. I don't know why I'm burdening you like this . . . I try to be positive . . ."

"It's easier to unload to someone not involved," Kane said. "It's cold out here. Shall we go in?"

The farmhouse was filled with heat and noise and laughter. Bob was teasing Mike and his team. Paul, uneasy, watched them, his eyes anxious. He was in a lower form and always felt at a disadvantage when Mike was around, although the older boy did nothing to upset him. Mike was taller, stronger, better dressed. Anne in her turn watched her son, wishing she could help him. He was still afraid of Damon, she knew.

The extra visitors left by lunch time, the team splitting up, some to travel with Mike, who, now nearly eighteen, had borrowed his mother's car, and some with the Berrys. Laughter echoed as they left.

Emma had excelled herself with the food. The Christmas pudding was brought to the table, the brandy flaming. She had a treasure store of old threepenny pieces, and Louise and Robin both found one in their slices.

"Good luck for the year ahead," Roz said.

Russell helped himself to crusty bread and a slice of Stilton.

"Do you realise it's the first Christmas dinner for three years that I've actually managed to eat right through without an emergency?"

"Don't tempt providence, Dad," Kate said. "You won't be able to walk if you eat much more!"

As if on cue the phone rang.

"What's the betting?" Robin asked as his father went over to answer it.

"You lose," Russell said, grinning, and held up the receiver as a yell of "Happy Christmas!" came out of it. Emma laughed and went over to speak to her sister.

That night Louise, lying in bed, put her lucky threepenny piece beside Mervyn's photograph. She thought over the past few months and how astonishingly her life had changed. It would change again in just a few weeks' time. Her baby would be a reality, lying in his new cradle, a living, breathing, crying, smiling human being.

There was a tap on her bedroom door and Kate put her head in.

"I saw your light shining across the yard. Are you OK?"

"I'm fine," Louise said, wondering if she should cross her fingers. She felt very uncomfortable indeed.

"I love living here. I just wanted to say thank you. I even love Mum now we're not on top of one another."

Louise laughed.

"I think Emma feels the same, and I expect your mum does too," she said. "That's families."

Kate walked over to the bed and hugged her.

"I love everyone today, but I don't expect it'll last," she said. "It's been a smashing Christmas."

Louise smiled at the closed door. Life had changed for Kate and Emma too. She switched off the light, wondering what the New Year would bring.

Thirteen

Christmas dinner had been a bad idea, Louise decided at about midnight. She had eaten little but the food had been rich and she had eaten too many mince pies. Emma's pastry was irresistible. The house was noisy with the wind rising, and rain beat against the windows. Sleep was impossible. She wondered if she would ever be comfortable again.

Dogs and cats were lucky, ridding themselves of their burden after only nine weeks. Nine months felt like eternity. Only nine more days. Her doctor had called in on Christmas Eve, forbidding her to make the journey to the hospital again before the birth. "Be glad you're not an elephant," he'd said, when she complained about the weariness of waiting. "Imagine being pregnant for two years." She had looked at him, unable even to summon a smile. Her sense of humour seemed to have vanished. Everything was an effort: it took several minutes to haul herself up the stairs, clinging to the banisters, and ending at the top out of breath. It was ridiculous. In the last few days her moods had been so volatile that she felt as if someone alien was occupying her body.

Emma, she knew, was watching her closely, anxious to see that she did not overtire herself. Even Kate insisted on walking with her to release Belle and Tarquin in the mornings. Jason was also afraid that they might knock into Louise and send her flying, as she was not well balanced now.

Still, she thought, it had been a good day, and everyone had worked hard to keep her from remembering past years. She appreciated their efforts. She had not, at first, wanted so many people, but now she knew it had been a good idea. Everyone had bought something for the baby except Emma, Russell and Roz who had given her, jointly, a gold locket on a chain into which she could put two photographs.

Unable to sleep, Louise was longing for a cup of tea, but if she went downstairs Emma would follow her, so she piled pillows behind her, and tried to read. But her own thoughts constantly interrupted her and she could make no sense of the book, having to read every sentence twice. She read until four, and then decided that she must go downstairs because she was cold. Central heating for the upstairs rooms was another improvement dependent on "one day when our ship comes home". It would be warm in the kitchen and she was thirstier than ever. She crept past Emma's closed door, trying to be silent.

The third stair down creaked and there was no way she could avoid it. The dogs followed her, tails waving. Louise was pouring milk into a glass when Emma appeared.

"I hoped you wouldn't wake," she said. "I'm sorry. I just couldn't sleep at all. The anchovies made me thirsty."

"Me too," Emma said, putting the kettle on the hob. "I've been lying awake hoping you'd come down. I was afraid if I did, I'd disturb you. That board outside your door always creaks."

Fern curled up in her bed. Mott leaned against Louise's knee.

"It was a good day." Emma made the drinks. "I hope it wasn't too much for you. You really ought to rest more. If it freezes, I want a promise."

"That I don't go out to Tarquin. I won't risk falling, I do promise, Emma." Louise laughed. "Maybe he can come in and see me!"

"He's getting a bit big for indoor visiting."

Louise walked over to the cake tin and took out a bun.

"Don't say it . . . it'll spoil my breakfast."

Jason knocked at the door and Emma unlocked it. He came

in, rubbing his hair, which was wet. A damp kitten followed him, complaining. Fern stood up, picked it up in her mouth, dumped him in her bed and proceeded to wash him, making him wetter than before. Smoke's complaints escalated.

Jason grinned.

"I suspect she thinks she's drying him," he said.

"Had breakfast?" Emma asked. Day had come without she or Emma realising it, though it was still dark outside.

Jason nodded, then went out again.

At just after five. Emma persuaded Louise to go back to bed. Another eight days and with luck the baby would be born. Louise, who was unexpectedly sleepy, went willingly, to Emma's relief. She woke at nine to the sound of rain lashing against the windows and drumming on the roof, and a ferocious wind that moaned around the house and thrashed the trees until the branches creaked as if they were crying for mercy.

She felt headachy. Showering helped, but dressing proved a penance and it was an effort to put on her socks and shoes. She had given up tights. She wore maternity trousers that did nothing for her morale and a loose top that made her feel as if she were wearing a tent.

She wondered, as she dressed, what Mervyn would think about a house full of people if he did come back. But she could not have coped with the farm alone.

Jason came in at eleven. By now he had done several hours work and was so hungry that Emma made him a second breakfast, well aware that his first consisted only of toast.

"Was Kate there?" Emma asked, dipping bread in beaten egg to fry for him. It was one of his favourites.

"Yes. She's gone off with Mike for the day."

He walked over to the sink to wash his hands, as if defying them to ask further questions. He did not sound pleased.

"My mum used to cook this in wartime," Emma said, turning it deftly, and adding an egg to the pan. "She called it eggy bread. It made one egg do all of us because they were rationed then. Sometimes Mum swapped her sweet coupons for the month for half a dozen eggs and she used to feel so guilty."

She scrambled an egg for Louise, who had not yet eaten. "Nothing fried for you, my girl."

"You don't know how lucky you are," Louise said as Jason began to cut up his fried bread. "When this baby's born, I'm going to eat all the things that give me indigestion now!"

He relaxed and grinned at her. Emma went to the stove to pick up the kettle. He cut off a minute slice and put it on Louise's plate. He glanced towards Emma and put a finger on his lips.

Louise smiled.

"Mike's mum's asked all the team over for the day. They asked me, but I've work to do and anyway, I don't fit in with them. I never did. They're still schoolkids, with mummy to look after them. Half my age, mentally. Such bores . . . I told them we could cope here without them for once. Paul's coming for a bit, because he wants to groom Chance and Corrie while Kate's with her parents. Bob'll come up later too. Says he and Kane need space, or they'll be quarrelling!"

He went back to work, the door almost torn out of his grasp as he opened it. Fern followed him. Mott refused to leave Louise.

Emma began to clear the table.

"This won't get the baby washed. Sit still for goodness sake. We don't want Junior rushing into the world early without time to get you to hospital."

"Heaven forbid," Louise said. She got up, with Emma's help, and sat at the table. "Give me the bread and butter and some things to put on it. It won't strain me to make sandwiches to put in the freezer. I can't sit and do nothing."

Emma cut slices of turkey and boiled some eggs. Paul appeared briefly, to get warm after grooming the horses. He stood beside the Aga, holding out his hands to the open door where flames blazed cheerfully.

"I've put Chance and Corrie and the sheep indoors," he said. "It's tipping down and the wind's rising. I can't stay. Mum's picking me up at the Keepgate."

By evening a full gale was blowing. The sheep huddled miserably against the hedges. Kane, who had been shown the recently acquired Jacob sheep on Christmas Day and, discovering that as Louise was short of grazing she did not want them in with her main flock, had offered to lend her one of his paddocks for the Jacobs, but they were not going until he was fully mobile again.

During the evening the wind worsened. Jason came across at ten, asking if he could sleep on the sitting-room sofa, because his flat seemed in danger of being blown down. He refused to admit that he was frightened, listening to the wind there on his own. Smoke was tucked into his anorak, and when Jason put the kitten down on the floor, he promptly walked over and curled up beside Fern. Later, the kitten woke and went back to his old bed in Kate's airing cupboard, cuddling up with a loud purr to his mother and sibling.

It was midnight before anyone even thought of bed. Louise, trying to settle herself comfortably, realised she was missing Kate, who had gone back home with her parents until New Year, when Roz planned a big party. The house seemed quiet without her.

By two o'clock the wind was a roaring menace that threatened the trees. A sudden crash sent Louise to the window, and as she walked across the room the lights went out. All the torches were downstairs and she was afraid to risk looking for them in the dark.

A moment later she realised that what she thought was indigestion most certainly was not. She shouted, hoping that Emma could hear her. Emma, who had woken and tried to switch on her light without success, blundered her way to the door, opened it and felt along the passage wall to Louise's door.

"The baby's decided it's time," Louise said.

"Where are you?"

"By the window. I was trying to see what had crashed."

There was a flash of light on the stairs.

"I've a torch," Jason said. He had been worried when he heard Louise call out. "Had a feeling we'd lose the lights tonight. What's up?"

"The baby's up." Emma tried to subdue what felt remarkably like panic.

"I'll phone. Only . . . you can't drive in this and an ambulance won't reach here, and it's too rough for the helicopter."

"Can you find some light for us?" Emma asked. "The cupboard by the kitchen door."

"Dear God," Louise said, as there was another crash. "Suppose the roads are blocked by trees?"

Jason came back with two big hand lamps, which gave some light to the room. Louise made her way to her bed and sat on it, doubled up. Emma followed Jason to the landing.

"No phone," he said. "Dead as a shot rabbit. I'll go down and ring from Kane's."

"In this?" The rain flung itself against the house as if trying to wash it away.

"No choice, is there?"

Emma returned to Louise.

"First babies always take ages. The contractions aren't too close, are they?"

Louise shook her head. She had other worries.

"Jason doesn't know how to start the generator and it's too heavy for me. And I don't know if there's any fuel. I never thought of power cuts."

Emma put the duvet around Louise's shoulders.

"You're best off up here for the moment. Like a drink? I can fill hot-water bottles. I can boil pans as well as kettles."

"It's an idea."

It gave Emma something to do but also gave her time for greater worries. As one gust after another rattled the front door, she wondered about Jason, making his way down the track towards the cottage, fighting the wind and soaked by the storm.

Jason had his own very considerable problems. He had to bend almost double to walk at times, as the wind hurled itself against him, driving rain into his face. It would be behind him coming back, which might make matters better.

Below him the whole village was dark. There should have been street lamps shining at the crossroads, and there were almost always lights on several of the houses. Now it lay black below him, and he was dismayed to realise that no one had power.

He had never known darkness so intense. Usually there was a glimmer of light, but now there was nothing. His torch cut a small swathe and kept him from tripping over the ruts and potholes. He dared not hurry or take the short cut across the fields. They needed him and a fall would be disastrous.

Kane's gate creaked when he opened it, and all the dogs began barking. He hammered on the door, and it seemed an age before anyone answered. Bob stood there, immense in violently striped pyjamas, his hair on end, stubble on his cheeks and chin. He blinked at the light.

"What in the world?"

"The baby's decided it's time to come and our phone's out."

Bob took the torch from Jason and went to their own instrument.

Kane, also in lurid pyjamas, was standing in the doorway of his bedroom.

"Look as if you swam here," he observed. Jason was very aware that he was dripping all over the floor. His hair was plastered against his skull. He wished he had grabbed a hat, but that would have been soaked anyway, and he had lost his sou'wester and not replaced it.

Bob returned.

"We're on our own. Our phone's dead too."

"Can someone explain the emergency?" Kane asked.

"Louise is pupping," Bob said. "Ever delivered a baby?"

"There's always a first time," Kane said, though he sounded grim. "It shouldn't be that much different to a foal. I've read of young children delivering baby sisters or brothers. If they can do it, I can. Hope it's not a breach. I doubt if we could use ropes."

He poured a glass of brandy out and handed it to Jason.

"Put that down you."

Bob, who had vanished, returned with two lamps and gave Jason back his torch.

"We'll be with you as soon as we've dressed. Don't see what else we can do. It would be madness to try and drive to the hospital in this and in any case it's likely there are trees down. She's better having the baby at home than in the car."

Jason, shivering, wished he could shed his soaked clothes. He doubted if even the best rainwear would have stood up to the torrent he had walked through. The slow minutes passed, seeming endless.

"Is there a generator at Bryn Mawr?" Bob asked, returning clothed but unshaven, his greying hair on end. He pulled a comb through it as he talked.

"Yes. But I don't know how it works, and Louise is out of action, and I don't think there's much fuel. It's not been one of our priorities."

"Ought to be, always. Two five-gallon cans in the shed," Kane said, swinging himself along on his crutches at a rate that startled Jason. "We'll take the jeep. I can't walk that far, and in any case there are the cans to carry. No point in us getting soaked. We need our wits about us."

The wind shook the jeep as it nosed its way up the connecting lane. Kane gritted his teeth, enduring the jolting that hurt his leg. Bob drove carefully but there was no way of avoiding the bumps. The windscreen wipers had difficulty clearing the glass. Jason was glad to be out of the rain, but worried about Louise. How long did babies take to come?

Suppose it was already there with only Emma to cope in the dark? The hand lamps helped but did not give nearly enough light.

The farm gate was blocked by a fallen tree. They parked and left the vehicle. Kane needed considerable help to negotiate the obstacle and cursed his leg but at last they were over it and in the yard. Heads down, they fought their way towards the kitchen door which blew out of Jason's hand as he opened it, and slammed back against the wall of the house.

"Merciful heaven," Bob said as he regained his breath. "I've never known a wind like this."

Emma, busy in the kitchen, looked up in alarm.

"You're stuck with me." Kane limped into the room. The break had healed, but it would be some time before that leg was strong. "Our phone's out of action too and there's no time to get down the village and haul the doctor out. The midwife lives nine miles away. If it wasn't windy . . . but it is."

"Jason and I will get the generator going," Bob said.

Louise was pacing the room when Kane arrived.

"I'm your only hope," he said. "No phones working and with this gale blowing, transport is out. No helicopter can make it and I'd sooner deliver the baby here than risk you in a car. I don't fancy acting as midwife in a layby or on the hard shoulder. Where's your bathroom? I want to scrub."

"Second door along."

Kane was relieved when the lights went on. The healthy thump of the generator was just audible above the wind. He had never known a night like it in his life.

"Bob and Jason are a long time," Louise said, half an hour later, trying to focus on anything but her own discomfort and not succeeding very well.

Out in the dark, Bob and Jason had their own problems. There had been a cry just as they left the outbuilding where the generator was stored. A thin wail that was carried to them by the wind.

"Louise isn't the only one giving birth tonight," Bob said.

"That sounded like a newborn lamb. Leave it out here in this and it'll be dead by morning."

They fought the wind across the field, shining the torches around the hedges, trying to pinpoint the sound.

"Could do with the dogs," Bob said. "No time to fetch them. There's a hell of a chill factor in this wind. Freeze the baby as it lies there. Hello, there we are. It's not been here more than a few minutes, I'd guess, and how it's ever going to stand up in this is beyond me. Do the sheep know you?"

"Yes," Jason said, well aware that if strangers handled a newborn lamb it was often rejected by its mother and died. He picked up the baby, which lay limp in his hands, and as he walked towards the yard the ewe followed him, bleating.

"I thought you weren't starting lambing till mid April," Bob said, as they struggled through the darkness.

"We aren't. This is one that one of the farmers gave us. He lives beyond the village. It's much lower there, and they lamb early. I didn't realise she was due so soon. Louise would have known but she's not been around the fields for the last three weeks. The Jacobs will be lambing long before ours too. Luckily there's only four of them. I'd hate to be out every night in this weather."

Bob fought the gate, which did not want to open. He was trying to avoid putting his scent on the lamb otherwise he would have held it while Jason climbed over the gate. The wind was a wild entity, with a force beyond anything he had ever known.

"Do you hear that?" Jason asked, as Bob put straw down on the floor of the stable next door to Corrie's.

"Sounds like terrified birds," Bob said. The cries of alarm were audible above the noise of the gale in the trees. "Never known anything like this before. More like a hurricane."

The ewe, fortunately, was used to Jason and was not bothered by his scent on her baby. They watched as the lamb struggled to stand and his mother licked him. It was almost an hour before he found the udder and began to suck.

167

"Safe to leave them," Bob said. "I should've bought a change of clothes. Can't see anyone's here fitting me. I'll go and steam by the Aga. Get yourself dry, lad."

Kane had wondered if Louise would be embarrassed at having her baby delivered by a neighbour. Not that they could help it if she were. He prayed nothing was wrong and that the child would be a normal birth. He did not know if he could deal with a breach presentation.

"No chance of painkillers, love," Emma said, worry flaring and refusing to die.

"I'll cope," Louise said, between gasps. "No choice, have I?"

"Not really. Like being on the motorway and wanting to turn round. You just have to keep going," Kane said. "Not long now. Come on girl, bite on the bullet and let's be having you. Good girl then. There's a clever girl."

He had lapsed into his surgery manner, babbling semi-nonsense, helping a reluctant bitch produce pups, and Emma grinned to herself as she realised that he was talking to Louise as if she were a dog and not a woman. Louise didn't care. She was lost to the world in her own dimension, dominated by pain and more pain and just as she thought that it would ease another shot through her.

She tried to distract herself. It was going to be a very long night. If only she could concentrate on what Kane was saying and forget the waves of pain.

He took her hand and held it. She gripped it with all her strength. Mervyn, Mervyn, Mervyn, said her mind, suddenly inexplicably angry that he wasn't here to help her.

"Not long now. It'll soon be over. Good girl. You're doing marvellously."

Jason, now dry, down in the kitchen, offered Bob a large towel. Emma, who found it easier on her own nerves to commute between kitchen and bedroom, stared at them.

"What have you been doing?"

168

"Rescuing a newborn lamb," Bob said. "It's wet out there, in case you hadn't noticed."

"I had," Emma said, vanishing and re-appearing with a large double blanket. "Get out of those clothes and give them to Jason to put in the drier. You'll catch your death."

"You sound just like my mother," Bob said, laughing. "All the same it would be a sight more comfortable."

She brought out two tins, one of which contained the remains of the Christmas cake and the other mince pies. She added bread, butter and a dish containing a variety of cheeses, plus a somewhat battered-looking turkey.

"There's still plenty of meat there, and stuffing as well. Can't see anyone getting any sleep tonight," she added, as the wind threw itself against the windows and rattled the bin across the yard.

"I don't have a roof," Jason said looking out of the window, as Emma went out of the room. "It's been lifted off as if it were a bit of cardboard. Bits of it are crashing about."

"Be a lot of clearing up tomorrow." Bob cocked his head. "Noisy business, having babies. Us blokes don't know we're born."

Jason grinned as the big man clothed himself in the pale-pink blanket. It made a most unlikely garment. The rumble of the drier added itself to the noise of the generator. The lights flickered briefly and then returned.

"Wind's dropping."

Bob, sitting in the big armchair, reminded Jason of a tribal chief. Emma, returning briefly to make more coffee for Kane, gave a deep sigh, as she poured some for herself, and took a mince pie.

"The rain's easing too," she said. "I hope I never spend another night like this." She could cope as long as she had things to do and feeding the men helped fill her mind and stifle her fears.

"How is Louise?"

169

"As well as can be expected. Kane's talking to her as he would a whelping bitch. Oddly, I think that helps. And idiotically, he's making her recite poetry to distract her."

She went out again. Bob, listening, made a face.

"Is it always like this?" Jason asked, distressed by the sounds from upstairs.

"Being in at the birth is not a habit of mine," Bob said, "but I gather it is."

He did not admit that his only knowledge came from watching actresses on TV. He stared into the fire. Suppose Louise haemorrhaged? Could Kane cope? Suppose the baby died at birth? Babies did. He reached his hand behind him to touch the wood of the armchair. Lot of nonsense but no harm in being safe.

He had a sudden unhappy vision of Mervyn returning to find his wife and child had died during birth. Someone would have to explain to him that they had tried to cope on their own without proper professional help. Made a botch of it. God help Kane, please, he said to himself. They ought to have foreseen this and made sure she was in hospital well before the birth.

There was another yell from upstairs.

"Why don't you go to bed?" Bob asked, knowing Jason was upset by the sounds.

"No roof, remember. And who could sleep here tonight? It seems to be going on for ever."

"It probably seems that way to Louise," Bob said. "It'd do some of the love-'em-for-a-night-and-leave-them-to-hold-the-baby brigade a power of good to help at a birth. Might make even them think a little; though some don't have brains."

Jason glanced at the clock. Time seemed to be standing still and the night was going on for ever.

Bob, gathering his blanket round him, went over to the drier and took out his clothes. He dressed in the passage and returned.

"A man doesn't feel at his best wearing nothing but a

170

blanket." He folded it neatly. "The rain's stopped and the wind's easing. Plenty of clearing up to do when it's light."

Jason, exhausted, was asleep in his chair. Bob hunted through the bookshelves in the next room, and found himself an old copy of Saki's short stories. He settled down to try and distract himself from the sounds above.

Emma came down for more coffee for Kane, and drank another cup herself.

"Much longer?" Bob asked.

"Probably a couple of hours. It's a big baby. I wish to heaven we had something to give her to ease the pain. She's being very brave."

"No complications?"

"Quite straightforward, and first babies always take ages." She pushed her hair back and yawned. "Brings back memories and I'm not sure I want to remember. I had a tough time with my first but I was in hospital and had all the equipment to help me. Even with that it was painful. Very."

She went upstairs, her footsteps dragging. It was a long night for all of them.

Mott, who had been under the table, emerged and came to have his neck rubbed. The dog had lain miserably outside the bedroom door, wanting to go in, and had reluctantly followed Emma downstairs, when she insisted. He lay, listening. Bob, after some thought, put a lead on both dogs and put them in the stable with Corrie and Chance.

By six o'clock the wind had almost died away. Bob heard the sound of a car, which had to stop outside the gate. Puzzled, he opened the door to see Kate and her father climbing over the fallen tree.

"What are you doing here?" Russell asked. "I've just dropped the team and they can't get in as everywhere's locked up. I came up to see if Jason had a key." Jason, who had wakened, took the keys that Bob offered to him. He had not bothered to undress.

"I'll get down there. Coming, Kate?"

"Not today." She turned her back on his astonished look, and went out of the room, just as another cry came from upstairs. She came back in again.

"What's going on?"

"No phone and the baby decided to make his entry early. Nobody but Kane to help." But turned to Jason and said, "He might need me. Can you manage on your own?"

Jason nodded, took his thick fleece-lined jacket and went out into the darkness, taking his torch.

Russell was frowning.

"I'd best get the doctor here," he said, "and if possible the midwife. Kane's hardly qualified. I take it the child's not born yet?"

"Emma reckons another couple of hours. It's been one hell of a night. How soon could the doctor be here, do you think?"

"Hopefully immediately I get to him. I don't know how many phones are out – ours is OK, but the midwife might be out of touch. Trees've fallen everywhere, bringing down power and the telephone lines. I'm on my way to a cow with mastitis, but she can wait an hour or so. Look after Kate, will you?"

He went out and a few minutes later they heard the engine rev as he reversed. The sound died away.

Kate avoided her godfather's eyes. She poured herself a cup of coffee, and sat at the table, staring into the fire. Spice appeared with both kittens, mewing for food.

"Want to talk about it?" Bob asked.

"No. Yes." She was fighting tears. "It's Mike."

"Mike?"

"He says he's in love with me. He tried to kiss me. Horrible wet lips and he put his tongue in my mouth. It made me feel sick. I like him, but not that way. I hit him and we had a row. He said he'd never cared for any girl before and we'll marry when we're older. I don't want to be involved with him. He's mad at me now and says I made a dead set at him and have no right to drop him. I didn't do either. I never thought of him like that."

172

First love and hit hard, Bob thought. Why did life have to complicate itself? He wondered about Jason, though he, he was sure, would never force himself on any girl. He was surprised at Mike, but young love and rampaging hormones were responsible for many acts of untypical behaviour. Also, Bob suspected, Mike thought himself irresistible, and would have received a severe shock. Which might do him good.

There was more noise from above.

Kate looked at her godfather.

"Is Louise dying?"

"Not by the sound of it," he said. "It's quite normal, Tich. It'll all be over soon. Then she'll forget. Women must or nobody would ever have a second child."

"It's not due," Kate said.

"Young animals, I suspect, come when they choose. They ignore dates. This little one is doing just that. After all, it's only a few days early. He was due around January the fourth and it's never accurate. Some are early and some are late."

"That must be worse," Kate said.

She did not want to stay with her godfather, but she did not want to sit alone in her attic, listening to Louise. She wanted to be home again and safe with her mother looking after her. She had thought that growing up would be fun, but it seemed fraught with all sorts of problems that she had never envisaged.

"Hang on. Don't worry. Everything's fine," Kane said, over and over. "Good girl. He'll come in his own good time."

He was not so sure of that. If he'd been in his surgery with a bitch he'd be performing a Caesar. He tried to listen to the baby's heart, wondering if he were becoming distressed and wished he had some hospital equipment.

The baby was now his chief worry. Labour had been going on for a long time. Were they going to make it with a live child? He avoided looking at Emma, afraid his eyes might reveal his fears to her. No need to worry her too.

*   *   *

Downstairs again, Emma looked at Kate in astonishment. Her granddaughter had been crying and looked defeated. Bob put a finger to his lips. Don't ask, his gesture said.

"Hi, Gran," Kate said, but there was no life in her voice. "Is the baby nearly here?"

"Hopefully." Emma too was beginning to wonder if all was well. Kane was doing his best but he could not do anything if the birth went badly wrong; and he had no facilities to help him.

"Russell's gone for the doctor," Bob said. "They should be back within the hour. With luck, they can reach the midwife but apparently there's a lot of disruption due to the storm."

Emma relayed the information to Kane who had come out on to the landing.

"Thank God for that," he said. "I'm not sure we can manage alone. She may need hospital treatment. The helicopter ought to be able to land now . . . but will it be in time to save the baby?"

Fourteen

L ouise was in a world where pain was the only reality. Pain that knifed through her body again and again. Pain that blotted out every other sensation. Tears streamed down her face. She clung to Kane's hand, using all her strength to try to combat a continuing agony. There was no life before pain. There was no life after pain. There was only now.

Emma bathed her face, and held her other hand and spoke to her soothingly, but the older woman might not have existed. Kane did not exist either. He had a hand that she could grip. Otherwise, he was not there.

"The baby will be here soon. Think of the baby."

The baby. He was the object of all this effort. Louise tried to imagine him as a reality, fighting for his existence, struggling to come into the world. She had to help him. There would be an end. Mervyn's son. She looked at the wedding photograph, trying to imagine what this legacy from his father would look like, but it was impossible to imagine.

Emma was willing the time to pass, praying for the final effort, for the moment of release. In hospital. there would have been pain relief. Here, Louise had to suffer as women in the past had always suffered. Even in her day, there had been gas and air. Probably methods had improved a great deal since then.

"Soon," Kane was saying, like a litany. "Soon. Try, girl, try. Give it all you've got. Good lass, then."

The soothing voice was automatic. There had been so many pups to help bring into the world in the past – when he was in practice and because he bred his own bitches but also, since retiring, he had had to take in bitches in whelp, thrown away because they had belied their pedigrees and mated with one of the local scruffs, come visiting unnoticed, because their owners would never blame themselves for lack of supervision.

Softly, softly, let the soft tone penetrate the suffering. Relax, Louise told herself. Remember the antenatal classes and remember how to breathe to help at each stage. It was easier to think than to do.

There was a brief break from pain.

Kane paused to drink a mug of coffee that Emma brought into the room. Louise didn't want hers. She had more important matters on her mind.

"No complications?" Emma asked in a whisper, as they stood by the window, looking out into the darkness.

"Seems fine. He just doesn't want to put in an appearance," Kane answered in an equally soft voice.

The wind had dropped and the thump of the generator filled the air. At least they had light, though it sometimes faltered and flickered. He wished the room was warmer. He must do something about that tomorrow.

"Is there enough fuel?" Emma asked, as the light dimmed and strengthened again.

"Plenty. I brought ten gallons. I always keep a store. Bob can get more in the morning, but the electricity ought to be back by them. They'll be working all night." He said hopefully. "Rather them than me. It's rough if you're up a pole trying to fix wires with frozen hands in the dark."

Louise was aware of the murmuring voices but too occupied with her own problems to listen. Come on, she said inside her head to the baby. Time you were here. She stopped and fought for breath as a contraction seized her with ever more viciousness. Breathe, said a disembodied voice from a long-ago antenatal class. She had only had time to attend three: there had been animals to feed; sheep to worm; shearers to arrange; rams to be put in. Tarquin would be able to sire

176

lambs next year. Think of the lambs – they would be wonderful. Dozens of little Tarquins in every field.

Breathe, said a voice above her. She *was* breathing. Push, push, push. As if she wasn't trying. She had to endure. There was no choice. She was on a rollercoaster in mid-air and she couldn't get off.

The pain was back. Think about something else. Trouble had had to have ropes attached to her hooves when she was born. Louise had a vivid memory of Huw, Mervyn and Russell pulling to get the calf free. Good job they didn't do that with babies. The cow had needed calcium afterwards. Eclampsia. Did women get eclampsia? She was sure some did. Had she taken enough calcium? Emma had insisted she take a supplement.

She heard Emma say, "Russell's gone for the doctor," but the words had no meaning. Minutes had become hours and hours were days and she had been here for ever.

There was a moment's pause, and then there was another voice in the room. Another man examining her.

"I don't like it. The child will be exhausted. We need to get her to hospital. I think it might be necessary to perform a Caesarean. We'll have problems getting her there. Too many obstacles in the fields for the helicopter to land close and I don't want her jolted along. We can move the animals, but not the pylons. I'll try forceps."

The words penetrated through the misery. No one was putting forceps on her baby's head.

The yell of "No!" sounded right through the house as Louise gave one more tremendous effort.

"Attagirl," Kane said, and handed the squalling bundle to the doctor, who smiled at the din.

"Lusty lungs. He doesn't seem unduly disturbed by his ordeal," he said. "He doesn't think much of his brave new world." He handed the baby to Emma to tidy. She walked to the other side of the room with him.

Louise lay back, exhausted. She felt as if she had been running for days.

"OK?" Kane asked.

She smiled, listening to the sounds her son was making. She felt sore, as if wild horses had been kicking inside her, but the agony had ceased. There was an odd unmistakable cry. The automatic newborn wail that sounded like a small machine. Emma washed the tiny face, wrapped the baby in a thick towel and brought him back to the bedside.

"He's perfect," she said.

He was red and angry, and small fists emerged from his covering, as if he were about to do battle. The crying ceased, ending in sobs. His thumb went to his mouth.

"Already?" Louise asked in amazement.

The doctor laughed.

"Judging by some of the scans they do that in the womb," he said.

Louise stared down at her son, unable still to believe in his reality.

"Enjoy him." Emma felt as if she had acquired a new grandchild. This one would be part of her daily life. "We'll tidy you both up in a minute."

There was a soft fine down on his head. His eyes looked up at her, unfocused. This was what she had been making all those long months. He opened his eyes and stared at her, and then, unbelievably, his right eyebrow, an almost invisible line, went up.

She had a sudden vision of Mervyn laughing at her, that one eyebrow raised. She must have imagined it. Mervyn ought to be here to hold his son. He had never even known that he would one day be a father. Suddenly the thought was unbearable, and she struggled to hold back tears. She should be rejoicing.

Bob and the doctor gave her a chairlift into one of the spare rooms, so that her own could be cleaned up. The midwife arrived, brought by Russell who, having left the doctor at the farm, had driven straight off again to fetch her, the phones still being out of action. He had been unable to reach their local nurse, and, anyway, Louise did not know the woman.

The midwife was busy and bustling, with a red face and a quick laugh which came at inappropriate moments. She supervised the first feed, brushed Louise's hair after she had washed her and found one of her honeymoon night-dresses and a little bedjacket loaned by Emma, and then bathed and dressed the baby.

"There's a lovely boy, then. Isn't he lovely, mother? Aren't you proud?"

Louise took him, hoping the woman would soon go. She could not bear the cooing voice. She wanted to be left alone with her son: to hold him, savour him, her only link with his father. Come home, she said to herself. Please come home.

Kane was exhausted and his leg was aching, a wild protest that dominated everything else. He made his way over to the battered old settee that was against the wall beyond the Aga, and lowered himself carefully, letting the crutches slide to the floor. Bob, seeing his grey face and pain-filled eyes, gently lifted the bad leg so that Kane could lie down. He put cushions behind the older man.

"Practising to be mother?" Kane's voice was almost a growl. "Stop fussing. I'm OK."

"I'd never have guessed." The doctor, who had just come into the room, accepted Jason's offer of coffee. "A good job you were around and not still in hospital, though I expect Mrs Jansen could have coped. Children have helped their mothers before now. It's not the best treatment for a man not yet recovered from a badly broken leg."

It was a moment before Bob identified Emma by her surname. He had persuaded her to go upstairs and sleep for a few hours. Jason had taken over her tasks and was cooking breakfast for all of them.

"I'll take a piece of toast and be off." The doctor drained his coffee mug, then rummaged in his bag and produced a small bottle of pills. "Here, these will help that leg of yours, but don't overdo them. I'd recommend resting. I know you. Don't rush to do things."

There came a sound of crying from upstairs.

"That little one is going to make his presence felt," the doctor said, as he went out of the door.

"We'd best get out of the way," Bob said. "You'll be better in your own bed and there are things to do at home."

Emma was downstairs by lunchtime. Kate had taken over her grandmother's tasks, and made piles of sandwiches, sure that meals for the next day or two would be unpredictable, with people coming and going and unable to keep to any specific time.

The midwife had gone, and left Louise to rest. Emma sent Kate up to see if Louise was awake, and to look at the newcomer. Kate behaved as if Louise had changed overnight into someone else, almost as if she were a visitor and not a member of the household. The baby was adorable. She wanted to pick him up and hug him, but he was asleep.

She was feeling hurt and bewildered and angry and wanted to talk to her grandmother but Emma was busy, with far too much to do, and a yearning for her own bed. Her rest had been far too short.

"Gran says would you like something to eat?"

Louise discovered she was ravenous. Also, although she was sore, she could move easily. She felt unbelievably light. She seemed to have enough milk for several babies. It must be near to his second feeding time. She glanced at the clock.

One p.m. He was due for a feed at two.

"I'd love some scrambled eggs and a coffee. Have one with me."

Kate returned with a tray, and took her own mug, perching herself on the window-seat. It was a grey day, the mountains hidden in dense cloud and rain in the wind. Several people had called during the morning to pick up their kittens and had

been told about the baby. The news would travel fast. Emma
rang Sheila Hunt, who promised to come up and help.

"So Ceredig Mervyn's here at last," Kate said, not knowing
quite what to talk about.

"It still seems unreal. Babies are so helpless, compared with
foals and kids and lambs, aren't they? They always amaze me,
able to run almost from birth." Louise looked out of the
window at the threatening sky. "They decided I don't need to
go to hospital. One of the nurses from the practice will come
in every day. I know her. The midwife was a bit
overwhelming . . . so gushy."

Kate laughed.

"She thought Gran was the cleaning lady and Jason and I
were your older children. Weren't we the lucky ones to have a
darling wee brother!"

"I hope I don't look that old," Louise said, laughing. "I'm
glad Bob and Kane had gone by then."

She had heard the jeep start up. It had a remarkably noisy
engine, and Bob had revved it. Since the wind had died away
outside sounds were remarkably clear.

"I can't imagine what she would have made of them,"
Louise went on, with visions of a gossipy woman telling
everyone what a strange household there was up at the farm
in the hills.

"Maybe she'd have thought that BFG was your
husband . . . I'm not sure what she'd have made of Mr
Merrit."

BFG. Big Friendly Giant. Louise puzzled for a moment and
then remembered this was Kate's name for her godfather. She
had never come across the book that led to that odd christening.

"Penny for them," Kate said, wondering what Louise was
thinking about.

"She knew about Mervyn. She said what a pity his daddy's
not here to see him. She sounded as if she was sure Mervyn's
dead." Louise looked down at her son, as if unable to believe

he was still there. "She isn't the soul of tact. You know, I'm going to be neurotic about this baby. Scared he'll suddenly stop breathing. Or maybe be deaf or daft."

"Nuts," Kate said. "He's as bright as a button. Just listen to him."

The small face puckered suddenly and he let out a yell.

Kate lifted him and handed him to his mother, shifting the tray. He was so unbelievably tiny. Louise tucked him against her and continued to eat with one hand. She was going to have to do a lot of that, she thought. He settled, putting his thumb in his mouth again, sobbing softly at intervals.

"I don't think you need worry," Kate said. "He makes the most astonishing noise for something so small. He sounds as if he's a very strong baby."

"Feeding time," Emma said, coming into the room. "Down you go, Kate. I've left the dishes for you to do. There's going to be a lot more work round here now Junior's made his appearance. Case of all hands."

Jason was in the kitchen, washing up his own dishes. Emma had told him to leave the rest. There seemed to be dozens of mugs that had been left around.

"You should have come to Kane's," he told Kate. "Half the team couldn't get there because of the storm. Mike didn't turn up either. I gather you and he had a bust up."

"I don't want to talk about it." Kate was suddenly angry again. She picked up her kitten and walked out of the room, shutting the door positively behind her. Not quite a slam, because of the baby.

And a very fine day to you too, Jason said to the washing-up bowl. He collected the dirty plates and mugs. Someone had to grow up, he thought. He glanced at the clock. There were definitely not enough hours in this day. The fallen trees across the road had also prevented any of the helpers from the school coming up to the farm so he was on his own, unless Emma could find some time to help him. Bob was not likely to come up today because he, too, would have the sole care of all the animals. Kane was too exhausted to help.

Jason made a rapid mental list of jobs to be done. Surprising how so small a creature could disrupt routine in such a big way. He had had a quick peep at the new arrival, on Emma's instructions, but babies were not exactly his thing. He hadn't known what to say, and had contented himself with asking Louise if she were OK.

He hoped she and Emma wouldn't coo. His gran had been impossible with babies and tiny animals, the one thing about her that really annoyed and embarrassed him. Women were inexplicable creatures. And what in the world had made Kate so tetchy?

The power was restored by four o'clock, for which everyone was more than thankful. The insistent thump of the generator was replaced by a wonderful silence.

Bob came up soon afterwards with a large electric fire for Louise's bedroom, and a guard to protect it.

"Kane says it's arctic in here. Won't do for a baby," he said, and walked over to the cradle to admire the newcomer.

"My father died three months before I was born." He looked down at the tiny mite. "Went down in an Atlantic convoy in 1942. My brother was three. Mum did a fantastic job for both of us." He held out his finger and a small hand clutched at it. "Amazing strength." He turned to face Louise. "We managed to move the tree by the gate. It's along the verge now. Be plenty of firewood. There are two other trees that ought to come down, behind the stables. I've arranged for some people I know to fell them tomorrow."

"Are they very dangerous?" Louise asked. She loved the trees that sheltered the farmhouse from the wind.

"They're old and another blow will bring them down, one across the stables and the two paddocks, and the other will fall on your roof. Can't risk that."

He turned as he walked to the door.

"I'll take Chance and Corrie and the Suffolks down to our

183

place while the men are working. The noise'll scare them, and the trees will have to fall across their space anyway."

"Will they do it in a day?"

"This lot will. I know them well. They do a lot of felling round here and are experts. You'll have enough wood for the rest of the winter and maybe next winter too. Jason and I will cut it, when we've time."

Babies, Louise discovered, did not know the difference between night and day. The orphan lambs had needed feeding three-hourly in past winters, of course, but there had always been two of them to share the chore. Ceredig needed feeding at midnight and again about five or six in the morning. However, he often woke earlier and cried, so she would feed him so that he would go back to sleep and give her some rest. The cradle was beside her bed. She left the light on, and looked down at him. Once fed, he slept peacefully, making surprisingly loud sounds of contentment.

Life was going to be very different from now on.

Fifteen

The tree fellers began work next day as soon as it was light. There were unfamiliar voices in the yard and men laughing. Louise looked out of the window as Bob drove away with the horses. There were eight men.

Emma came in with a breakfast tray.

"You can rest and come down later," she said. "I'll carry the baby for you when you do come. I've put the nursing chair, and the carry cot in the sitting room. It'll be more peaceful there when he needs to be fed and changed. The kitchen's like Paddy's market with the school children coming up to help. They're very good, but I seem to make an awful lot of coffee and bake an awful lot of cakes."

She looked out of the window at the men working outside.

"I expect they'll need me to brew up, too. The children are going at lunchtime and won't be back till tomorrow. Sheila's bringing them. There are only three, but they are so energetic it feels like an army."

The practice nurse arrived at ten to make her patient comfortable and bath the baby. One of Louise's Christmas gifts had been a little hammock-type folding bath on legs.

"Nice warm room," Megan O'Malley said approvingly. The big electric fire provided more comfort than Louise had ever known in the bedroom.

It was good to see a familiar face. Megan always took her blood pressure and gave her advice when she went to see the doctor. Born to a Welsh mother and an Irish father, the nurse had a ready tongue and a happy laugh.

"Shocking weather," she said. "Makes driving a nightmare. Not only trees, but floods."

"Floods?" Louise said.

"The little river decided to take a change of bed with all that rain." She undressed the baby and put him in the bath, deftly soaping his small body. She lifted him on to a towel that had been warming in front of the fire, wrapped him and held him up and kissed him.

"He's a bonny boy. There now, lamb, doesn't that feel nice and clean and don't you smell lovely? All baby powder."

She handed him over to Louise for his feed, and then she tidied up. Louise thought how odd it was to relax and let other people do her chores.

The nurse folded the towels and put the nappies in a big bucket, with a lid, that she had brought upstairs with her.

"You can get up and go downstairs when you feel like it, but don't you go doing too much. Let others take the weight. Doctor says he'll look in later. I'll be up every day for a bit."

The farm had never been so noisy. The men were using electric saws, and the screech provided a constant background which was worse than the generator had been. The baby seemed oblivious and Louise did wonder uneasily if perhaps he was deaf.

It was a bright day with frost in the air. Bob came up to help Jason, leaving Kane to supervise what he called his chain gang. Kate and Paul stayed on at the cottage to groom the mare and her foal, and Kate, recovered from her sulk, and feeling ashamed of herself, prepared lunch for the three of them, leaving Bob free to stay up at Bryn Mawr, where there was an immense amount of tidying to do after the storm.

Jason's roof had first priority. The tree fellers helped them put a huge tarpaulin over the rafters, to keep the contents dry. It would have to do until the builders could come and finish repairs. So many houses had been damaged that there was a waiting list, in order of priority. The tarpaulin added to the noise by flapping loudly every time the wind blew.

Emma made up a camp bed for Jason in the annex to the scullery.

Louise, looking out of the kitchen window when she did come downstairs just before lunch, found the view unfamiliar. The two trees from the back and the one which had fallen by the gate were now being sawn into manageable lengths to tuck in the barn for Bob and Jason to tackle later.

"Easier in winter than summer," Emma said. "No leaves."

The paddocks still had to be cleared and re-fenced because the men had removed the posts and wire to prevent it from damage from falling branches. Louise could see down the hillside to Kane's cottage, high above the village. It had been hidden before. She looked up at the hills, now capped with snow. Walls separated the fields, many filled with sheep, and, far below, there was the unfamiliar sight of water spreading where none had been before.

"We can semaphore to each other with flags," Bob said, looking over her shoulder. "Looks so tiny from here, doesn't it?"

There was something missing.

"Where are the dogs? I thought they were in the kitchen."

"They kept trying to come upstairs," Emma said, putting down plates of shepherd's pie in front of them. "It didn't seem a good idea, so Jason put them out in the stables."

"They need to meet the baby."

"After lunch," Emma said. "If you don't eat now you won't have time before his Lordship's next feed."

It was nearly four o'clock before there was time to bring the dogs in. They had been unable to understand why they were suddenly banished from a home that had been theirs for the past six months. Life outside was part of a distant past.

They were both anxious. Mervyn had inexplicably disappeared and now Louise had abandoned them. Though Jason and Bob walked them, they escaped on every conceivable occasion to sit at the kitchen door, looking up, hoping it would magically open and let them in.

Mott, dragged away forcibly by Jason, had bared his teeth, but was too well mannered to bite. For all that, he could not control the low growl. He wanted to find Louise and he did not want to spend another night in the stable.

Released, the two dogs sped hopefully to the back door, and this time Jason opened it. Louise was in the kitchen. Mott raced to her, crouching, crying, almost sobbing a welcome. He pushed against her, knowing he must not jump up. She knelt and he licked her cheek, over and over.

Fern, also chastened by her banishment, joined in, both dogs waving their tails in an ecstatic greeting that seemed as if it would never end.

Louise let them exhaust their enthusiasm and settle down. Emma brought the baby in, and the pair, who had been lying on the hearthrug, revelling in the warmth, sat up, their expressions astounded, especially when Ceredig gave a tiny wail.

Louise sat in the big chair, and took her son. The dogs came to her, and then sniffed at the baby. Gently, meticulously, their busy noses covered every inch of him except his face – Louise prevented that.

"That," said Louise, "is my puppy. You're expected to look after him."

Two heads tilted sideways.

"You're not having them back in the bedroom, I hope," Emma said.

"They'll have to stay in their beds down here."

"They'll probably welcome that after two nights outside in the stables." Jason said. "They've been black determined to come back in. I had to drag Mott off the step every night."

Louise had never known the day pass so quickly. No sooner was the baby fed than it was time for their own meals. The little sitting room was cosy, with a wood fire burning, and a guard around it, which Kate had brought from her own home at her grandmother's request.

She went up early to bed, wondering how doing nothing very much could be so tiring. The dogs, told to stay in the kitchen, looked at her mournfully, but understood.

By the end of the week, they did not even try to follow Louise upstairs any longer, and Fern had constituted herself nursemaid. Every time the baby cried she ran across to Louise and gave a small warning bark as if saying, come on, your puppy needs you.

"You know something," Megan said, when she called in for the last time. "That little bitch of yours gets between me and the cot every time I come. She's protecting the baby. You've got a good nursemaid and guard there."

Louise had not realised that Megan was never allowed to pick Ceredig up but, in fact, either she or Emma had to do so and hand him to the nurse if Fern was in the room. Mott watched all the time, as if noting everything that had to be done.

"Our Kate's up at the crack of dawn these days," Emma said, in mid January. Louise had just returned from letting out Tarquin and Belle, which she now did after the six o'clock feed. She ignored Emma's and Jason's protests.

"She's in the stable, grooming Corrie and talking to her," Louise said. "She adores that mare, and likes to tend her before she goes down to the kennels. It's amazing that the team still turn out every day, especially this weather. There've been some very cold mornings."

"I miss the children now they've gone back to school," Emma said. "Still, they do come at weekends and that gives us a bit of a break. I'm glad we aren't lambing yet, though Russell says they've begun on some of the lowland farms."

"Tarquin has a full fleece at last, and no longer looks piebald," Louise said. "I was afraid it wouldn't grow over his injuries, or where they'd shaved him, but you'd never guess he'd been so badly hurt."

January proved a quiet month. There was little snow or

frost and no gales, which was a relief, as it was almost the end of the month before the men came to repair Jason's roof.

Emma had forgotten how much chaos surrounded a baby. Kate was astounded. She had been too young to notice the upheaval when Jock was born. Louise found it impossible to understand how such a small entity could cause so much work and untidiness. The house suddenly seemed to have shrunk, without enough space for anything.

Bob made a stand for the cradle, to lift it from the floor, lest the kittens got into the room and jumped on the baby. Anne Berry provided a cat net to drape over it. Tiny clothes seemed permanently to be either washing or drying or waiting to be put on their small owner.

Ceredig himself contributed to the overall disturbance. Although he only cried to be fed or changed, he had a lusty roar, and with four-hourly feeds Louise felt as if she was for ever tending him. There seemed to be no time at all for herself.

Kate, bewildered by her own reaction when Mike had tried to kiss her and in need of someone who would understand, felt neglected. Mike avoided her, dashing off in the opposite direction if he saw her coming towards him. She was sure the other girls were giggling and knew all about the incident.

Damon brooded, glaring at Kate when they met. She wished she was not afraid of him, but she was sure he had not forgotten her involvement. He now had a pedal bicycle on which to come to school, instead of his moped.

Babies, she discovered, were not sweet or easy or quiet. This one cried at night. His last feed was at midnight and the next wasn't due until about five thirty, when Jason started on his own chores, but around two a.m. he woke and shouted, and Louise, half asleep, and desperate for more rest, gave him an extra feed.

The books said to leave him, but even Jason, in his now re-roofed flat, could hear him. By the end of the month Kate was visiting her parents and sleeping in their house at the weekends, in order to avoid being wakened.

Mike avoided her and for that she was thankful. He no longer came with the team when they came to help with the dogs, a procedure that continued even when Kane was able to move around without his crutches.

"Thought the boy had more guts," Bob observed.

"All show. Good-looking and he relies on that. He's been rejected, and it's hit him hard. Soft-centred. I know his sort." Kane had taken an instant dislike to Mike, who he regarded as a dandy, and was relieved by his absence.

Sheila Hunt organised a rota of sixth formers to come up at weekends and every day during the holidays. She brought little groups from the lower forms, and the children paid to go round the farm, at their teacher's insistence. The school paid a good fee for each visit, being given a sum of money to supplement the children's contributions.

The smaller children were overawed by the cows, but loved the calves. Jason bought four rabbits, which had their own enclosure and which could be cuddled. If he had time, he gave the children talks on how to look after them. The working teams freed him at weekends.

Paul was there often, treating Chance as if he were his own. Kate, retreating into herself, spent more and more time with Corrie. The mare seemed to give her immense comfort.

Louise, with Sheila Hunt's encouragement, was making plans, for more visits, not only from other schools but for a playground for the children, a farm shop and a cafe, but she did not want to start any of it until Mervyn came home. She was still sure that he would, one day. He'd hate to see so many changes made without consultation. The small alterations she did make could all be done away with if he didn't like them.

Meanwhile she needed money. Prices for farm animals had never been so low. Even those for pigs had fallen and farmers incomes were being halved. At the last auction there had been no bidders at all and everyone had taken their unsold stock home again. The banks would not be patient for ever.

She built up the flock of chickens, and bought more ducks. Mervyn couldn't object to that.

By early April Ceredig was beginning to settle. He had not been a placid baby in his early months. He seemed to Emma to cry more than any of hers or Roz's ever had. He had a temper, and his small rages kept them all busy. The children were fascinated by him and always asked to see him.

"Charge for that," Sheila Hunt said, with a grin, not meaning it. She was delighted to be among animals again, and came up whenever she was free, spending most of her weekends doing various chores. She was determined that Louise should triumph and not be forced to sell the farm.

Louise thought that she was coping well. Days were never a problem. The black times came when she had been wakened by the baby in the middle of the night and could not settle again. She wondered how it felt to sleep for six hours at a time. At least, when she was awake, she could look at the baby, and watch his small movements. He was angelic when asleep, and was beginning to smile now and make different sounds. He was happiest if they propped him on pillows so that he could see them at work.

He was most definitely not deaf, and he now knew everyone who visited regularly. Jason was amused when he realised he was being greeted with a smile and a coo. The baby loved to lie on the floor on a rug and kick, and was trying to sit himself up. That often lifted right eyebrow was a fact now, reminding Louise perpetually of both Mervyn and her father-in-law.

"No problems there," the doctor said. He called in when passing or when he came to buy some newlaid eggs. He was always afraid that Louise might have had bad news. No one in the village believed that Mervyn was alive, although no one ever voiced that opinion in her hearing.

Ceredig, as he grew and took more notice of life around him, proved of absorbing interest to all of them. He was fascinated by the cats and dogs and if propped on his pillow would lie quiet while Jason's and Kate's kittens romped together. They had been named Smoke and Panda.

Mott observed him as if puzzled, but Fern was more positive than ever that it was her duty to fetch Louise the moment Ceredig began to wail.

The little bitch was in whelp, the pups due early in May. Louise had not intended it to happen, but they had been so busy with the baby they had not noticed that Fern was in season, and Mott had taken advantage of their lapse of attention. Not that that mattered, but Mervyn had intended to mate her to the county's winning trial dog.

"Puppies will help the bank balance," she said. "Even though they aren't sired by Dai the Post's champion, they'll still be worth around £400 each. But how in the world are we going to find time for them?"

"I can help with the puppies," Kate said. She now picked the baby up when he cried and rocked him, no longer terrified that she'd drop him. She had hated his lolling head and the way it had to be supported. He had looked as if he might break his neck, now he could hold it up.

By the first week in May, lambing was at its peak. Sleep was again a luxury, as most of the ewes gave birth at night. Emma and Jason made two-hourly checks, taking them in turn. Bob came up to help, and Kane was called in for the awkward ones. Russell was for emergencies and was happy about that, knowing Louise would not accept reduced bills but could not afford enormous sums for her animals.

Ceredig loved watching the lambs. There was always excitement in the fields, with youngsters butting each other and frisking around in the sunshine.

The baby was fascinated by Tarquin, and Louise always carried him when she went to look at the ram, who ran to the gate, calling to her, wanting his head scratched. He was now over a year old and a magnificent animal, fulfilling all that they had hoped. Mervyn would love him when he came home.

They settled into an easy routine, except for Kate, who worried all of them because she was plainly unhappy at school. She no longer brought friends home, or stayed on late. She spent too much time in her room, with Spice and Panda as her only companions. When she wasn't there she was in the paddock or the stable with Corrie. She tolerated Paul who could not bear to be away from Chance, but she did not confide in him. He was as baffled as everyone else by her desire to keep her distance from people.

Now the baby slept better at night, she did not go home at weekends.

"It'll pass," Emma said, although she did not sound hopeful.

The second Monday in May started wet, but cleared to a blue sky flecked by small clouds. Louise sat down to do her accounts. There weren't too many unpaid bills. She felt a small thrill of achievement: Mervyn would be proud of her.

"Your father won't know this place," she said to the baby. He smiled at her and lifted that one eyebrow and she picked him up and hugged him. His brown eyes were his father's eyes, as was his curling chestnut hair. She put him back in his cot and looked out of the window. The mountains were hazy, their flanks still outlined by long trails of snow that lay in the hollows and had not yet melted.

She looked up as a car drove into the yard. Sleek and long and black, it spoke of men from the ministry. The driver was unknown to her, not one of the men who had been before, but she was quite sure that he was from the Foreign Office. The MAFF officials did not dress in elegant suits, or drive such expensive cars.

A tall man, with dark hair greying at the temples, got out of the car. He looked around him, a slight frown on his face. She went to the door.

"Mrs Pritchard?"

She nodded.

"May I come in? We have corresponded, I'm Major Moulton. You've met my assistant before. John Summers."

"I'm sorry to ask you to come through the kitchen door," Louise said, aware of Spice and her kittens, the baby in his carry cot, the clothes that were neatly piled but not yet put away.

Emma, who had been hanging out the washing, came in, took one look, and decided so elegant a visitor ought to be in the sitting room, which was at least tidy.

"Do go into the other room. Would you like some coffee?" she said.

"Thank you. It's quite a drive here. I would indeed," the major said, as he followed Louise into the other room.

"You live alone here?" he asked, walking to the window and staring up at the hills. A city man, he found the immense space forbidding. "It's very isolated."

"I've two friends living with me and Jason, the farmhand, lives over the cow byres. They've moved in since my husband vanished. I don't know what I'd have done without them."

She looked at him as he turned to face her, suddenly anxious.

"You've news?"

Emma came in with the coffee. She had found the silver tray and used the best china. Louise loved the delicate pattern of greys and blues, but she rarely used it. The visitor looked at Emma.

"Are you bringing yours in here too?" he asked.

Emma looked at Louise, who nodded, suddenly afraid.

There was an uneasy silence.

"I do have news," the major said. "I'm afraid it's not good news."

Neither Louise nor Emma could speak.

"A young man came into one of the hospitals in Bosnia. He had been injured by a landmine and had to have his leg

195

amputated. When he recovered from the operation he kept saying it was a judgement on him. He told the doctor that his father and he had been part of a group who had stolen a lorry from Food Aid last June."

Louise was conscious of a stray sunbeam that glittered on the tray. Her hand shook and she put her cup down, its rattle against the saucer almost deafening.

"Both the drivers were shot."

"They left them?" Louise did not recognise her own voice.

"They took their clothes and left them. No one knows what happened after that. They hid the bodies. We searched but there's no sign of them in the area he told us about. It's been a fighting zone for most of the time. I'm sorry . . . I can't say how sorry."

He held out a gold watch on a wristband of gold. Louise had given it to Mervyn on their wedding day. She took it, tears springing into her eyes. She stroked it, her throat suddenly blocked.

"He was wearing this."

She looked at the inscription: With all my love, Louise.

She felt numb. Those months of hope . . . the long waiting . . . the effort to carry on as if nothing had happened . . . now she had to make new plans. A new way of life . . . yet she was halfway to that already.

"We'll help in any way we can. Your husband was insured?"

Louise nodded. There would be more than enough money now. The farm was no longer threatened. But she had no proof of death. The watch could have been stolen from a living man. She looked out of the window up at the tops of the mountains, hidden in faint cloud. The sun ought not to be shining. If she sat very still she would wake up and discover she was dreaming.

"You'll stay with her?" he asked Emma as he went out, leaving Louise sitting silent. She felt as if she would never move again.

"Of course I will," Emma said. "She'll cope . . . it's been a shock . . . she never gave up hoping."

"I hate this abominable world," he said, as he opened his car door. "I'm for ever breaking bad news to someone. I feel guilty when I go home to my wife and our children . . . why should I be happy when so many are suffering?" He started the engine and looked up at her. "I could have sent my assistant, but he's young . . . and I wanted to see the place for myself, and make sure she wasn't alone."

Emma, only a year away from her own loss, had no answer. She had begun to enjoy herself again, without feelings of guilt, and though there was a gap in her life, it was beginning to fill.

"I think we have to snatch what happiness we can," she said. "Louise had to know . . . and it's not your fault, or your guilt."

He smiled at her.

"At least she's in good hands," he said. "I was afraid I'd find her on her own. She needs her friends."

The day passed slowly. Emma rang Russell, who told both the doctor and the vicar. The doctor, coming in the afternoon, brought a bottle of pills. Louise thanked him and put them in the drawer of her bedside table. She didn't intend to take them.

She didn't want to see the vicar. She rarely went to church and was afraid he would sermonise. A quiet, elderly man, he sat drinking coffee, and playing peep bo with the baby, who was fascinated.

"He'll be a comfort to you," the vicar said. "I wondered if you'd like a memorial service in the church? A tribute to your husband. He died bravely. Later, perhaps a plaque in the church wall."

Louise, when he had gone, resumed her work. Work deadened pain. She spent some time with Tarquin, wishing Mervyn could have seen him now he was full grown. Mott followed her, anxious. Fern, her pups only two weeks away, spent more time resting than before. Emma was now giving her four small meals a day and Mott had to have a taste too. He didn't see why she should be fed when he wasn't.

"It was stupid to hope. I should have known," Louise said at bedtime. Emma had sat with her, knitting, during the evening. Kate had come home early and had spent most of the evening with Corrie and Chance, grooming them as if they had never been brushed before. She didn't know what to say and in the end had said nothing and felt guilty about it.

"We always hope," Emma said, "and you couldn't be sure."

But now she was sure.

Sleep refused to come. Louise got up at two and went downstairs. Ceredig was fast asleep and she would hear him if he cried. She needed light and she needed a drink. She needed distraction. She took out the account books that she had left that morning and began to work on them.

She looked back at the previous year, wondering how they had fared by comparison. Mervyn's writing triggered tears. It was a long time before she was able to dry her eyes. She went over to the stove to make coffee.

The door opened.

"Kate?"

"I couldn't sleep. I kept thinking of you . . ." She crossed the room and hugged Louise. "Why is life so horrible?"

There was something in her voice that made Louise look at her.

"It oughtn't to be horrible for you," Louise said. "I'll get by. It happens all the time to people and they get over it: road accidents; plane crashes; people drowned at sea . . . there are sorrowing relatives everywhere, all the time. Life goes on. It's just a shock, at first, even when you expect it. I've always known that there might be a chance that he'd never come home. I just didn't want to face it."

She poured hot water on to the coffee powder. They had been neglecting Kate, she thought, both Emma and herself so busy that, though they had sensed something was wrong, they had done nothing about it, hoping it was a minor misery that would soon be over. She felt a sudden pang of guilt. She was not the only one with worries.

"Kate. Is there a problem?" she asked, as she stacked the papers in the file, ready to resume her task in the morning.

Kate hesitated. She had hidden her feelings for so long. She wanted to talk, although it was never easy, but quite suddenly she knew she had to bring her misery into the open.

"Mike made a pass at me. I liked him, but not like that and I tried to push him away. He wouldn't let go . . . he wouldn't listen. He was horrible." Now she had begun, she could not stop. "Mike's telling everyone I only like women, not men. That's why I'm here. He says I have a crush on you. It's not true. It's just that I don't want to be involved with anyone. I'd rather steer clear till I've finished my A levels. Three of my friends are doing badly because all they can think of is their boyfriends. I want to go to vet college. I want it more than I want anything else and I need high marks. I haven't time to waste."

Louise stared at her, completely lost for words.

"I've been trying to catch up on what I missed at the beginning of this term."

"Missed?" Louise asked. Surely Kate wouldn't play truant.

"I was still frightened by the lot that raided Kane. Mike won't have anything to do with me now and his friends left me alone too. I just mooched round the town for the first two weeks instead of going to school. Then I met Mrs Hunt in the shopping mall one Saturday morning. She'd missed me. She persuaded me to go back. The headmaster did speak to them, but I don't trust them.

"So far, Damon hasn't done anything to upset me. But he's said he'll get his own back. His parents have cut out all his pleasures, and he's got to pay them back for their share of the vet's bill. A lot of the girls are avoiding me as if I'm bad news – I don't have to have a boyfriend to prove I'm normal, do I?"

"Of course not. That's ridiculous," Louise said.

"Was your first date with Mervyn?" Kate asked.

"No. It was with a man from college who asked me to a dance. I hated the dance and he got drunk and tried to kiss me, and I stubbed my cigarette out on his hand. That was the end of a not at all beautiful friendship."

"I don't want boys close to me," Kate said, worry suddenly flaring. "I don't like being touched by just anyone."

"Nor does anyone with any self-esteem," Louise said. "My mother used to say I was worth far more than a bunch of flowers, or a not very special meal and a trip to the cinema. Girls today seem to have a very low sense of their own value."

"Most of them only think of dates and boyfriends," Kate said.

"It's a matter of chemistry or magnetism." Louise was glad to think of something other than her own tragedy. "I could never have lived with a man who didn't make me feel he was vital to me. And only Mervyn did that. The others were passing fancies, and I reacted as you did . . . I hated them trying to touch me or to make me think they were all I needed for a perfect life."

She walked cross the room and hugged Kate.

"Oh, love, love," she said. "The only thing wrong with you is that you have far more sense than the other girls."

"Do you mean that?" Kate asked.

"I think you're terrific," Louise said.

Kate looked happier.

"Will you be OK now?" Kate asked, suddenly sleepy. She felt as if a burden had been lifted. Her worries, compared with those of Louise seemed so insignificant. There was a whimper from upstairs.

"I'll be fine," Louise said, and was relieved when Kate picked up her kitten and went up to her own room.

Ceredig needed changing. She sat rocking him in the chair that Paul Berry's father had made for her. Mervyn watched her from his photograph. She kissed the baby when he slept and tucked him into his cot and looked down at him. A year ago they had thought they would never have a son. She touched the warm cheek, and then went to her own bed and fell into an exhausted sleep.

Sixteen

Nothing seemed real. Louise realised that although she had known, all through the long months, that there was a strong possibility that Mervyn was dead, she had never believed it. There was always hope and now there was none. She had to re-plan her future: Mervyn would never come back to help her.

The memorial service was held on the following Sunday. Most of the villagers were there. Some of them came to speak to Louise afterwards, and admire the baby. He, to her relief, had slept throughout the ceremony. During it she realised she must make plans for his christening. No use waiting now.

Nobody knew what to say, but at least they could tell her that Ceredig was bonny and those who had known Mervyn said he was the image of his dad. She felt remote, an onlooker, as if she were on a stage and none of this was happening.

She needed to work and she needed to think. There were things she ought to do, but she put them off. They had waited almost a year. A few more days wouldn't matter. She didn't want to write to the insurers yet. It seemed so mercenary. The money couldn't make up for his loss. Also she was not sure what proof they would need. There might be long time-consuming arguments and delays and she could not face that yet.

Letters of condolence arrived and she and Emma devised a formula for answering them. People sent flowers as well as sympathy. She was thankful when the post ceased to bring such offerings although she did appreciate them, especially those who wrote of Mervyn and little things they remembered about him.

Louise was doing her best to make sure that she did not inflict her sadness on anyone else. The baby and the animals were her lifeline: they often made her laugh.

The morning after the memorial service she went out to release Tarquin and the ewes, holding Ceredig in her arms. It had snowed overnight. She sometimes wished they had a lowland farm and a kinder climate, but she and Mervyn had always loved the hills. There was only a slight covering of snow, but Mott raced out into it and dug, sending the flakes flying. He had always adored snow and behaved like a puppy when it came. The baby watched him, laughing, secure and warm in his mother's arms.

Fern was no longer playful. She was ungainly and had no desire to run and she sat by the paddock gate. Jason came towards Louise, and Ceredig crowed to him.

He laughed.

"Do you realise that every other time we've met here Tarquin has already been outside? I've never known if Ceredig was greeting me, or him. Today I know he does greet me, too. Shall I hold him?"

Louise handed the baby over, and went to open the door of the shelter where the sheep spent the night. Mott took up his position. Fern appeared to have resigned her duties, other than ensuring that Louise was always aware of even the least whimper from her son.

Dog and ram greeted one another, nose to nose, a daily routine now. Placidly, the sheep walked into their paddock. Louise watched Tarquin as he came towards her. He stopped. Jason watched, amused, knowing the routine. A sideways step and a little prance, and then he pushed against Louise, almost a butt but never quite. He wanted her hands on him, he loved being stroked. The older children, under supervision, were allowed to do that too, but these moments in the morning were special. If Jason let him out, instead of Louise, he

ignored Mott and ran to the kitchen door and tapped on it
with his hoof. If he was allowed out in the yard he still
followed her around, chasing after the dogs.

"Reckon he'd herd the sheep," Bob said one morning,
laughing, as the ram followed Mott who was shepherding
the ducks to the pond and who had decided, for reasons of his
own, that they had forgotten the way. Kate had thrown corn
out for the chickens to eat and overdone the amount. The
ducks had made the most of an extra opportunity.

On the third Monday in May Louise was alone for the first
time since she had been told that Mervyn was dead. Emma
and Kate had gone out to celebrate Russell and Roz's silver
wedding anniversary. Mrs Hunt had offered to babysit so that
Louise could go too, but Louise had felt she would dampen
the evening. They would be back before eleven. Nobody
wanted a late celebration because there was work tomorrow.
They left before five, having a long drive to a restaurant the
other side of the town.

The house felt surprisingly empty. There were shadows
hiding the mountains. A rising wind irritated the animals,
and moaned round the angles of the buildings. Mervyn used
to laugh and say it sounded like a woman wailing for her
demon lover. It was a most eerie noise. No wonder people
used to believe in banshees, Louise thought.

The other sound she hated was the screaming of the jays.
That too was a ghostly noise. She glanced out of the window.
Buzzards soared over the sheep field. She welcomed the pair:
they kept down the rabbits.

She glanced at the clock. They had been gone just over an
hour. Time seemed to be standing still. In the past few
months she had never been alone for more than an hour or
so. Every sound was magnified: the rustle of a leaf became a
footfall.

Jason was out in the fields. One of the older ewes was
having trouble giving birth and he and Kane were staying with
her. Bob had gone alone to the party but Kane had stayed

behind because he did not feel that Jason was experienced enough to cope with complications.

Louise suspected Kane was glad of an opportunity to avoid a big social occasion. He was always shy in a crowd, and avoided the farm when the school parties were there. They were good for the baby, though. Ceredig loved the children. It still amazed her that so young a child could show such joy when people greeted him. He was changing daily, and far more placid. Also he now slept from midnight to six a.m. He was asleep now.

"Early colic," the doctor had said, when Louise confessed her worry that he was unduly fretful. "It happens to a lot of young babies, but they seem to grow out of it around five months."

Ceredig loved watching, his eyes following any person or animal near him. He kicked vigorously, exercising himself, threw his arms around and grabbed at anything near him. She went over to the carrycot. He would soon be too big for that. She touched his warm cheek. There were days when she could not believe he was real, and was afraid she might wake and find she had dreamed him. If only Mervyn had known.

She looked about her, wondering at the changes that had come into her life in the past year. The kitchen had always been her favourite room. Here she and Mervyn had sat, the Aga door open, the firelight warm and welcoming. It was impossible to believe that he wouldn't come through the door again, eager to tell her of a new calf or lamb. Here they had planned and dreamed.

On their last night together it had been very warm. They had taken their supper outside, to watch the sun set on the mountains: a wonderful red sky, with black streamers of cloud. They had gone inside when darkness came and Mervyn had suddenly realised he should have had a hair cut. Louise had trimmed it, very badly, with her nail scissors and they had laughed at the odd effect.

"I won't take my cap off," he promised.

"Not even to sleep?"

It was the last time she had been able to curl up close to him in their big double bed. He had been due to meet Chris early. They had said goodbye by the paddock, where a very small Tarquin jumped with delight in the early sunshine, and then ran to Belle for a feed.

"Our future," Mervyn had said, admiring his cherished new lamb. He had kissed her and was gone.

"There's more of a future than he knows," she had told the dogs as he drove away. She crossed off the days on the calendar. Mervyn'd be home in a week and she could tell him he was to be a father.

She pushed away the memory.

She made coffee, wondering how Jason and Kane were faring in the field. The ewe was close to the cottage; with luck they could observe her from indoors. Emma had made a pasty, and put a potato to bake in the oven. Sheila Hunt, who had a greenhouse, had brought up a lettuce from her early crop.

Make a meal. She had not put the hens or the ducks in for the night and Tarquin and the ewe were still in the paddock making the most of the lighter evenings. Kate had put Corrie and Chance in the stable before she had gone out.

Louise had plans for the farm but she had not wanted to go ahead in case Mervyn came home and did not approve. It was time to move on. She fetched a notebook and began to work.

The pot-bellied pig and her babies were part of the children's corner that Paul and Jason were building. They could expand that. It would be fun to have pygmy animals: goats and pigs, and Kate wanted a miniature horse. One had been advertised in the last week's farming magazine. They could convert the whole field, and put swings and slides and tunnels in part of it, to make an adventure area for the children. Sheila Hunt wanted to bring up groups of them, out of school hours, especially those who had nowhere to play. It would be fun for Ceredig when he was bigger.

206

There was a rap on the door.

Who could that be?

She opened it, and then laughed as she looked down at Tarquin. She had forgotten to put the padlock on the latch of his gate. "You've spoiled them," Kane had said, but had laughed as he said it. It was not of vital importance. He had also laughed at Louise earlier in the year: she had read that lambs benefited in cold weather if they wore woolly jumpers, so she, Emma and Kate had knitted some and fitted out those born early, when there was danger of ice and snow. Louise felt they had proved a point as they had no losses.

She was glad of the interruption.

"Come on, pest," she said.

The ram came briefly into the kitchen while she cut off a crust of bread. She walked towards the door. Tarquin suddenly decided he was a dog today and stayed at heel at her side, his nose on the food which she held tightly in her closed fist. He followed her into his shelter.

"You'd do anything for grub," she said. "You're a pig, not a sheep."

He nosed her pocket, looking for more. She laughed, pushed him in and shut the door. Belle never challenged the dogs but Tarquin was sure he was their equal, if not their superior so Louise had had to develop a low cunning in dealing with him. Kane was right: he was thoroughly spoiled and Louise wondered what Mervyn would have made of her methods.

She went back to her half-eaten meal, but before she sat down, the phone rang.

"Louise? It's Kane. This is going to be an all-night job. Don't worry if Jason doesn't come back till morning. She looks as if she has triplets and she's very slow starting. Are you OK?"

"I'm fine," Louise assured him, glad that he had phoned. Nothing like an ex-vet for a neighbour, she thought, knowing that, as Russell was unavailable, Kane would be able to cope.

There was a locum at the surgery for the evening and the night, but he was very young and she valued experience.

Kane, his accident long forgotten except for occasional recurring aches in his injured leg, had proved to be a very good neighbour indeed. Bob now spent all his time either at the kennels or helping on the farm, and Kane was a frequent visitor, telling her when she could cope easily with a health problem and when she needed to call Russell. Kate and Jason still went to the cottage with the team to help out.

Kane and Bob came up to the farm almost every Sunday for the lavish midday meal that Emma insisted on preparing. Roast meat, roast potatoes, several vegetables and a creamy dessert that everyone was sure they ought to resist, but never could. Sheila Hunt, whose elder children now lived on their own and whose youngest son was at college, often came too, bringing with her a supply of cakes and buns as her contribution. Louise suddenly wished she had invited the school teacher to spend the night at the farm. It would have been company.

She had so much help. Life was so odd. None of this would have happened if Mervyn had been here, she thought. She looked out of the window. The wind was dropping. There was far less movement in the trees. Weather changed so fast, here on the hills.

Fern, uncomfortable, asked to go out. She needed frequent trips into the little field behind the farm where the dogs were always exercised. Mervyn had fitted security lights which enabled Louise to watch the little bitch. Her mother had started to whelp in a corner of that field, some years ago. It was only by chance that Mervyn had found the first puppy as Dally had panicked and run indoors. It had been her first litter. Fern was one of the pups from her last litter. Mott had been bought from another farm.

Louise could not settle. She tidied the kitchen. She made coffee. She finished the ironing. She wished that Ceredig would wake, but perversely, he slept soundly. Time to think about Fern, who was lying on the rug, now very obviously in whelp. Louise had no intention of selling pups that knew nothing of the world, and had only seen a shed or barn or kennel, so that when taken to their new homes everything they met terrified them, so they were always born in the utility room beyond the kitchen. It had once been a scullery, and the floor was tiled and easily cleaned.

She went through to look at it. The walls needed re-doing. It was a small room, which also housed the washing machine and the deep freeze. She fetched a brush, and a tin of white-wash and began to work, leaving the connecting door open so that she could see the baby.

Fern should whelp the last week in May, Russell thought . . . The litter would be ready for sale at the beginning of August, which was a good time: winter was not too near and they would be house trained before the nights grew dark. She might need to keep one or two puppies back because people went on holiday then. Perhaps not such a good a time. She did not like pups to be sold after eight weeks because by then they were part of a family pack, and it was not the right family.

The newly whitewashed walls were satisfying and she was, at last, tired. It was time to put Fern's rug in the whelping box and get her used to it. She didn't want newborn pups in the kitchen. The bitch might resent visitors and the last thing she wanted was an eager child picking up a puppy and getting bitten by its mother.

She'd put the rug in the box tomorrow as it might be necessary to sit with Fern, who ought to have been introduced to her whelping quarters earlier. Louise had not had time to think about that. She cleaned her brush and put away with the tin of whitewash.

She closed the door and went back to the kitchen. That had passed nearly two hours and she felt a sense of achievement. Something to show Emma and Kate and Jason when they all got in.

She let Fern out again. The sky was clear and the wind had dropped. There was a haze in the air, and two faint stars. This time Mott followed. She watched the dogs. There was a chill in the air and she was glad when they decided to come in.

Frost in May. The fruit blossom would suffer. They had had the same problem last year and a sparse crop. The apples were cookers and kept well and were very useful throughout the winter. Not many this year either, at this rate.

Spice and her kittens were asleep, curled together in Emma's chair. Louise checked her son, who lay on his side, his small thumb in his mouth. His hair, growing fast, stuck up from his head in small spikes, just as Mervyn's had done in the mornings before it had been brushed.

The phone rang again.

"Louise . . . it's Jason. Look, I'm sorry. I forgot to say I hadn't had time to feed the lambs. Can you do it, or shall I come up?"

"No problem," said Louise, using his own favourite phrase, and he laughed.

"We're still waiting . . . Kane says any moment now."

It was almost ten. The baby was still asleep, which was unusual. He turned over and murmured.

"Stop fussing," she said to herself.

She went out to the lambs in the smallest of the five barns. There were several: three orphans, three who were each one of twins, and two that were part of a group of triplets. None of the ewes had enough milk for more than one baby. Bob had built a rack and she slotted the bottles into it, watching the lambs line up, as they ran for their food. She was later than Jason would have been and the milk was soon gone.

When she got back in she ate her sandwiches and glanced at the clock. It was the longest evening she had spent for months. How could time go so fast when you were busy and so slowly when you were on your own? She fed both dogs and let them out into the yard. They showed no desire to stay outside.

Fern went over to Louise and nudged her leg as the baby began to cry. Sometimes she wondered if the bitch were telepathic as she often alerted Louise before she heard a sound. Maybe the baby made small waking noises that only the dogs could hear.

By the time she had changed and fed him it was late but she did not want to put him back in his cot. She held him to her, happy in his warmth and closeness, revelling in his smile and his contented noises.

She put him down on the hearthrug on a blanket so that he could kick freely. The two dogs watched him. Spice and her two kittens had long gone up to Kate's room. The cat had her own ideas about bedtime.

The knock on the door startled her.

"Who's there?" she called.

"Only me. I've got my arms full."

Jason's voice reassured her. She turned the key and let him in. He was holding one of the tiniest lambs she had ever seen.

"Mattie had twins. The first is a big fellow and pretty tough. This little one looks as if she's lost out. She wouldn't move so Mattie shook her, tried to lift her by her scruff, and even kicked her. She is alive, but she hasn't even attempted to stand yet."

Mattie was one of their bottle-fed lambs, now three years old, and a major nuisance if ever free in the farmyard. She had been reared in the kitchen and still thought it was part of her territory. If the door was shut she butted at it or kicked it, and had to be bribed with bread to go back to the flock. She was a genius at finding escape routes and kept Jason busy mending her break-out points. She had never given up her attempts at getting human attention. She stole Jason's sandwiches if he did not watch out.

"She needs warmth," Jason said, as if he had been dealing with newborn lambs for all his life. "It's cold in the barn."

Louise was delighted to have another human being in the house. She settled Ceredig in his cot. Babies were all very well, but you couldn't hold a conversation with them. It was almost eight months since she had been alone every day. She now depended on company.

Jason settled the lamb in the big cardboard box that Louise lined with an old blanket. He put it close to the Aga and looked down while she prepared a bottle.

"She had problems with the second lamb. It was lucky that Kane was there . . . He had to pull it out. I didn't want to come back till I was sure she was OK. He's taken her and the big lamb down to his place for the next few days to keep an eye on her. The ewe was exhausted."

Louise took the teat out of the boiling water and fastened it on

"Do you think she'll feed?"

"Find out," she said, handing him the bottle. Kane had milked several of the ewes soon after birth and they had a supply of first milk.

Louise glanced at the clock. Emma and Kate were late. It must have been a good party. Jason must be hungry. She took out a pack of sandwiches and defrosted it.

Jason lifted the lamb's head to help her suck better. Mott had come to watch. This was part of his life, curled up beside Mervyn in the fields at night, waiting for the ewes to give birth.

Louise made coffee for both of them. She must change to decaffeinated – maybe caffeine was one of the things that kept her awake. She wondered how many cups she drank a day. Perhaps she was addicted: she seemed never to relax, these days.

She took one of Jason's sandwiches.

Unexpectedly there was a whimper from the cot, followed by an impatient nudge at her leg. She stroked Fern.

"I wonder what she'll do when she has her own pups. I'm sure she thinks I'm either deaf or a dreadful mother. She can't bear him to make the slightest unhappy sound."

"I suspect she'll have problems," Jason said. "She'll prob-

212

ably try and put the pups in his cot so she can watch them all together."

"Heaven forbid," Louise said, with an uneasy feeling that it might be true.

She picked the baby up and rested him against her shoulder, patting his back, which produced a burp that made Mott put his head on one side, listening.

The lamb opened her mouth as Jason squirted milk from the teat on to her lips. She began to suck, though not with fervour.

"She doesn't seem to have much strength," Jason said. "I'll sleep on the sofa, and feed her every two hours. I'll fetch my alarm clock."

"No need," Louise said. She put her son back in his cradle and, producing a small bedside alarm from the dresser drawer, set the hands and the little trigger that would sound the bell. Mervyn always used it in lambing time when he needed to wake every two hours. She held it in her hand, remembering, and then put it on the table.

The lamb struggled to its feet. She made several attempts before she succeeded in remaining upright for some minutes and then decided to lie down again and sleep.

"That's something," Jason said, beginning on more sandwiches. "I'm famished."

Louise brought out the cake tins and helped herself to a couple of scones.

"I need to lose weight," she said, wondering whether to put them back, but she needed comfort so she buttered them, spread strawberry jam on them and fetched the clotted cream from the refrigerator. Emma made it twice a week, having a considerable weakness for it herself.

"Have you got to go out again tonight?" Louise asked Jason. "Are any more due?"

"Bob and Kane said they'd cope. Bob's going round them twice during the night, at two and four. He came back from the restaurant early, thinking we might need help. I'll go at six.

Kane said he'd look round at midnight and take any ewe that
seemed to be near down to his place. He doesn't think any will
produce for a couple of days, but he's moved those due in the
next week or so down to the field nearest his cottage. Hope
he's right. Give us a rest."

There was mist over the low-lying ground and above the river
as Emma drove back to the farm. The mountains were hidden,
the horizon flattened. Trees seemed to rise from nowhere,
standing in mid air. Above the mist the sky was clear, and
moonlight gave an eerie haze to trees and bushes. Emma
drove slowly, her vision obscured. Kate had decided to stay
the night with her parents. The party had been an outstanding
success.

Emma was glad to turn into the yard. She was tired. It was
well after midnight. She cut the engine. Louise was still up, to
her surprise. As she opened the door the lamb opened her eyes
and bleated.

"She's the feebler of twins. Jason's going to sleep here and
give her her two-hourly feeds," Louise said.

"Good party?" Jason asked.

"A lovely party. They're inundated with presents as Peta's
been telling practically everyone who came for treatment in
the last few weeks. Your rose bowl was the centrepiece, filled
with red roses. They loved it."

Going up to bed late, Louise fed her son again just after
one, hoping that he would not wake for at least six hours.
That would give her time to do some of the early morning
chores. She lay awake, listening to the soft sounds from the
baby. She could not help wondering what Mervyn would have
made of the situation at the farm if he came home. Changes
seemed to have come about without her making any effort.
Tomorrow she'd start work on the farm shop. That would be
an attraction for the parents who brought their children up to
see the animals at weekends.

She'd make a go of it yet.

"You'll see," she told an invisible bank manager. "This farm will be profitable, without the insurance money."

She might have to wait seven years without having proof of death. Mervyn's watch was on her bedside table. She held it. Tomorrow she would put it safely away for his son.

Seventeen

S heila Hunt arrived next morning just as Emma was making the coffee for the mid-morning break.

"I know it's early, but I thought you could do with an extra pair of hands."

"I can," Louise said. "I can also do with some distraction."

She had been thrust into a new dimension: everything now depended on her because Mervyn would never be there to consult. There was no need to wonder if he'd approve of what she had done.

She had spent a restless night, thinking. Ceredig's inheritance depended on her.

"I need to think. We need to make much more money. I rang to ask about the insurance but they've not had such a situation before and said they need time to take advice. They need proof of death. How do I get that?" She picked up her coffee mug. "So I've no idea when, or even if, Mervyn's insurance will come through. I suppose in seven years' time . . . I think that's the period after which death can be presumed . . . it's a long time."

Sheila Hunt perched herself on the arm of the big chair.

"You can open to the public as a working farm with a farm trail. My parents didn't open all the year round – just from Whit to mid September."

Sheila's face brightened as she became more enthusiastic.

"Their landlord was very keen on the idea. Lambing's more or less over by the time the first visitors come but the lambs

216

are there for people to bottle-feed and, of course, you charge for that."

Emma opened the cake tin.

"With people coming for a farm trail you can open a farm shop." Sheila helped herself to a large piece of cake. "I'm anybody's for a good old-fashioned fruit cake – you could sell them. So few people bake these days."

"I'd love that," Emma said. "Maybe we could sell home-made bread. Buy even more hens and sell the eggs to shops."

Sheila drained her mug.

"If Jason had a room in the house you could do up the flat over the barn and let it to summer visitors. They do make money. My father did it, he had two large caravans as well – you'd need planning permission for the alterations and the vans, but I'd think you'd get it."

Sheila Hunt had triggered ideas and she and Louise had spent their spare time that day trying to work out various plans, and making a list of the animals they already had.

"A farm trail would need notices," Jason said during their evening meal. "Arrows pointing to chickens, pigs, lambs, children's playground, pets' corner."

"I can do some of those and Leila Green would probably help me," Kate said. "She's a wizard at drawing. I think she'd like to make up to you for what happened. It would help her. She's not that bad . . . it was Damon . . . she had a crush on him. She's been trying to make friends with me this term."

"Toilets?" Jason asked.

"We can have portaloos in one of the sheds," Louise said. "Later on if we make enough money we can build and have showers and a laundry room, but we can't do it yet."

Kate was becoming interested.

"We've a school newspaper. The editor does all kinds of things on the computer, and has a colour printer. We could do leaflets and brochures and get them put in shops and pubs, and in dad's surgery and the doctor's surgery. What about cartoons of farm animals, as postcards to sell?'

217

Everyone was talking at once. Louise became excited and her mind raced ahead.

"We could start keeping rare breeds. I could join the Rare Breed Society and get help and advice from them. It's something I always wanted to do. It's such a shame to let rare breeds die out." She had filled half a notebook with ideas and suggestions. Then she said, "I'd like a Gloucester Old Spot."

"What's that when it's at home?" Jason asked.

"A breed of pig. And maybe some of the old breeds of sheep, chickens, ducks and geese. Animals people wouldn't see anywhere else."

"One of the farms down the valley breeds rare birds for collectors," Jason said. "They have an incubator."

"We'd need to build up slowly," Emma said, "and to think hard. There are snags as well as benefits."

"But some things you could start now," Sheila Hunt said. "The major part needs careful planning but you should be able to open a trail next year."

Ideas spilled out of them.

Louise had already been in touch with the Food and Farming Education Service who were adding them to the list of farms which children could visit. The children had grabbed the information packs when they had arrived at the school and Sheila had had to send for more.

Louis began to see more possibilities that she had first imagined, especially on the next Sunday when Kane and Bob came for the midday meal too. Emma always made a feast of Sunday lunch.

"A baby elephant?" Jason suggested. "Ostriches? A herd of bison? Then we could start selling organic meat."

"Where would we put them?" Emma asked. "Do be sensible."

Jason laughed and winked at Kane.

"Only joking. But we could maybe have unusual small

animals. There was an ad for a pygmy goat in the local paper. Someone wants to sell it."

"You can ring up and ask. That wouldn't cause much of a housing problem," Louise said. "They're entertaining animals."

"I'm really keen about the miniature pony," Kate said. "It'd be great fun. And I saw an ad for two racoons, free to a good home. They'd be a terrific attraction."

"You can't have anything exotic," Kane said, "because that involves a zoo licence, which is expensive and you'd need special cages."

"Paul's making Ceredig a little Noah's Ark with animals," Jason said. "What about an ark instead of a Wendy house in the children's playground? We could find an old rowboat that was no longer watertight, which wouldn't matter on dry land, and build it up and make animals for it."

"A Welsh dragon's nest in the tea barn," Kate said. "With hard-boiled goose eggs painted in rainbow colours. The little ones would love it. I've got a pattern for a dragon. It's quite big. I was going to make it for Ceredig."

"You could have that at the end of your treasure trail, sitting on the prize," Kane said. "We'll have to work that out, and where the nest is going to be."

"I could train youngsters to train their sheepdogs." Louise said. "I'm going to teach Ceredig as soon as he can understand . . . turn out the best trial dog in the district."

"Why not keep Fern's pups and sell them as trained adults?" Kane asked. "Might cost a bit at the start, but you'd get far more money for a trained sheepdog."

"I suppose in between we will still have farm animals and keep on with them?" Louise said, suddenly afraid they were straying more and more from the real purpose of Bryn Mawr.

"You can combine the two," Bob said. "You already have plenty of help from the school. They'll be fascinated. They may even come up with ideas of their own. It's better than turning the place into a golf course, as they've done on some of the lowland farms."

"You might give work experience to some of the school leavers who can't find jobs," Kane said. "There's a scheme that would help with that. It would give them something more to do than sitting at home, fretting. I've a couple of girls who want to help me. I'm about to look into it."

Everyone was eager and wanted to be involved. Paul and Jason decided to expand the children's corner. Bob decided he would be responsible for improving the play area to make it a big attraction and thought he would start by visiting various places to see what was possible.

The next few days sped past. Louise looked at the calendar. It would soon be the anniversary of Mervyn's disappearance and her own birthday. Though there was a small corner of her mind that was dreading both, knowing they would re-awaken memories, she was so busy that by the time she got into bed she immediately fell fast asleep.

The end of May produced a heatwave. Fern was waddling around miserably, reminding Louise of her own last weeks of pregnancy. Mott appeared bewildered by his companion's refusal to join him outside. He walked up to her and nosed her, looking puzzled when she growled at him, as if saying, for heaven's sake leave me alone, can't you see I have other things to think about? After a few abortive tries, he sighed deeply and went to find Louise.

"He finds women unpredictable," Jason said, grinning.

"Don't we all?" Kane, who now spent several hours a day at the farm, grinned too.

In the evenings Fern, so far from being remote, developed a need to be close to Louise, as if asking for sympathy. She lay by her chair, looking up at her anxiously, but she still contrived to alert her mistress if she didn't hear the baby at once.

"I don't know whether it's because she's pregnant herself and is more sensitive to him, or whether she's bonded to him, but she's much quicker off the mark than I am if he does cry, in spite of her size. I wonder if she knows what's happening to her yet," Louise said, watching the little bitch lift herself wearily and go to her water bowl.

Kate was busy revising, but had been induced by Emma and Louise to cut the number of hours and take time off. She was anxious to do well in her exams, although the vital ones were not until next year. She spent much of her spare time with Corrie, talking to the mare, who was a willing listener, and not likely to pass on secrets.

Paul cycled up after school every day to look after Chance, who now skittered to greet everyone, adding his small noise to his mother's more fervent welcome.

On the last day of May, Russell called in to check on Trouble who once again had mastitis.

As they came out of the cow byre into the brilliant sunshine Russell looked across at Fern. The little bitch was lying in the shade; the sun was so hot the ground was baked. Jason was busy carrying water for the animals. The vet went over to her and knelt and stroked her. She licked his hand.

"There shouldn't be any problems but it is her first litter. She's very big and could be up to a week early. Mott could easily have mated her several times since none of you were aware she was in season, so we don't know the exact date. If you need me, ring. Never mind what time it is."

Louise thanked him.

Working out of doors was a penance in the blazing sun. Jason was so tanned that he looked Italian. The baby was fretful, and had a heat rash which Louise treated with calamine lotion. They were all thankful when the weather broke and it became cooler, although there had been no rain as yet. A pleasant breeze stirred the dust in the farmyard but Jason had no time to hose it down.

On the first Saturday in June Kate decided to prepare the evening meal to give Emma a treat. She dished up, and they sat down to eat. It was too hot for heavy meals and they had cold chicken, green salad and a rice salad. Ceredig, who had been fed half an hour earlier, was sound asleep.

Fern had disappeared. Emma, not wishing her out of sight, went to look for her in the whelping room. The little bitch looked up at her anxiously. She had stolen one of the baby's cot blankets from the basket in which the laundry waited to be put in the airing cupboard. It was all around her, shredded into one inch pieces.

"Oh, Fern, Fern!" Emma said, and the collie wagged a tentative tail.

"I think we're going to have pups by morning," Emma said, returning to the others. "I'm afraid we're a blanket short. She's made a nest of it. I've never seen anything torn up quite so small."

"I'll stay with her," Louise said. "She knows me best. I'll call if I need either of you. Bed, Kate, and no revising. Your exam's not till Monday."

"I have nightmares," Kate said. "I'm sitting there, with the paper in front of me and all I write is my name. My mind is a total blank and so is the paper."

"Dreams go by opposites," Jason said.

Emma lifted Ceredig and took him upstairs. Louise settled, placing the armchair so that she could see into the whelping room. Fern was restless, unable to understand what was happening to her, and asked time and again to go outside into the yard but, once out, wandered round as if sure she needed to go only nothing was happening.

It was well after two before there was any sign of any pup, and then there was only the top of the head. Fern, who had been struggling to give birth, was becoming exhausted. Louise, now thoroughly worried, rang through to Russell.

He answered her sleepily.

"I'm sorry," she said. "I think the first pup's head's too big to pass down through the birth canal. She's stopped trying

222

and she's getting tired, and I suspect it will have to be a Caesarian."

"Could Emma get her here?"

"I will," Louise said. "Jason can come with me and watch over her. There's no point in you coming up. You need the surgery and its equipment."

Kate appeared in the doorway.

"I couldn't sleep and wondered what was happening. No need to wake Jason. I'll come. If there are real problems we might not be back till morning and Jason's needed here."

Kate ran upstairs to dress and tell her grandmother they were going out. Emma put on her dressing gown and came downstairs.

"I can feed Ceredig in the morning. I'll keep my door open so that I can hear him," she said.

"There's plenty of goats' milk. I'll stay and bring Fern back, if it's possible and she isn't too weak for the return journey. If I leave her any longer she may be."

Kate had already put one of the plastic dog beds in the Land Rover, covering it with clean newspaper and then a special fleecy dog blanket which let anything wet through, leaving the surface dry and bitch and pups comfortable.

Fern followed Louise outside, and was lifted into the bed. Kate sat on the floor beside her.

It was months since Louise had driven at night. The headlamps picked out the hedges, and trees swam ghostlike into view, then vanished. She went slowly down the rutted lane, trying to see the potholes and avoid them.

At last they reached the surgery. There were lights on in the porch, the waiting room and surgery, and as they drew up Russell was already outside and immediately lifted Fern from her bed. Louise and Kate followed him in. He laid the little bitch on the operating table, and examined her. She was exhausted by her efforts and seemed almost unaware of her surroundings.

"No chance of that one coming the usual way. I hope the others aren't as big," Russell said. "Are you going home?"

"I'd like to stay till you've finished and then take her back if it's possible," Louise said.

Peta was already busy with the apparatus for the anaesthetic.

Roz, tying her dressing-gown girdle, appeared in the doorway.

"Come and have coffee. Kate, see to it, love, will you? I'm going to get dressed. I might be needed."

Louise sat listening for sounds from the operating room. It was over half an hour before the sitting-room door opened, and Russell appeared, looking worried.

"Roz, can you come? There's a bit of a complication. Louise, you'd better go home. I'll have to keep her here for at least two days. I'll ring as soon as we've finished."

"She'll be all right?"

"I hope so. Nothing's ever certain in this world. You know that as well as I do and it's no use saying yes, when all I can say is maybe."

It was a silent drive back through the darkness. A barn owl flew beside them, just above the ditch, for a couple of miles and then turned away. A thin rain began to fall. Louise needed to concentrate on her driving. Visibility was poor.

Kate sat and prayed. Please let Fern be all right. Please.

It was six o'clock when they got home. Emma had fed the baby and Jason, the cows already milked, was eating his breakfast. Ceredig, propped on his pillows, was watching. He held out his arms to his mother, who picked him up and hugged him.

"I wonder if all this would have happened if Mervyn had been home," Louise said. Her thoughts were with Fern. Would she and her pups survive?

Jason had a sudden memory of his grandmother.

224

There's no luck aboot the hoose,
There's no luck at a'.
There's no luck aboot the hoose
When the guid man's awa.

His gran had loved Robbie Burns, as she always called him. He knew better than to say the verse aloud. It was less than four weeks to Louise's birthday. A year ago, she had expected her husband home. Now she knew that would never happen. If anything happened to Fern . . .

It was Sunday so Louise suggested Kate went back to bed, but she shook her head. She couldn't have slept. She took over the breakfast-making from her grandmother.

"Sit down and have yours," she said, cooking for both of them. She made coffee. Louise sat, cradling the mug in her hands to warm them, willing the phone to ring. There must be some news by now.

It was after eight o'clock and the instrument still remained obstinately silent.

Eighteen

L ouise, unable to stand the uncertainty, rang the surgery just after nine. Roz answered.

"We wanted to be quite sure before we phoned in case we gave you false hopes. We're pretty certain now that Fern will be OK. She gave us a fright, though. There were eight pups, but the first one died soon after birth. I did my best, but I couldn't bring him round – it was too much of a struggle for him. The other seven are healthy."

"What was the problem ?" Louise asked.

"She stopped breathing, briefly, on the operating table, but we managed to resuscitate her. I had to help clean and dry the pups, as she was out of action. A couple had difficulties getting started."

"She really is all right? She won't stop breathing again?"

"No. I'll bring her up later this morning. She's done much better than we expected and she'll be happier in her own home."

Emma came into the kitchen

"Did I hear the phone?"

"Fern's fine," Louise said. "They had a panic, but she's OK now."

Clouds shadowed the sun and the breeze was cool. The mountains were dappled with shadow but it was still clear on the far side of the valley.

"Rain soon," Jason said, coming in for his morning break. "Any news of Fern?"

"Mother and pups doing fine," Louise said.

"Great. Let's celebrate," Jason said.

But Louise had begun to distrust providence. "I'll do that when all the puppies are sold and paid for," she said.

The following day Kate came home over an hour early, bringing Paul with her.

"They said we could come home as there were no exams this afternoon. Bob gave us a lift. Can we see the pups?" Kate looked hopefully at Louise who had gone to collect Fern and the puppies earlier that day.

Fern scratched at the door which connected the kitchen to her new quarters. She went to the kitchen door to be let out into the yard.

"A quick peep." Louise watched Fern investigate outside.

"More Mott than her," Kate said a few minutes later, as she looked down at the assorted bundles. Fern was almost white, with three black paws, black ears and a black cheek on her left side. Mott was black and white, with more black than white and the pups were the same.

Fine weather brought more visitors than ever before. Bob and Jason converted one of the smaller barns into a tea room. They sold farm produce at one end and Emma's cakes always sold out.

Kate and her friends had fun at the weekends acting as waitresses, which they did with even more enthusiasm when they discovered that people tipped them. Parents enjoyed coffee and cakes while their children played with the tiny animals, supervised by Bob or Kane or Sheila Hunt.

Not all visitors were either welcome or well-intentioned. Looking out of the window on the Saturday before her birthday, Louise saw a group of strangers walking determinedly across the yard. One of them, a grey-haired man, knocked on the door.

"We can't walk the footpath on your land," he said. "It's overgrown with brambles, thistles, nettles and young trees, and the fields are a disgrace."

227

His voice was accusing, and Louise was annoyed.

"Which fields?"

He pointed.

"That's not my property. It belongs to another farm. Nothing to do with me, or the cottage on the other side of it."

"Where's the owner? What on earth is he thinking of?"

"He's dead," Louise said.

"Someone must own the land."

"So far as we know it belongs to his son who emigrated to Australia. Nobody knows his address. Letters are sent back labelled addressee unknown."

"Something ought to be done about it."

"If you feel so strongly, go and clear the fields yourself and restore the path," Bob said. Nobody had noticed him come across the yard behind the little group. He had been teaching Jason how to drive the tractor.

The group, baffled expressions on their faces, turned away.

"I'll be making a complaint," the grey-haired man said.

"You do that," Bob said. "But not to us. We'd like the fields in order as much as you would. The weeds spill over on to our ground and we have a constant battle with them. But if too many farmers get bothered by intrusion, there won't be any of us left. And there'll be nowhere to walk, as all the land'll go back to the wild. It's only taken eight years for those fields to get like that. In another twenty . . ." He shrugged. "And shut the gate when you go out," he called after them, as nobody showed any sign of doing so.

"I'm glad you were here," Louise said. She sighed.

Farming as she knew and loved it would never be the same again. She felt as if she were becoming a theme park, geared to entertain people, rather than to provide them with food. There were days when she longed to be back with the milking herd, and days spent with animals that provided a good living, just her and Huw and Mervyn. No use wasting time in regrets.

*　　*　　*

228

Louise was often silent these days, lost in her own world. Emma was increasingly aware that the sixteenth, the date on which Mervyn had vanished, was coming close. She determined that Louise should have a party on her birthday, a week later. She tried to keep her attention on that.

Everyone was trying to ensure that there would be little time for memories.

Ceredig cut two teeth, making as much noise as possible about it.

June 23rd was a Saturday. It dawned bright and fine, and Fern decided to give Louise an impromptu birthday present by bringing her small family out of the scullery and putting them on the kitchen rug. The pups were now just over three weeks old. Mervyn would have loved them, Louise thought.

"They are a time waster," Louise said. "I could watch them for ever, especially now they've begun to develop distinct characters."

Ceredig, in his baby chair, was kicking and shouting, entranced by the puppies.

"Never thought of pups as a baby minder," Jason said. "He does love watching animals, doesn't he?"

"In the blood." Louise had a sudden memory of her husband leaping out of bed just before he went away, saying gaily, "What a day! You can hear the grass grow," and then racing down the stairs, taking them two at a time, to go and gloat over his new ram lamb. Tarquin had followed him everywhere that day, together with both dogs and Demon the drake. So much had happened in the year since Mervyn had disappeared. She put sad memories away.

Roz had promised to come to her party, and Russell had said he'd look in if he could. Kane and Bob had been invited as well as Paul and his father and the woodwork master and his team who intended to finish roofing the new houses for more small pets during the morning. Anne Berry was working and wouldn't be able to come.

Sheila came up during the morning to help with the party

229

preparations. Kate, with only one more exam, joined in, and Louise promised to keep out of the way. She had been inundated with presents, many of them summer clothes for the baby.

Kane and Bob helped Jason with the chores, so that he would be free during the afternoon. There was a riotous atmosphere, everyone determined that Louise should enjoy herself.

The afternoon was the busiest she had known. She was afraid that Ceredig might not like the bustle, but he loved having people around constantly and appreciated the extra attention. After tea school children began to arrive, bringing presents. The baby was propped up by pillows while everyone ate, and spent his time kicking and chuckling. Russell arrived just as Louise started to cut her cake.

There was a chorus of "Happy Birthday to You".

Nobody noticed the heavily bearded man who walked in and stood staring in astonishment. A moment later Mott exploded from his corner, and ran round the newcomer, crying, wagging his tail, trying to leap up and kiss his face in an ecstasy of welcome. Fern flew into the room from her own quarters and joined him.

He stood, in the sudden silence, looking like a sleepwalker who had been roughly awakened.

Ceredig, upset by the change in the atmosphere around him, began to cry.

Louise knew she was looking at a ghost.

Nineteen

Everyone stared at the newcomer.

He appeared bewildered. He stood quite still, looking at the dogs, who seemed to give him confidence. They had known him. Nobody else seemed to. They sat, their eyes watching him.

As Louise stood still, the cake plate in her hands, his voice cut into the room. It was hoarse and he spoke as if in a language that was strange to him.

"Will someone tell me what's going on?"

He lifted one interrogative eyebrow.

Emma grabbed the plate as Louise dropped into the chair beside her, her face white. This was no ghost.

"Mervyn!" She was too shocked to move.

"This *is* still my home? Who are all these people?"

"It's my birthday," Louise said, her voice faint. "They threw a party for me."

Nobody knew what to say.

"It seems you couldn't wait for me to come back. Whose child is that?"

"Ours. Yours and mine. He's Ceredig Mervyn Pritchard."

Mervyn had no eyes for anyone but his wife. He had expected to find her alone, in the familiar house, and instead everything had changed, both inside and out. There were baby clothes, toys and equipment everywhere. The room was full of people.

Even the outside appearance of the farm was altered with new buildings and different animals. He had been longing to come back, had expected an enthusiastic greeting and instead Louise had become a stranger, in a strange place, with a strange child. He felt dispossessed.

"How can it be my child? I've been away a year."

"He was born on December 29th, six months after you were reported missing," Russell said. "Come on, old man. Let's go into the other room and have a quiet talk. I think you've a lot of catching up to do."

He took Mervyn by the arm and led him out of the room.

"Time we were all off," Kane said, and led the way out into the yard, followed by a subdued group of people.

Louise was shaking.

"I never even kissed him. He's changed," she said. "He was never like that."

"He had a shock," Emma said. "He expected to find the farm as it was. Life moves on, but he's lost in time, remembering everything as it was the day he left."

"Do you want Gran and me to go home with Mum and Dad?" Kate asked.

"We can't put things back to the way they were," Louise said. "The farm needs your money to survive. If you just go to your rooms . . . I hope Russell can help."

She was near to tears. She had never imagined that there might be problems for them both if Mervyn returned home. Only now did she realise how much her own life had changed since the day she found Jason in the barn.

Emma and Kate cleared up quickly. It was time for Ceredig's feed. As soon as the room was tidy both went upstairs.

"Can I come and talk to you?" Kate asked her grandmother.

"I'd be glad of company. I wonder why no one told Louise he was safe and coming home?" It was not a question that either could answer.

Kate was concerned.

"I thought she'd be pleased to see him . . . excited, happy . . ."

"She's been accepting the fact that he was dead," Emma said. "At first, she hoped. Then they killed her hope. I don't think she even recognised him at first and when she did it was a terrible shock. A dead man come to life. A year is a long time. Think of all that's happened here . . . and how difficult it will be to help Mervyn catch up."

"He was so angry."

"That doesn't surprise me. He left a quiet orderly farm, just Louise and Huw. He walked into a party . . . a new baby . . . a wife who's changed . . . a farm that is nothing like the one he left . . . a room full of people, most of whom he'd never seen before. He feels threatened."

"I thought being grown up would free people from problems," Kate said.

"They just get bigger." Emma sighed. "Mervyn's come home to new obligations . . . children change your life for ever." And grandchildren, Emma thought. There's still that same tug. "We don't ask for the changes, and rarely see them coming. We have to survive and learn to live with them, whatever happens." She sighed, wondering how on earth the situation would resolve itself. "Louise only made the major changes after she was told Mervyn was dead . . . she would never have done it if she knew he would be home. As it is, they will benefit the farm, but they aren't easily reversible."

Emma was trying to sort out her own feelings, and wondering if she and Kate would have to leave. Would Mervyn accept strangers in his home?

She would have to look for a flat. She wanted to stay in the area. Meanwhile what was she going to do with the rest of her life if Mervyn did not want her to stay on? Louise needed her, now she had the baby . . . there was far too much for her to do, even with Mervyn home. Would he recognise that? Would he go along with all their ideas, and allow Jason to stay and Bob to help? What kind of man was he? And how had he changed in the past year?

She looked out of the window. The sun shone on the

mountains, and cloud shadows fled across the windswept slopes. She had come to think of this as her home, and she did not want to leave. She took up her knitting. Whether she stayed or went, Ceredig would grow and need larger clothes for next winter.

There was uncertainty too, downstairs in the kitchen, where Louise, still shaken, sat, unable to collect her thoughts. Suddenly the knowledge of all the things she needed to tell Mervyn overwhelmed her . . . how could she bring him up to date on everything that had happened while he had been away? Or explain her own feelings during that time?

"Hot sweet tea," Roz said, anxious to do something practical. She had to stay until Russell left as she had got a lift up to the farm. There was nothing she could think of to say that would help. She too could see trouble ahead: not just breakers, but great reefs. How would he react to all the changes? How would he live with a baby in the house, demanding attention and time from the wife who had been as free as he before?

"You've had a shock."

"I wanted him home so badly," Louise said, listening to the soft sounds of voices from the dining room. "But I'd begun to get used to the idea that he was dead. It's not like I imagined . . . Roz, I ought to be jubilant . . . and I'm frightened. He's never lived with a baby."

She sipped the tea, her mind filled with so many new worries.

"He's having to accept a ready-made baby. He missed my pregnancy and the preparations, and Ceredig's first few months. And all those changes to the farm. I hadn't realised how much we've done. How do I explain them? He must feel as if everything he knew has been taken away from him . . . even me, with a baby as well."

They sat in silence, worry dominating Louise. When Ceredig cried she jumped up and took him outside. Jason, sure that this was the end of his own stay on the farm, was sitting on the wall.

"Will I have to go?" he asked.

Louise stared at him. Her thoughts had not taken her so far. There were three people dependent on her now for homes. What would Mervyn say to that? She would fight for them. She needed them. She looked at the clouds drifting over the sky, at the mountains, which seemed unchanging and yet changed with every flirt of the weather. Life suddenly seemed more unpredictable than ever. And she had thought that impossible.

Mervyn had been appalled when he walked into a crowded noisy room full of people he had never seen before. The baby was not real to him. He could not absorb the fact that he now had a son. His head ached, and he had not eaten since early that morning. He had been pitchforked into a kind of hell, having expected a heaven, and a devoted wife running to greet him.

After a year spent in a remote country cottage, where horses and carts were the only transport, he had found the seething roads and the noisy crowds unbearable and had longed for Louise and the peace of his own home. But he felt a stranger here. He was faced with problems that he had never imagined. He stared around him at the sitting room, looking for differences, and relaxed when he realised nothing here had been altered. There was still the odd shaped crack in the ceiling that always reminded him of a pig's head. Both he and his father tried to remove it, but it always returned. Idiotically it now comforted him.

Russell began to explain, realising he had a daunting task.

"The Foreign Office has been trying to find out what happened to you. They could tell us nothing till early May, when a lad with a landmine injury was hospitalised. He was the son of one of the men who hijacked you. He said both of you were dead. He was wearing your watch. They brought it back to Louise."

Mervyn stared at him.

"Dear God. When did they tell her?"

"A few weeks ago. Up to then, she'd been hoping. When she realised she was on her own she had to make plans to keep the farm going. She's been putting off making changes, waiting for you to come back. The bottom's dropped out of the market for farmers since you went away. And she didn't know if the insurers would pay up . . . she had no real proof of your death."

"No wonder she looked so startled when she saw me. She must have thought I was a ghost."

"I wonder why the Foreign Office didn't warn her that you were coming home? It would have been kinder to both of you."

"The Foreign Office?" Mervyn spoke as if he were using an unfamiliar language which, he realised, he was. Although he hadn't been able to master his rescuers' language, he had learnt to communicate with them in basic terms. Only in the past three weeks had he heard English spoken again.

He looked foreign even to Russell, who had known him since their schooldays: he was bronzed, and both his hair and his beard needed attention. His clothes were sufficiently unusual to cause second glances as he passed. Nobody would take him for a Welshman at the moment.

"What has the Foreign Office to do with me?"

"When you and Chris were reported missing they thought you had been kidnapped and expected a ransom demand. Since they didn't get one they've been trying to find out what happened to you. What did happen to you both?"

"A band of brigands jumped us, tied us up and put us in the back of the lorry. They drove it up a terrible mountain road and overturned it. They took the food, and left us by the roadside. Chris was so badly injured that he died. I had concussion. I didn't even remember my name until about three weeks ago. I had no idea anyone had been looking for me. It just didn't occur to me. I suppose that was stupid." He frowned. "To me it seems as if I've only been gone for three weeks . . . it's impossible to explain. I can't believe it's a year. The hijacking is still more vivid than the life I've been leading all that time. All that shouting and shooting . . . they beat us both. It was terrifying."

Russell was concerned. Concussion and memory loss could have odd repercussions, such as wildly swinging mood changes and sometimes irrational behaviour.

"What have you been doing ? Do you remember or has that gone now you've regained your own memory?"

"Marika and Georg . . . they found us lying by the road-side. They buried Chris. They were about to bury me when I regained consciousness – they'd thought I was dead too, at first. They took me in their cart to their home . . . a tiny cottage up in the hills. I don't even know where it was. They farmed in a small way. Sheep."

Roz appeared with coffee and sandwiches and a slice of birthday cake in an effort to restore normality. Mervyn began to eat and Russell followed his wife back into the passage.

"How is Louise?"

"Recovering, but she's bewildered. It's not the way she expected . . ."

"Mervyn's like Rip Van Winkle. Time's stood still for him, but here they've moved on through a very difficult year. I'll try and help . . . I don't know if I can but I don't want to leave him. Can you take the car and do surgery, and then perhaps Peta can come back for me, or Bob will drive me home."

Mott followed Russell back into the room and settled by his master's feet, leaning against his leg. A moment later there was a whimper and a scratch at the door. Russell opened it and Fern walked in, carrying a pup in her mouth. She put it on the rug and looked up at Mervyn. He was too busy with his own thoughts to do more than cast a cursory glance at her.

"It's hard to take in," Mervyn said. "Louise must have been three months pregnant when I went away. Why didn't she tell me?""

"She was saving the news until she was sure and the critical period had passed. She lost both the others, if you remember, around the twelve-week mark. She intended to tell you on her birthday – a present to you. Only you didn't come back. The pregnancy and then the baby complicated her life enormously."

"Where's Huw?"

"He had back trouble and the doctor told him he had to retire, or end up completely crippled. He is over seventy."

"So much happening and I never knew."

You don't know the half of it yet, Russell thought, remembering the afternoon that Kane's dogs had been released, and the agonising wait to see if Tarquin would recover. Louise had had as difficult a year as her husband, though perhaps he would never realise that.

Fern, who had vanished, returned with another pup in her mouth.

"She's determined you'll see them all," Russell said, laughing.

Mervyn's smile was tentative, but he picked up the pup and held it against him. He still looked shocked.

"I think it would be a good idea if we got rid of that beard, and you put on your own things; you look like a total stranger to all of us." Russell was trying to work out ways of making the situation easier for both his friends.

An hour later, showered, clean-shaven and dressed in familiar clothing, Mervyn looked more like the man that Russell remembered. Both trousers and shirt were too large for him.

While he was changing Roz had retrieved the pups and both dogs were lying on the rug by the Aga, with small bodies clambering all over them.

Russell and Mervyn walked into the kitchen as Louise was trying to persuade Ceredig that food went into his mouth and not all over the floor. The baby seized the spoon and dropped it.

She looked anxiously at her husband, trying to determine his mood. There was a great deal of grey in his hair, and he looked far more than just one year older. He was thinner, and so tanned that his skin looked dark.

"It's going to take a lot of getting used to and a lot of catching up," he said. "I seem to have lost part of my life."

He sat in the big chair that had been his father's, and took the mug of coffee that Louise offered him. After a moment, she brought him a slice of birthday cake. He looked at it, and then up at her, his right eyebrow rising .

"A year too late," he said. "I don't know what's been happening anywhere in the world, let alone here. It was so remote where I was. My hosts were refugees. They'd left their own home, because of the war. Both their sons were dead. They had so little. They were trying to make a new start in life, farming sheep in those remote uplands. I knew about sheep . . . I didn't forget that." His mind went back to the remote hillside and the two friendly people who had become almost his proxy parents. "They called me Peitr. They healed my injuries and in return for food and bed I became their shepherd and taught Georg all I could. We couldn't really communicate . . . their language was difficult and I only learned basic words."

He stroked Fern, who was sitting with her head on his knee.

"It's an odd life, and a desperately poor one. They do almost everything by barter, and hardly ever use money. Georg went down the hill to the nearest shop about once every six weeks and, as far as I could gather, he didn't even show himself. What he needed was brought to him by friends. He was afraid of being discovered and both of them killed. They belonged to the wrong group of people. I never understood what was going on. I did realise I would be killed as well if we were found. I caught their fear. It's going to be hard to let that go."

"We thought you were a prisoner," Louise said. "I had

visions of chains, and torture, and the government were expecting a ransom demand. Then they said you were dead."

"The bandits obviously thought so, otherwise they'd have finished me off. Chris moved before they shot me and they made quite sure he never would again. I decided to act dead, even if I wasn't, but as it was I must have passed out. I wasn't a prisoner on the farm. I could have left whenever I liked. Only where could I go? I was no one. I remembered nothing of my past life. I don't even know what made my memory come back but it was there, suddenly, and I knew who I was and that I ought to be here."

"How did your hosts react?"

"They were concerned. Of course I must go to my own home, they said, your wife will be so unhappy. But it wasn't that easy – I had no papers. The thieves had taken everything, including my watch and my passport and all the contents of my pockets. I was a nameless man when Georg found me. He told me they'd stripped both Chris and me naked, and tied my hands and my ankles."

"How did you get back?" They were all curious.

"I suspect as an illegal immigrant. A friend of Georg's rode with me for four days across country and then left the horses we used at a farm. I was smuggled over the border. I don't even know which countries I entered." He looked out of the window at the mountains. They were old friends. The hills in which he lived for the past year had been high and forested and there had been no horizons.

"And?" Louise asked.

"Then I was taken by car for miles. That took another three days. We came into France. At least that was a language I recognised."

"What about customs at the borders?"

"We never entered at any point where we could be investigated. It was always a matter of finding an entry and going in at night. I began to feel like a criminal, although all I was doing was trying to return to my own country."

"Why didn't you contact an embassy?" Russell asked.

"It just never occurred to me. My first companion on my way home spoke a little English and told me I had no need to worry. I'd be able to get here, but had to co-operate, and I must never tell anyone what route we took. Come to think of it, he probably thought I was a criminal of some kind." For the first time Mervyn smiled. "That's only just crossed my mind. I was so confused. I've only been myself for three weeks. Up to then I was someone completely different . . . takes some getting used to."

"Didn't anyone question you at Dover?"

"I was lying under a pile of boxes, in a small compartment they'd made. It never struck me as odd till now. I just took everything for granted. My mind wasn't functioning properly. I simply needed to get home. Like a dog that's lost it's master."

His hand went down to Mott's head. The dog had not left him for a moment since he came home.

"We went through customs without a problem. Then I was transferred to another lorry as co-driver. I went across London in a taxi – the taxi-driver never asked for payment. Then I came here by train. Someone gave me a ticket, and enough money for a bus fare from the station to the village. I walked up."

For a moment there was silence. Roz turned to her husband to ask if he was ready to leave when there came a shrill neigh and a scream, followed by pounding feet and shouts. Louise put the baby in his cot. She raced after the others.

Corrie, in the field, her foal close against her, was standing, wild eyed, a twelve inch long gash gaping on her shoulder. She was staring at a blood-covered figure lying on the ground.

Jason, in danger of being kicked, was trying to herd her towards the gate to calm her, lest she trampled her victim. Mott ran into the field, barking. Corrie turned towards him. He dodged out of her way, and she followed him to the farthest corner of the field, intent on charging him, but he was too agile for her to catch him.

Roz ran in to phone for an ambulance. Russell, torn between the intruder and the mare, went through the gate. He kicked the blood-stained knife away.

"It's Damon," he said, as he bent over the silent figure. "She's kicked him on the head."

Kate and Emma, hearing the uproar, had also appeared.

"He said he'd hurt Corrie," Kate said, almost in tears. "I didn't believe him. He's always threatening things. Everyone at school laughs at me because I love Corrie and her foal so much. He said he'd make me suffer for telling on him. I didn't think he'd come up here. He knew about the party of course. Everyone's been talking about it. Is Corrie all right?"

She was flushed and tearful.

"Nothing that a few stitches won't remedy, though she isn't going to care much for people now," Roz said. "We'll have to tranquillise her before we treat her."

"Have I come home to a war?" Mervyn asked.

"Not exactly." Some birthday, Louise thought. "This began months ago when this lad and his cronies thought Kane was a vivisectionist and released all his animals. A couple of the dogs got in here and killed a number of sheep . . . and attacked Tarquin. Kate told the authorities who they were and has been victimised ever since."

"Tarquin?" Mervyn stared at her, appalled.

"He's fine now. He was badly hurt but Russell did a marvellous job on him. He's turned into everything we hoped for."

Mervyn looked at her and saw signs of hardships she had endured during the year. He had, on his journey home, imagined the farm going on as before with everything running smoothly. Life was no safer here than it had been in Georg's country. Jungle predators everywhere.

He looked at the mare. She was shivering, the foal tucked up against her, scared by all the noise. Mott lay watching her.

"Are we breeding horses now?" Mervyn asked.

"They're Kane's. At livery here." How in the world, Louise thought, do I bring him up to date?

The ambulance and the police car arrived together. The two men were familiar faces, drinking companions with Russell when they all had time. They grinned with pleasure when they saw the newcomer.

"Mervyn! We thought you were dead! It's good to see you, they need you here. What's been happening?"

At last he was welcomed. He was back in his own place. In charge. They were all waiting for him to speak. He was barely aware of the significance of the change in his feelings. He explained and Russell handed over the knife.

"Maybe that young man will have learned his lesson," the elder of the two policemen said. "He's well on the way to being one of our wildest."

"If he survives that kick," Jason said. "She's done a lot of damage to his head."

Louise was seized by a new worry.

"Are we liable?"

"Not with the evidence we have here," one of the policemen said. "He brought it on himself. The mare was gashed by this knife. The blood will match. That's no wire-caused wound."

"He told me he'd pay me out one day," Kate said. "He said he'd teach me not to interfere, not to tell tales."

She was shaking, and Russell put his arm round her.

"He'll not be troubling us for some time," the younger man said, as the ambulance drove Damon away, still unconscious.

Russell went over to the mare, who no longer resisted attention. She stood, head down, accepting his presence.

"I saw him come," Jason said, as they walked towards the house. "I was too far away to do any good. I saw the knife glint. He went for Chance, but Corrie wasn't having any. She charged him, which is when he cut her."

"Maybe just as well you weren't near," Mervyn said, knowing how he would have reacted in the same circum-

243

stances. He looked at Jason. He was becoming aware that his return was going to cause problems for those who had helped Louise. "I can see you're a major asset here. I hope you'll stay, as it seems Huw won't ever be coming back."

"Kate and Emma live here, too," Louise said. "Emma's Roz's mum. Her husband died last year. She's living in the little suite we made for your mother. Kate's moved into the attic. There was so much empty space with you away."

Kate was looking at him. He had changed so much. Gone was the enthusiastic and eager Uncle Mervyn she remembered and in his place was a stranger.

"You've grown up while I've been away," Mervyn said, looking at long legs, soft skin and dark eyes that were observing him with some anxiety. He remembered suddenly that Kate was his goddaughter. "It'll be a change to have a full house. Louise and I used to rattle around in all that space. It was meant to be occupied."

Kate glanced at her grandmother, echoing her sigh of relief.

There was a wail from the baby who had woken to find himself alone. Louise lifted him, and he lay in her arms, looking at all the people around him.

"We might as well finish the remains of our party," Emma said. The two policemen joined them, laughing and joking.

"We may have cleared up a crime wave." The older man was jubilant. They had had their suspicions but this was the first time they had positive proof.

Quite suddenly, the atmosphere changed and they were celebrating Mervyn's return.

Ceredig, overcome by the noise of too many people, began to cry.

Louise lifted him. She walked across the room and put him in Mervyn's arms.

"Time you knew your father," she said.

Two pairs of brown eyes regarded each other intently. The baby smiled and wound his hand tightly round Mervyn's finger. He was used to being petted and cuddled by people he didn't know at all. Neither Louise nor her husband noticed when everyone else went quietly out of the room.

"Hello, son," Mervyn said, raising one eyebrow.

The baby looked at him, considering and then copied the action. Mervyn laughed, a happy sound that echoed through the room.

"Blow me. He copied me. No doubt whatever that he's mine. Dad did that too. I picked it up from him."

"It's not a copy. It's inborn. He's done it right from the start," Louise said.

Mervyn held out a hand. Louise took it and then leaned against him. Beardless and dressed in his own clothes, he was familiar again. He smiled at her.

"Happy birthday. I haven't a present for you. I didn't remember. We've a lot to learn about one another again, but now I know I've come home."

"I have the only present I need," Louise said.

Mervyn looked down at his son, and then put his arm around her. "And so have I."

Fern, anxious not to be left out of any action, picked up one of her pups and deposited it firmly at Mervyn's feet. It was time he recognised her contribution to the family. He had neither acknowledged the pups nor praised her yet.

He laughed, and handed the baby back to Louise. He knelt and picked up the puppy. She had her father's markings and her mother's pretty face. She tucked herself against him, snuggling into his arms, delighted to be noticed.

"I'm going to do something that was in my mind before I went away," he said. "We're not selling these pups at eight weeks. We're keeping them and training them. A trained dog can fetch a fortune. A thousand pounds or more. I gather from Russell that things haven't got better in the farming world, but worse, and that Kate and Emma and the horses are part of your attempts to keep us going."

He put the pup back with the rest of the litter, and walked over to his wife. The baby watched, interested, as they stood,

Joyce Stranger

holding one another close, knowing that this was just a beginning. Both had a great deal of adjusting to do in the days ahead.

Jason, on his way to his flat, glanced through the window into the lighted room, and smiled to himself.

The guid man was home. Maybe the luck would now change.